THE CURSE OF THE BRONZE LAMP

THE
CURSE OF THE BRONZE LAMP

Carter Dickson
(John Dickson Carr)

Carroll & Graf Publishers, inc.
New York

Reprinted by agreement with William Morrow and Company, Inc.

First Carroll & Graf edition 1984

Carroll & Graf Publishers, Inc.
260 Fifth Avenue
New York, N.Y. 10001

ISBN: 0-88184-101-3

Manufactured in the United States of America

I

In the drawing-room of a suite at the Continental-Savoy Hotel, Cairo, a girl and a young man waited for the telephone to ring.

That was not the beginning of the story. But it was the beginning of the terror.

Cairo, they say, is much changed nowadays. But at the time these things happened—on a brilliant warm April afternoon, ten years ago—life flowed with its old pleasant serenity.

Against the strong blue of an Egyptian sky, the white stone of that hotel stood out with hard intensity. Its shutters, its little iron balconies at the windows, gave it a vaguely French appearance, splashed with the colours of awnings. Trams clanged along the Shari Kamil into Opera Place; a mob of tourists besieged the American Express office just below; high lights winked on the stream of cars that drew up at the hotel door among rosewood-trees and dwarf palms. But the sounds—and scents—of an older Cairo stirred across from that city of mosque-minarets against the sun.

These sounds came only dimly to the suite on the second floor of the Continental-Savoy. The shutters were closed, so that only thin level slits of light penetrated into the drawing-room.

And the young man said:

"For the love of Mike, Helen, sit down!"

The girl stopped pacing, looking hesitantly at the telephone.

"Your father," the young man added reasonably, "will phone as soon as there's any news. And there's nothing to worry about anyway."

"I wonder," said the girl.

"A scorpion bite!" said her companion. His tone was not exactly contemptuous, but it was clear he regarded a scorpion bite as nothing very serious—in which, medically speaking, he was quite right. "I mean to say, Helen!"

The girl partly opened one of the shutters, so that a little

5

more light came into the room, and she stood looking out with her face in profile against it.

You could not have called her beautiful. And yet she had that quality which caused many men—including Sandy Robertson, who watched her thoughtfully now—to fall over their own feet and talk inanely after only two whiskies.

Sex-appeal, so called? She had that, yes. So have most healthy and pretty girls in their late twenties. Intelligence? Imagination? The hint, under that mild and smiling nature, of a hidden intensity which might sweep over her to the point of danger in any of the affairs of life? There, possibly, we come closer to the explanation.

She was a blonde. The soft yellow-shining hair contrasted with the faint tan of her skin, which brought into relief the luminous whites of the dark brown eyes. You could note the wide mouth, a little uncertain of itself. You could note the uncertain gestures: the beginning of a smile, then doubt.

Too much imagination! Too much intensity!

But there it was, and Sandy Robertson for one had no wish to change it. She could work with a spade at the diggings, as hard as any hired *Reises*. She could discuss rubrics and canopic vases as learnedly as Professor Gilray himself. Yet that small lithe figure, in blouse and leggings, lost none of its femininity.

You may remember, in those years 1934-35, how the attention of the world was directed towards that valley on the west bank of the Nile called Bîbân-el-Mulûk, the Tombs of the Kings. A small party of British archæologists, headed by Professor Gilray and the Earl of Severn, uncovered a buried tomb in the sand.

Working through two seasons, trom October until the broiling heat of May stopped them, they penetrated through granite blocks into the ante-chamber, the side-chamber, and the tomb-chamber. They found, among treasures which dazed even the Egyptian Government, the sarcophagus of yellowish crystalline sandstone. With infinite labour they brought to light the mummy ot Herihor, high priest of Ammon, who had ruled as king over Egypt at the end of the Twentieth Dynasty.

It rang with astounding noise through the press ot the entire world.

Tourist crowds poured into the camp. Newspaper correspondents haunted it. There were photographs of Professor Gilray, of Lord Severn, of Dr. Budge the anatomist, of Sandy Robertson, and, above all, of Lord Severn's daughter —Lady Helen Loring—whose presence gave this expedition the romantic interest it needed. Then came the last hearsay thrill, the last twist of the knife.

Professor Gilray, of Cambridge, had been the first person to enter the tomb. And Professor Gilray, towards the end of the second year, was stung in the hand by a scorpion. . . .

It is very easy to start the whisper of superstition. It is also good copy.

Standing now by the window in that hot drawing-room at the Continental-Savoy, Helen Loring swung round. She was wearing a white sleeveless tennis frock, with a scarlet-and-white silk scarf caught round her neck; and the sun made a gold shimmer behind her head.

"Sandy. Have you . . . seen the papers ?"

"That," Mr. Robertson announced firmly, "that, my sweet, is rubbish."

"Of course it's rubbish ! Only . . . "

"Only what ?"

"I was wondering whether I oughtn't to cancel my reservations for to-morrow."

"Why should you ?"

"Do you think I *ought* to go back to England, Sandy ? With Professor Gilray in a nursing-home ?"

"Can you do any good by staying here ?"

"No. I suppose not. All the same . . ."

Sandy Robertson, seated astride a chair with his face turned towards the back of it, studied her out of semi-gloom. His hands were folded on the top of the chair-back, his pointed chin propped on them.

A small, thin, wiry man—hardly as tall as Helen herself— he looked older than his thirty-five years and would probably continue to look just like that until the age of fifty. His hair, of the colour that gave him his nickname, bristled above a faintly lined forehead and dark, clever, roving eyes. His face had that humorous ugliness, with a twist to the mouth, which women often find attractive.

"Your father," he said, "wants you to go home and open up the house. We shall be following," . . . he hesitated, . . . "just as soon as we've wound up this business with

7

the Egyptian government. I repeat, my dear, what can you *do* here?"

Helen sat down in a chair by the window. Each time he looked at her, Sandy Robertson's expression—he knew it was well hidden by the gloom—took on an edge that was grotesquely like physical pain. But his manner grew elaborately casual.

"All the same, before you do go back to England . . ."

"Yes, Sandy?"

"Have you given any thought to that matter I mentioned the other night?"

Helen looked away, making a slight gesture as though she wanted to avoid the subject but didn't quite know how.

"I own," pursued Sandy, "to being absolutely worthless. If you did me the honour of becoming my wife, you would undoubtedly have to support me."

"Don't talk like that!"

"Why not? It's true."

After a pause he went on in the same unruffled tone:

"In ordinary circumstances, I might urge my social advantages. My golf, bridge, and dancing are all first-rate. I've picked up a smattering of Egyptology. . . ."

"More than a smattering, Sandy. Do yourself justice."

"All right. More than a smattering. Because *you're* interested in it, whereas you're not much interested in the other things. You are serious-minded, Helen. Ve—ry serious-minded."

For some reason, no woman in her heart quite likes to be called serious-minded. Helen Loring looked back at him rather helplessly. Affection, doubt, embarrassment, a conviction that Old Sandy never quite meant what he said, struggled together inside her.

"On those grounds," continued Sandy, "I guarantee to keep up with you. On those grounds, my pet, I guarantee to master any subject from Esperanto to tropical fish. I . . ." He broke off. Suddenly, and with shattering harshness in that half-darkened room, his tone changed.

"What the hell am I doing," he added, "talking like a bloody Noel Coward play?"

"Sandy, *please!*"

"I'm in love with you; and that's that. Oh, and don't say you're 'fond' of me, because I know that already. The

8

point is, Helen, what about the usual somebody else ?" He hesitated. "Kit Farrell, for instance ?"

Helen tried to look him in the eyes, and couldn't.

"I don't know !" she cried.

"You'll be seeing Kit, I expect. when you get back to London ?"

"Yes. I imagine so."

Sandy brooded, again lowering his chin on his clasped hands.

"There are some people," he said argumentatively, "who call Mr. Christopher Farrell a ruddy collar-advertisement. *I* don't, because I know his sterling worth. But it's all wrong, I tell you ! The whole situation is wrong !"

"How do you mean, wrong ?"

"Well, look at it ! Here's Kit Farrell, with plenty of good looks. Here am I, on the other hand, whose face wouldn't only stop a clock—it would make the clock run backwards and strike thirteen."

"Oh, Sandy, do you think that matters ?"

"Yes. I do."

Fierily embarrassed, Helen again looked away.

"*He* should be the social hound," persisted Sandy, "and *I* should be the grubber in legal chambers. But is it like that ? Oh, no. It's just the other way round. That bloke is interested—really interested—in Whistleby *v.* Bouncer, 1852, Law Report What's-its-name. And you," he wound up this tirade by throwing the accusation at her, "you're serious-minded. When was the last time you laughed ?"

Perhaps to his surprise, Helen did laugh.

"As a matter of fact," she answered, "I think it was this morning."

"Oh ?" said Sandy suspiciously, as though he rather resented anybody else who made her laugh.

"Yes. There's a man staying here at the hotel . . ."

Sandy smote his forehead.

"Please, you idiot ! This man is old enough to be my grandfather !"

"What's his name ?"

"Merrivale. Sir Henry Merrivale."

Despite the worry in her dark brown eyes, Helen leaned back and regarded a corner of the ceiling with a reminiscent pleasure which lightened her whole face. There are persons who could have told her that the presence of Sir Henry Merrivale, though often productive of exasperation and sometimes of fury, never fails as a remover of gravity.

"He's supposed to be here for his health," the girl explained, "though there's nothing wrong with him, actually. And he says he's leaving to-morrow, because the effect on his blood-pressure of being so constantly swindled is undermining all the good work of the climate. In the meantime, he's compiling an enormous scrapbook. . . ."

"Scrapbook ?"

"Of his own activities. From bundles of press cuttings for years back. Sandy, that scrapbook is absolutely priceless ! It . . ."

On its small table beside the grand piano, the telephone rang shrilly.

There was a slight silence, as though neither Sandy nor Helen Loring quite wanted to move. Then the girl sprang up and ran towards the phone. Though her face was in shadow when she picked it up, he could see the shining of her eyes.

"Your father ?" he asked.

Helen put her hand over the mouthpiece of the phone.

"No. It's Dr. Macbain from the nursing-home. Father's . . . on his way here."

The telephone went on talking thinly, though he could distinguish no words. It seemed to go on at interminable length, scratching the nerves; you would have imagined that thirty messages could have been conveyed in that time. Finally Helen replaced the phone on its cradle, with a loud jarring click that showed her hand was not steady. Then she spoke.

"Professor Gilray is dead."

Outside the windows, the late afternoon light had begun to die. It would shortly be time for the *mahgrib*, the sunset call to prayer, sounding and echoing from the minaret of every mosque in Cairo. The room—odd how you noticed it now !—had recently been redecorated. The smell of paint and furniture polish, even the fustiness of yellow satin upholstery, seemed to get into the lungs with stifling effect.

Sandy sprang up from his chair.

"That's impossible !" he shouted.

The girl merely shrugged.

"I tell you, Helen, it's impossible ! A scorpion bite ? It's no more dangerous than . . . than . . ." He searched his mind for suitable comparisons, but found none. "It must have been something else !"

"He's dead," Helen repeated. "And you know what they'll say now."

"Yes. I know."

"There's already a rumour about a curse attached to the tomb. I even read an article warning me about that bronze lamp." Helen clenched her fists. "After all the trouble Father's had already, it does seem a bit thick."

Distantly, a door opened and closed. Slow footsteps approached through the outer room of the suite. The door of the drawing-room was opened, and closed behind him, by a man who seemed to have grown older in a few hours.

John Loring, fourth Earl of Severn, was a middle-sized hardy man, stringy of body and bony of hand, whose face had been burned to leatheriness by the sun. His iron-grey hair and cropped grey moustache looked mouse-coloured against it. Two deep furrows in his cheeks, one on each side of the moustache from nostril to jaw, gave him a severe expression which his nature belied. He went over and sat down, stoop-shouldered, on a yellow upholstered sofa. It was some seconds before he lifted his eyes to ask, in a mild voice:

"Did Macbain phone you ?"

"Yes."

"Bad luck," said Lord Severn, breathing noisily. "Couldn't be helped."

"But a scorpion bite ?" demanded Sandy.

"It's a question," said Lord Severn, "of what the doctors call the toleratory condition. Some people can throw it off as no worse than a bad mosquito bite. Others can't. Poor Gilray couldn't." He put his hand inside the jacket of his light summer suit, feeling for the region of the heart. "To tell you the truth, Helen, I don't feel any too well myself."

At the alarm that showed in both their faces, Lord Severn essayed a light tone.

"This old ticker," he patted the region of the heart, "has been going on a long time. Bound to be a bit rocky sometimes. And we've had a lot of trouble, what with one thing or another. Especially as . . ." His mild eyes grew unfathomable, as though he refused to believe something in which he must believe. "I think," he added, "I'll go in and lie down."

Helen ran forward.

"Are you sure you're all right ?" she cried. "Hadn't I better ask the doctor to come up ?"

"Nonsense !" said Lord Severn, and got to his feet. "I'm tired, that's all. I want to get back home. The sooner you can get things ready there, Helen, the better for me."

Helen hesitated. "I was just telling Sandy that I wondered whether I ought to go to-morrow. And now, with Professor Gilray dead. . . ."

"There's nothing you can do," her father pointed out. That odd, unfathomable look returned to his furrowed face. "Besides, in a sense, you'd be in the way. Not that you haven't been helpful, my dear ! I only meant . . ." Lord Severn made bothered gestures, as though of apology. "Poor Gilray !" he said. "My God, poor old Gilray !"

Shadows, presaging the swift tropical night that would come at one stride, had gathered over the city. Its usual hum, a muted clatter-and-babble, died away before a new note, a sonorous note—the muezzin's call to prayer.

Allah is greatest ! I testify that there is no God but Allah ; I testify that Mohammed is the prophet of Allah ; come to prayer ; come to salvation ; Allah is greatest ; there is no God but Allah !

A thin thread of sound which became many sounds, it rose and fell over a secret land. Lord Severn glanced towards the windows.

Kindly, a little absent-minded, he shook his head.

"Who can a man trust ?" he muttered, as though he were repeating a quotation. "It's a great question. Who can a man trust ?"

He turned round, still fumbling inside his jacket over the region of the heart, and walked in a dispirited way towards his bedroom. The door closed after him. Helen and Sandy looked at each other in perplexity, while the muezzin still called in the twilight.

2

At two-thirty on the following afternoon, outside the Main Railway Station, occurred a truly memorable row. It is still mentioned with respect by Arab porters and hotel-commissionnaires, even in that city of memorable schlimozzels. And opinion is still divided as to whether the fault lay with the taxi-driver or with Sir Henry Merrivale.

The Main Railway Station lies to the north of Cairo. It is not far from the centre of town, as distances go. But this depends on your means of locomotion.

In a city where tram-lines interfere with camels, and camels with tram-lines; where the driver of your two-horse Victoria doesn't know his way, and has to be directed with screams; where almost any sort of traffic block can be caused by a combination of dogs, donkeys, tradesmen, and beggars; then it is as well to start early when attempting to catch a train.

So it happened this afternoon that there sped north, clanking and rattling along the Shari Nûbâr Pasha, a motor taxi-cab.

This cab was an ancient Ford whose original colour no man could discern. On its roof were fastened two large suitcases and a small one. It had a taxi-meter which didn't work—or, at least, the driver said it didn't work. It had as driver a dark-skinned young man with a guileless countenance, dark liquid eyes, the patchy beginnings of a beard like hair escaping from a mattress, a dirty white cloth wound round his head, and a dream of much fine gold in his mind.

Finally, it had a passenger.

This was a large, stout, barrel-shaped man in a white linen suit and a Panama hat. From under the brim of the hat, which was turned down all round like a bowl, there peered out behind shell-rimmed spectacles a face of such terrifying malignancy that even Cairo beggars might have hesitated.

He sat bolt upright, his arms folded in majesty. On the seat beside him lay a large leather-bound volume with the small gilt letters Scrapbook. From two articles whose tops could be seen projecting from the breast pocket of his coat—a pair of long-bladed scissors, handle uppermost, and a large tube of liquid glue—it could be deduced how he meant to spend his time in the train.

So far, conversation between driver and passenger had been conducted in a mixture of English, French, and whatever scraps of Arabic the latter could remember. Now he leaned forward to tap the driver on the shoulder.

13

"Oi !" said the stout gentleman.

The taxi-driver had a soft, liquid, purring voice, the very honey of flattery.

"You spoke, O lord of the morning ?"

"Uh-huh," said the lord of the morning, casting around an evilly suspicious glance. "Is it," he added in French, "that we proceed towards the railway station ?"

"But, behold !" cried the taxi-driver, sweeping out an arm with the air of one who conjures it there. "See before you the railway station itself ! We have proceeded with expedition, kind gentleman."

He proved this by putting on a burst of speed that sent the taxi screaming on two wheels into the square called Midan el-Mahatta, and nearly drove the stout gentleman's head through the offside window. Though their fifty-mile-an-hour approach to the station rather suggested that the driver meant to plunge into the booking-hall, he yanked on his brakes at the last moment. Then he turned round, eager-eyed like a dog, for approval.

The stout gentleman did not say anything.

Slowly, his hat crushed down over his eyes, Sir Henry Merrivale crawled out of the taxi.

"The station, O lord of the morning ! The railway station !"

"Uh-huh," said his fare in a strangled, far-away voice. "Make descend my baggage. How much ?"

The taxi-driver smiled a melting, guileless smile.

"Do not look at the meter, kind gentleman," he said. "This is only drollery. It is broke."

"So am I," said his passenger, "after stayin' in this goddamn country for nearly a month. How much ?"

"To you, kind gentleman—only fifty piastres."

"*Fifty piastres ?*" said Sir Henry Merrivale.

A curious purple colour crept over his broad face. Indeed, it compared not unfavourably with the purple part of an extremely bright necktie which the jolting of the taxi had thrown outside his coat. The scissors and the tube of glue hung half-way out of his breast pocket. Trying unsuccessfully to hold the scrapbook under one arm, H. M. clutched his hat to his head with both hands.

"Fifty piastres," he breathed, "nearly ten bob, just for drivin' here from the Continental-Savoy ?"

"It is not much, I know." The taxi-driver seemed

14

heart-broken at his own moderation. "It is not much, O lord of the morning! But then," he brightened, "there is always the tip."

"Listen!" said the stout gentleman, pointing a finger in the other's face. "Do you know what you are?"

"Pardon, kind gentleman?"

Feverishly H. M. searched in his inside pocket. He produced, and thrust into the taxi-driver's hand, a sheet of paper closely written with Arabic characters. Prior to leaving, H. M. had requested from his friends a collection of choice Arabic swear-words to take back to England. Over a number of whiskies the night before, these willing philologists had compiled a series of epithets so vile, so obscene, so rich in many-flowered insult, as to freeze the marrow of a Moslem's soul.

A spasm contorted the taxi-driver's face.

"Who?" he demanded, indicating the list.

"*You!*" said H. M., again pointing a finger in his face.

"This is me?"

"That is you," said H. M., "*avec* knobs on."

The taxi-driver uttered a hoarse scream.

"Now may Allah, the merciful and all-compassionate," he cried in Arabic, "look down upon this offence to me and all my house!"

And he leaned forward, swift as a snake, and plucked the long-bladed scissors out of H. M.'s pocket.

Any Western onlooker would have been forgiven for thinking that his purpose was simple assault with the scissors, using their points. But the Eastern mind has refinements of craft and guile. The taxi-driver's eyes had already been fixed—almost with an expression of greed—on H. M.'s bright-coloured necktie. And now he leaned forward, smiling, and with one deft chop of the scissors cut off H. M.'s tie just below the knot.

"Is it thus, O offspring of a dissolute camel," he inquired, "that you attempt to evade your just debts?"

Now in the action of having a tie sliced off before one's eyes there is something so peculiarly insulting, so degrading in its studied deliberateness, that no ordinary reprisals will suffice. It cannot be avenged by any mere blow, any common-place kick in the pants.

H. M.'s subsequent behaviour, then, can be justified.

A large left hand shot out and grasped the taxi-driver by

what passed for his collar. From his pocket H. M. whipped out the tube of glue. Before the hysterical driver quite realized what was happening, his fate was upon him.

With a fiendish expression, and using the tube as a kind of squirt-gun, H. M. sent a stream of liquid glue spurting into the driver's left eye. Then, with a slight twist of the wrist, he sent an equal stream with unerring aim into the right eye. In conclusion, as a kind of flourish, he drew across the driver's face a design rather suggestive of the Mark of Zorro.

"Haah !" said Sir Henry Merrivale. "So you want money, hey ?"

As another shriek bubbled from the driver's lips, the pattern was completed. H. M. replaced the glue tube in his pocket, and fished out instead an English five-pound note. He plastered the bank-note fairly and squarely, with a hand like a government stamp, over the driver's face. And he did this just as two flash-bulbs glared, and several Graflex cameras of the press recorded the scene for posterity.

"Sir Henry !" called an agitated feminine voice.

H. M. whirled round.

Neither he nor the driver had noticed that they were now surrounded by a wild-eyed crowd. Spectators poured across the square. Hotel-touts, Arab porters with their metal arm-bands, loped out of the station. Three more taxis, followed by a Victoria with neighing horses, piled up in a crush behind the first. And Lady Helen Loring, in the midst of half a dozen newspaper reporters, was appealing to him.

"Please, Sir Henry ! *May* I have a word with you ?"

Still dizzy from wrath, H. M. controlled himself.

"Sure, my wench ! Sure ! As many as you like. Just as soon as I . . ." Here he broke off. "*My luggage !*" he bellowed. "*Come back with my luggage ! Make descend my luggage !*"

In fairness to Abou Owad the taxi-driver, it must be stated that his instant flight was not due to any lack of courage.

It was simply that his almost blinded eyes had seen approaching a real five-pound note. True, it had been presented to him in a somewhat unorthodox way. But the fact of its being glued to his face implied possession; and it therefore behoved him, argued Abou Owad, to scram out of there before the passenger reconsidered.

Pausing only to drop the scissors and detach a corner of

the note from one eye, he put the car into gear and clanked away with three suitcases still on the roof. The cry from fifty throats about this luggage—following H. M.'s bellow —drove Abou Owad into his last frenzy.

Leaving the steering of the car to its own devices, he swung himself like a monkey to the car's roof. Fifty throats shouted a warning as he laid hold of the luggage. But Abou Owad, a wild bare-legged figure against the blue Egyptian sky, paid no attention.

The first suitcase he threw was caught by an Arab porter. The second landed squarely at the feet of Sir Henry Merrivale, now in a state past describing. The third suitcase struck the station wall and broke open, showering the pavement with shirts, socks, shoes, underwear, toilet articles, and a copy of *Razzle*.

"May thy sons be drowned in the *kanif* !" shrieked Abou Owad—and abruptly disappeared inside just in time to avoid swiping a milk-cart dead amidships.

The ensuing five minutes are best left undescribed.

Someone—probably Argus News Service, Inc.—handed H. M. his shorn necktie. Someone else—perhaps Mutual Press—gave him the scrapbook. Arab porters zealously repacked the damaged suitcase, with such good effect that at least one set of silver-backed brushes and one pair of gold cuff-links have never been seen since. The great man seemed a little less ruffled when he found himself on Platform Number One, beside the three-hour Express to Alexandria, looking down at a remarkably attractive brown-eyed girl in a grey travelling suit.

"Are you . . . are you all right ?" asked Helen.

"Candidly speakin'," answered the great man, "no. I expect I'm goin' to die of a heart attack at any minute. Feel my pulse ?"

The girl obediently did so.

"Awful," said H. M. darkly. "Murderous and flamin', that's what it is. All the same, once I get out of this ruddy country . . ."

"You *are* taking this train to Alexandria ? And then on to England by plane ?"

"That's right, my wench."

The girl lowered her eyes.

"As a matter of fact," she confessed, "I . . . I asked them at the tourist-office to book me the seat next to yours. I need advice, Sir Henry. And you're the only one who can advise me."

"Well, now !" said the great man. He gave a modest, deprecating cough. Observing that one of the attendant pressmen was about to take another photograph, he removed his hat—revealing a large bald head—and glowered ahead into vacancy with a stern, stuffed, heroic look, until the flash-bulb glared and the camera shutter clicked. Then he became (reasonably) human again.

"You were sayin', my wench ?" he prompted.

"I suppose you've read in the papers about the death of Professor Gilray ?"

"Uh-huh."

"And about a certain bronze lamp ?" said Helen. "All the other finds from the tomb are now in the Cairo Museum, of course. But the Egyptian Government presented me with the lamp as a kind of souvenir."

At those galvanizing words, 'bronze lamp', the waiting circle of the press moved in again.

"Excuse me. Lady Helen," began International Features smoothly.

Helen turned to face them. She obviously dreaded the flow of questions which, while perfectly polite, were as tenacious as the coils of an octopus. She was trying to keep her head, trying to smile, trying to pretend that this was only a pleasant little farewell party.

"I'm sorry gentlemen !" she said, raising her voice and standing on tiptoe as though to reach the back row of the reporters. "But, honestly there isn't anything more I can tell you ! And the train's starting at any minute !"

A smooth-voiced chorus deprecated this.

"There's plenty of time, Lady Helen !"

"Sure there is !"

"Just one more picture, Lady Helen !"

"Couldn't we have a picture of you holding up the bronze lamp and looking at it ?"

Helen laughed on a very false note. "I'm sorry, gentlemen ! The bronze lamp is in my luggage."

"What are your plans when you get back to England, Lady Helen ?"

"I'm going to open Severn Hall."

"Severn Hall ? Has it been closed ?"

Backing away a little towards the train, Helen put her hand

18

on the door-handle of the first-class compartment beside which she was standing. An obsequious porter darted forward to open the door for her. She seemed to welcome, with a flush of eagerness, this slight change of subject.

"It's been closed for ages !" she cried. "The only servant there is old Benson, the butler; but I expect he can get together some kind of staff. He . . ."

"But your father's staying on in Cairo. Is that it ?"

"He's following later ! He . . ."

"Is there any truth in the report, Lady Helen, that your father's too sick to be moved ?"

There was a sudden silence in the gritty shadow-and-dazzle of the train shed, a silence so tense with expectancy that you could hear a train whistle distantly up the line.

"*Gentlemen ! Listen to me !*"

"Yes, Lady Helen ?"

"There is absolutely *no* truth in the report. You can say that from me. My . . . my father's perfectly all right. Mr. Robertson is taking care of him."

Argus News Service spoke innocently.

"Then he does need to be taken care of ?"

"I mean . . . !"

"*Is* he ill, Lady Helen ? What about the report ?"

The girl breathed deeply, as though measuring the intensity of every word. Her eyes, almost pleading, moved about the group.

"I repeat, gentlemen. You can say from me that there is not a word of truth in it. This foolish, poisonous, nonsensical story about a curse attached to the tomb, and even to the bronze lamp . . ."

She broke off again, breathing deeply.

"You can say from me," she went on, "that the thing I shall enjoy seeing most when I get back to England is my own room at Severn Hall. I'm going to put that bronze lamp on the mantelpiece; and I'm going to . . . . at least, I'm going to try . . . to write an account giving the real facts of the expedition. When I get back to that room . . ."

A voice on the outer edge of the group spoke agreeably.
It said:

"You will never reach that room, mademoiselle."

3

IN the startled pause that followed, the reporters instinctively craned around and moved back to let him through. And he sidled through their ranks with a fluid smoothness of movement.

He was a very thin man of indeterminate age, perhaps forty, perhaps less. Though well over middle height, he seemed less by reason of his stooped shoulders. On his head he wore the red tarbush, with tassel, which used to be a sign of Turkish citizenship. But his shabby suit of European cut, his white necktie, his French accent in pronouncing English words, all were as indeterminate as a complexion between white and brown.

So he came sidling to the front, smiling and smiling and ducking, but his little black fevered eyes never left Helen's face.

Helen found her voice.

"Who spoke then?" she cried out.

"*I* spoke, mademoiselle," answered the newcomer, appearing so suddenly just under Helen's nose—or, rather, just over her head—that she jumped back. Helen stared at him in confused perplexity.

"Do you," she hesitated, completely at a loss, "do you come from a French newspaper, or something?"

The stranger laughed.

"Alas, no." He upturned the palms of his hands with a sort of comical whimsicality. "I have not that honour. I am a poor scholar of—shall we say?—mixed blood."

Then all the whimsicality fell away from him. A desperate appeal shone out of the little black eyes, and animated his whole cadaverous body. He partly stretched out his hands towards her before letting them fall. His voice, a soft hypnotic bass out of that lean throat, sharpened to a higher pitch.

"And I entreat you," he said, "not to take this stolen relic from the country."

"Stolen relic!" cried Helen.

"Yes, mademoiselle. This bronze lamp."

Again Helen looked around helplessly, angry almost to the point of tears.

"May I point out, Mr. ... ?"

"I am Alim Bey, at your service," replied the stranger. Inclining his head forward, he lightly touched his finger-tips first to his forehead and then to his breast. "*Nahârak sa'îd!*" he added formally.

Helen answered him mechanically.

"*Nahârak sa'îd umbârak*," she said. Then she made a fierce gesture, her voice rising. "May I point out, Alim Bey, that this 'stolen' relic was presented to me by the Egyptian Government?"

Alim Bey lifted his shoulders.

"Forgive me. Had they a right to present it?"

"Yes. I think so."

"It is unfortunate," said Alim Bey, "that we differ." He brought the palms of his hands together, pressing them hard. "I ask you, mademoiselle, please to reflect! You say this lamp is a small thing. I say no."

And then, dominating her, he went on with a rush of words which would not be checked.

"By the light of that lamp, in the black night, a high priest of Ammon saw the dead and wove the spells. This body you tore from its sarcophagus,"—his hands described a gesture of desecration, a brutal and vulturish bit of pantomime,—"this body you tore even from its wooden coffin, was no mere king. No. Let me repeat that he was a high priest of Ammon, skilled in arts beyond your comprehension. He will not be happy."

For a space while you might have counted ten, nobody spoke.

Alim Bey's moving hands, his mad-gleaming eyes that turned on the reporters, emanated such a power of earnestness that momentarily it struck the grins from their faces. But this last was too much. From the press went up a cynical, subdued whoop of delight.

"Wait a minute!" interposed Argus News Service. "You mean ... magic?"

"*Real* magic?" demanded International Features, with every evidence of deep interest.

"I wonder," Mutual Press said thoughtfully, "whether old Pushface could take a rabbit out of a hat?"

"Or saw a woman in half?"

"Or walk through a brick wall?"

"Or ... ?"

21

And the smile returned to Alim Bey's face, but it looked suddenly evil under the grit and dazzle of the train shed. He joined heartily in their amusement, which sounded uglier still.

"You are pleased to joke, messieurs," he told them without offence. "But you will return to me! Yes. In a week, or two weeks, perhaps, you will return to me . . ."

"What for?"

Alim Bey spread out his hands.

"To apologize, messieurs, when this young lady is blown to dust as though she had never existed."

The guard's whistle, thin and shrill, echoed from the other end of the train. Two or three doors slammed like pom-pom guns. The guard's voice, soaring up hoarsely in three languages, conveyed an urgency like that of the muezzin.

"*Quatr yesâfir! En voiture! Get in!*"

Sir Henry Merrivale, who had been surveying this scene in majestic silence, with the corners of his mouth pulled down, intervened for the first time.

Taking Helen firmly by the arm, he impelled her into the carriage. He clambered in after her, and closed the door with a bang. Pausing only long enough to stick his head out of the window and say: "Phooey!" into the face of Alim Bey, H. M. sank down glowering in a corner seat. It was Helen herself, looking a little flushed and dishevelled, who remained at the window to hear a chorus of farewell as the train glided out.

"Good-bye, Lady Helen! Good journey home!"

"Thanks for your help, Lady Helen!"

"Watch out for the goblins, Lady Helen!"

"Don't let old Pushface get you!"

"It's all nonsense, I tell you!" cried Helen, gripping the edge of the lowered window as though she were being torn away from that group. "I'll *prove* it's all nonsense!"

"She will never," said Alim Bey, "reach that room alive."

The blurred voice reached her faintly. A last glimpse she had of him—the red tarbush on his head, shifty-eyed and urbane—as the train carried her away. She stood for a moment at the window, gripping its edges.

Then she turned round and sat down in the corner seat opposite H. M., in an otherwise deserted compartment.

Sun blazed in as they cleared the station; heat pressed down, woollen and prickly; and the rumble of train-wheels sank to a steady clicking. H. M., his scrapbook on the seat beside him, watched Helen as she shook herself angrily, took off her hat, shook back the heavy yellow hair she wore in a short bob and, with a curiously hysterical look around her eyes, at last burst out:

"Who on earth *was* that man ?"

H. M. sniffed.

"I dunno, my wench. An escaped lunatic, most likely."

"Blown to dust as though I had never existed !" Helen clenched her hands. "It's so . . . so ridiculous !"

"Sure it is, my wench. You're not," a small sharp eye fastened on her, "you're not takin' it very seriously, I hope ?"

"No ! Of course not !" cried Helen. And then, uncontrollably, she began to cry.

"Now, now !" roared an acutely embarrassed great man, peering over his spectacles for assistance that did not come. "Now, now, NOW !"

Glowering, muttering direful things about the nature of woman, H. M. lumbered over to sit down beside her; and she promptly cried on his shoulder. There he sat, stern and stuffed and heroic, acutely conscious of the arms round his neck, while the emotional storm exhausted itself. But still he continued to expostulate.

"I got no tie," he said in accents of tragedy. "And my blood-pressure is something awful. Listen, my wench ! There's a pair of scissors in my breast pocket, goddam it ! You'll cut your eye out ! You'll . . . oh, lord love a duck !"

Helen recovered herself.

"I'm awfully sorry," she apologized, slipping away from him and taking the seat opposite, where she tried to regard him with wry humour out of a tear-stained face. "Case of nerves that's all. Don't pay any attention to me."

Opening her handbag, she drew out mirror and handkerchief, and made a mouth of distaste.

"I shall lose this tan," she commented, with desperate lightness, "in three or four days. I always do. But these," she tried to smile, and held out the palm of her hand, "these calluses . . . A hand like a navvy ! . . won't go so easily."

H. M. glowered at her.

"Looky here, my wench. You said you wanted advice. Is that so ?"

"Yes."

"I'm the old man," said H. M. "You tell me."

Helen hesitated.

"It's an accumulation of things, really. I don't need to explain, of course, what our party has been doing for the past two years?"

"Diggin' up old Herihor? Burn me, I should think not! And there's been trouble?"

"Trouble with the Department of Public Works! Trouble with the newspapers! Trouble with tourists! Do you know, for instance, that twelve thousand tourists visited the tomb and the laboratory this season?"

"And what'd these tourists do? Pinch things?"

"Some of them tried to," Helen admitted, her forehead wrinkling. "But, even ordinarily, the responsibility of caring for all that valuable stuff, after the heart-breaking work of moving it and cleaning it ... !"

H. M. eyed her malevolently.

"Looky here, my wench. I've been readin' about old Herihor's treasures until I get fed up and start to gibber. *Is* this stuff as valuable as the newspapers say it is? Jewels and whatnot?"

"No jewels," smiled Helen. "that we should consider valuable nowadays. They used only things like polychrome glass, and lapis-lazuli, and calcite, and obsidian. But most of the possessions and body-ornaments are solid gold; and their antiquarian value .. !"

She drew a deep breath, her brown eyes fixed on the past.

"An American named Beaumont," she went on, "offered us sixty thousand dollars for the gold mask worn by the mummy. He offered equally fantastic sums for things like a gold dagger and a gold perfume box. And he wasn't even a collector or an archæologist, either. All he wanted to do was display them at home as being the property of an Egyptian king more than a thousand years before Christ.

"We simply *couldn't* make him understand that the things weren't ours to sell" She brooded. "There was some trouble about that, too; I don't understand it even yet, but I know it's worrying my father. Towards the end. you know, I felt I had to get out of Egypt or go mad! And then ..."

"Uh-huh?" prompted H. M. "And then?"

"Well," Helen confessed "there's a man."

"So," said H. M., "and you're in love with him?"

Helen sat up straight.

"No! That's just it! I'm not in love with him! Or at least, I don't think so."

She shook her head impatiently, an impatience that was directed against herself, and looked out of the window.

"His name's Sandy Robertson," she continued. "I like him enormously. And I'm running away partly because I don't want to hurt him by saying no."

Then Helen's eyes challenged H. M.

"That sounds silly, doesn't it? Running away just because you don't want to hurt somebody's feelings? But did you ever think how much of our lives we spend, dodging and twisting and making things difficult for ourselves, to avoid hurting somebody's feelings? Even people with absolutely no claim on us?

"Sandy said last night that the whole state of things is wrong. And it is, Sir Henry! It is! There's a great friend of mine at home—Audrey Vane, her name is; she'll probably meet the plane when I get to England—who's completely mad about Sandy Robertson. And he only laughs at her. He treats her like I don't-know-what. Whereas, on the other hand there's a man named Kit Farrell . . ."

Abruptly Helen checked herself, again shaking her head and lifting her shoulders.

"Anyway," she added, "that's a persona issue. It doesn't matter."

"It matters a whole lot," said H. M., "if I'm supposed to be advisin' you."

Helen looked at him in surprise.

"Advice?" she cried. "But I don't want advice about *that*!"

"Then what's on your mind, my wench?"

"Look," said Helen.

Their train had rattled out through pleasant suburbs, past gardens and villas that conveyed a peacefulness of shade and cool water. Far away to the left, past dust-grimed windows, you could now make out the shape of the Pyramids, no less aloof and lonely under a fiery sun, and, still farther beyond, the blue Libyan mountains.

Helen got up. From the well-filled luggage-rack she took down a small suitcase, which she put on the seat beside her. She unlocked it with a key from her handbag, snapped back the clasps, and took out a cardboard box carefully bedded between two layers of underclothing. From the box, and its packing of cotton-wool, she lifted out the bronze lamp.

It was not large, standing no more than four inches high. In shape it resembled a flattened chalice-like cup, the bowl round and bulbous, lined with alabaster. Though its bronze had darkened, there was about it none of that dry and dead appearance we associate with museum pieces; Lord Severn had been too careful about the cleansing. The sunlight made a living entity of the picture carvings which fretted every inch of the bowl.

Helen handed it to H. M. who adjusted his spectacles and turned it over in his fingers.

"Y' know," he said, after a long pause, "this thing sort of makes you creep by sheer weight of antiquity. How old *is* the blighter?"

"A little over three thousand years."

"It's rather a rummy-lookin' sort of lamp, ain't it? How did it work?"

"They filled it full of oil, and then put in a floating wick. You see the pictures carved around the sides?"

"Well?"

"Scenes from the Book of the Dead," said Helen. "Not pleasant ones." She was silent for a moment. "We found it in the inner coffin, close by the mummy's hand."

"And it's not usual to find a lamp there?"

"That's right. Some special value or significance was attached to this."

H. M. weighed the lamp in his hand.

"Not much bigger 'round," he said, "than a ruddy ash-tray. Not much heavier than a big ash-tray, either. What's the hocus-pocus about it?"

"So far as I know, there isn't any. But . . ."

"But what?"

"I want to get away from emotional tangles," said Helen. "I'm going to do exactly what I told those reporters. I'm going down to Severn Hall, as soon as Benson can get it ready for me. I'm going to put the lamp on the mantelpiece in my room, as a proof that the curse is rubbish. I'm going to bury myself there while I write the full story of our expedition. Does it surprise you to hear I have a literary bent?"

26

"No, my wench. I can't say it does."

Helen was looking at him in a curious way, a very curious way.

"But suppose something did happen to me?"

An expression of ghoulish amusement crossed H. M.'s face, and Helen bent forward earnestly.

"Please! I'm perfectly serious!"

"All right. So am I. What's goin' to happen to you?"

Helen glanced out of the window, as though wondering how to approach something.

"You heard what that man said," she pointed out.

"Alim What's-his-name?"

"Yes. 'Blown to dust as though she had never existed'. Of course it couldn't happen. I know that. And yet . . ."

Her voice trailed off. H. M. eyed her with sudden sharp interest. arrested by the change that had come over her.

Helen was staring out of the window, apparently at the dim line of the Pyramids moving past in the distance. Her body was rigid. her delicate mouth partly open. What she saw there what held her transfixed and hardly breathing, would have been difficult to determine. Then she nodded to herself. She brushed the palms of her hands together, slowly. When she turned round to face him again, it was with a bright. blind absorbed look which scarcely saw him.

"Sir Henry," she began, and cleared her throat.

"Uh-huh?"

"Please forget everything I've been saying to you."

"*What's that?*"

'I said I needed your advice. That was true, a few minutes ago. But I don't want it." Suddenly her voice rose in a quaver like terror. "I don't want it! I don't want it! I don't want it!"

4

APRIL in England came with a cold drench of rain which sponged out even the memory of Egypt. And nowhere was the chill felt more than at Severn Hall.

To reach Severn Hall from London is a pleasant enough journey if you have a car. But by train it is a tedium of changing; something over three hours, via Swindon and Purton, to Gloucester. At Gloucester you take a bus or taxi, and drive south-west in the direction of Sharpcross until the high stone boundary-wall of the vast estate looms up for what seems like miles along the road.

You enter the grounds through open iron gates, past a lodge, and up a winding gravel drive. It takes nearly two minutes to negotiate that long drive, even in a car. And then you look, with astonishment, on Severn Hall.

This passion for the 'Gothic' was started, about the middle of the eighteenth century, by a certain Mr. Horace Walpole. Mr. Walpole bought a modest villa at Twickenham, and gradually set about enlarging it in what his romantic soul imagined to be a medieval manner. Darkling towers, stained glass—'lean windows fattened by rich saints'—a profusion of antique armour and weapons, gladdened his heart at Strawberry Hill. Mr. Walpole presently wrote a novel called *The Castle of Otranto*. And he began a literary fashion which, with the assistance of Mrs. Radcliffe and 'Monk' Lewis, lasted well into the nineteenth century.

Our great-great-grandmothers thrilled to these romances. 'Is it horrid?' asks one of them eagerly, in Miss Austen's gentle satire. 'Have you read it? Are you sure it is horrid?'

Gentle-eyed heroines were pursued by wicked counts through the corridors of mouldering castles. The Gothic in architecture became a fad with those who were romantic enough or wealthy enough. And one of these, about the year 1794, was the wife of the first Earl of Severn.

Lady Severn thereupon devilled her husband, who was making money hand over fist, to build a house which should be worthy of his newly acquired peerage. Lord Severn didn't like the idea much, being a plain man who would have preferred something more in the line of comfort. But he was deeply in love with his Augusta—whose portrait still hangs at Severn—and he threw himself with determination into the resulting architectural beano.

Severn Hall, when completed, was something like Strawberry Hill itself, but much larger and more encrusted with battlements. It had arabesques in stone, it had rooms of medieval draughtiness, it had stained glass.

"So damned much stained glass," complained the second

Earl, about the beginning of Victoria's reign, "that a man can't see out of his own windows."

And yet it appealed to generations of that family. Even its mock dungeon, with manacles—where you could shut up a snoring guest after his third bottle of port, and watch him turn green when he awoke in the morning—appealed to some imaginative strain the Lorings never quite lost. If the present Earl had kept it closed for several years, it was mainly because the state of his health compelled him to spend so much time abroad.

But now it was being opened again.

On this rainy afternoon, Thursday the twenty-seventh of April, Severn Hall bloomed again with fires and lights. There had been a frantic short-time effort to put the place in order. In the butler's pantry at tea-time, looking benevolently on Mrs. Pomfret the housekeeper, sat Mr. Benson the butler.

"Newspapers!" said Benson, shaking his head. He ended almost on a sigh. "Newspapers. newspapers, newspapers!"

"Yes, Mr. Benson," said Mrs. Pomfret obediently.

The butler's pantry was at the end of a narrow passage backstairs, shut off by a green-baize door which opened out at the rear of the main hall. Mr. Benson sat at his ease in a rocking-chair, while Mrs. Pomfret preferred to sit formally on the edge of a straight chair.

Privately, Mrs. Pomfret wondered why she had been invited to the butler's pantry at all. It hadn't occurred in any of her previous positions. She wondered uneasily whether this might be an indication of 'goings-on'.

Mr. Benson didn't look like that sort of man. But none of them did, first off.

If Mr. Benson had been taller, she thought, he might have been a fine figure of a man; certainly a fine figure of a butler. As it was, being short and plumpish, he had to do the best he could with his own natural dignity.

He sat back comfortably in the rocking-chair, radiating good nature. Mr. Benson's thin grey-white hair was brushed with great nicety. His light blue eyes, his pinkish complexion, his broad mouth, all expressed the same combination of good nature with dignity. Black coat, striped trousers, dark tie sombre against wing collar, these were as sleek and correct as his polished nails. After a weighty pause, as though for consideration, he spoke once more.

"Shall I tell you something, Mrs. Pomfret?"

"Yes, Mr. Benson?"

"I am not, I think." said Benson judicially, "a superstitious man."

Mrs. Pomfret registered shock.

"I should hope not, Mr. Benson!"

"And yet I was relieved—I admit it!—when I heard her ladyship had arrived back in England."

(Now for it! Confidences!)

A little shiver went through Mrs. Pomfret. It was not caused by the spatter of rain against the windows, or the faint white lightning that showed the sodden park outside—though pity the poor gardeners who had to work on a day like this! A bright coal fire burned in the grate; in fact, every room in the house had its roaring fire to drive out the damp. Firelight illumined the snug pantry, gleaming on the display of silver plate behind glass-fronted cabinets.

And Mrs. Pomfret leaned forward.

"If one might be so bold as to ask a question, Mr. Benson . . . ?"

Benson held out his hands towards the fire. "By all means, Mrs. Pomfret! By all means!"

"Why," asked Mrs. Pomfret, "does her ladyship stay in London? According to the newpapers, or at least the one I read, she's been back for nearly a fortnight."

"To be correct," said the meticulous Benson, taking a tiny diary out of his inside pocket and consulting it, "since the fifteenth of April."

"Then why doesn't she come on here, if she's not afraid of anything?"

At those ominous words 'afraid of anything', some of the benevolence faded out of Benson's manner.

"Her ladyship won't be very comfortable, I'm sure," pursued Mrs. Pomfret. "A wretcheder lot of servants I've never seen! And the plumber taking so long, and being so insolent! And the grounds, if you'll pardon my saying so, hardly in decent repair! But at least . . ."

"At least?" prompted Benson politely.

"Well!" said Mrs. Pomfret, hardly knowing herself what she meant.

"We have been in residence," Benson pointed out, "only

three days.   And," he coughed, "Mr. Kit Farrell is in London."

"Ah !" said Mrs. Pomfret.   "Might one enquire whether her ladyship and Mr. Farrell . . . ?"

"No, Mrs. Pomfret."   He was kindly but firm.   "It is perhaps better *not* to enquire."

Mrs. Pomfret sat up straight.

"No offence intended, I'm sure !"

"And none taken," beamed Benson, all amiability again. "As for her ladyship, Mrs. Pomfret, you need have no fear. She will join us in her own time.   I can also assure you, knowing her as I do, that she will warn us in good time to prepare a suitable . . ."

On the sideboard beside the fireplace, the telephone rang.

Was there, Mrs. Pomfret wondered, a shade of anxiety in his manner as he got up to answer the phone.   In any case, she had one of those inspired previsions which she was to talk about to the end of her days.

Mrs. Pomfret also got to her feet, contemplating her own image in the mirror behind the clock over the fireplace.   A well-preserved woman of fifty, not unattractive, and only another woman would have known that her chestnut-coloured hair was dyed.

She heard Benson say: "Telegram ?   Will you read it out, please ?"   She heard Mr. Golding at the post office laboriously reading, a thin sound in that overheated room.   She heard Benson repeating it.   But Elizabeth Pomfret, with a sense of shock which frightened her and which she did not like, had already guessed what it was.

" 'Driving down with Kit Farrell and Audrey Vane.' " Benson backed away, still holding the phone, so that he could see the clock on the mantelpiece.   " 'Expect me before . . .' "   He broke off.   "Before what time, did you say ?   Five ?"

Another rain-laden gust of wind rattled the windows.   A drop hissed down the chimney into the fire.   And the little clock on the mantelpiece, as though diabolically inspired, began to strike five.

"Oh, dear !" said Mrs. Pomfret.

Benson was still craning to look at the clock.

"What time," he demanded, "was this telegram handed in ?   Never mind !   Thank you !"

He replaced the receiver and put down the phone on the

sideboard. He was still staring at it when a bell pealed again, and Benson had snatched up the phone for a second time before he seemed to realize that this was the house telephone on the wall. When he answered this, Mrs. Pomfret could now distinguish the heavier voice of Leonard, the lodge-keeper at the front gates.

Again Benson put back the receiver. His colour came and went like that of a much younger man.

"We must not lose our heads, Mrs. Pomfret !" he said. "We must not lose our heads !"

"What . . . ?"

"That was the lodge-keeper. Lady Helen and Mr. Kit and Miss Audrey drove through the gates just now. They'll be here any minute."

Now this, from the standpoint of an old-school servant, was really serious. Mrs. Pomfret was shocked.

"Mrs. Benson ! We must assemble the others !"

"There isn't time for that," cried a thoroughly human Benson. "We shall be lucky to get to the front door before her ladyship. We must hurry ! We . . ." He paused, and looked very hard at her. "But I hope, Mrs. Pomfret, that this disposes of any notions you may have been getting ?"

"Notions, Mr. Benson ?"

"A fortune-teller named Alim Bey prophesied that Lady Helen would never reach this house alive. Well ! She *is* here."

"If you'll pardon the correction, Mr. Benson, that was not exactly what the fortune-teller said."

"How do you mean ?"

"The fortune-teller, if the newspapers report him correctly, did not say her ladyship would never reach this house alive. He said she would never reach *her room* alive."

Benson's eyebrows went up.

"This is surely a quibble, Mrs. Pomfret ?"

"I merely wish to be accurate, Mr. Benson."

"My God, Mrs. Pomfret, what could happen to her now ?"

It was the housekeeper's turn to raise her eyebrows at such language.

"Really, Mr. Benson. And might I suggest that it is you who are delaying us, after insisting we must hurry ?"

"Yes," agreed Benson. "Yes. We must hurry."

His old urbane self again, he went over and opened the door to the passage, ceremoniously gesturing her to precede him. But, as she went out. he stopped her.

"Mrs. Pomfret !"

"Yes, Mr. Benson ?'

"To a person of your experience—and, if I may say so, your breeding—I shall not venture to offer any advice. But, when you are presented to Lady Helen, I hope you will, er, express pleasure at being here ?"

"Naturally, Mrs. Benson !"

"That is so, is it not ?   You like the house ?"

"Frankly, Mr. Benson, I don't. It's a *horrible* house."

Benson was honestly surprised.

"Full of nasty things," explained Mrs. Pomfret, "and all about being dead.   Not, of course, that I shall say anything about it to her ladyship.   No, Mr. Benson !   I trust I know my duties better than that !"

She marched out into the passage.   And, at the same moment, lightning blazed into it through the glass panel of a door at the rear.

It was a narrow interior passage, carpeted in coconut matting, and with faded yellow-brown paper concealing its stone walls.   No amount of airing could ever take away its fustiness.   At the front end was the green-baize door leading to the main hall.   At the back was a glass-panelled door which admitted daylight.

As the lightning ran along that passage, picking out with white clarity the dark surfaces of three or four pictures which hung on the walls, Mrs. Pomfret stopped short.

"Mr. Benson !   Look there !"

"Really, Mrs. Pomfret . . . !"

"It's gone," said the housekeeper.

"What's gone ?"

"A big painting, hundreds of years old, that hung on the wall over there.   It was there at lunch-time.   I saw it. And now it's gone."

Benson's lips drew together.

"You must be mistaken, Mrs. Pomfret."

"I'm not mistaken, thank you.   You can see the oblong of cleaner paper where it's been hanging.   Look !"

"Perhaps it was moved by one of the maids."

"Without my orders ?"   She was withering.   "Or yours ?"

"For the last time, Mrs. Pomfret, I must entreat you to hurry! Her ladyship may be at the front door now. I shall not be entirely happy, and I admit it, until I see Lady Helen again. This matter of the painting, if it is of any importance, can be dealt with later. Will you kindly go ahead of me?"

"Nasty things!" said Mrs. Pomfret.

It indicates Benson's state of mind that he so far forgot himself as to seize his companion by the elbow and impel her forward. Mrs. Pomfret disengaged herself with silent rebuke. And, as rain-whips stung against glass and the terror gathered round Severn Hall, they moved together towards the green-baize door.

5

THE car was a long, blue, low-slung Riley, one of those coupés in which you mash your hat over your eyes every time you get in or out. Mr. Christopher Farrell, sitting at the wheel as they swung through the entrance-gates of Severn Hall, even had to keep his head down when he drove.

By this time, it is to be recorded, Kit Farrell was a badly worried young man.

Beside him in the front seat was Helen. He glanced at her surreptitiously. Then he contented himself with studying the ghost of her reflection in the windshield, while the wind shield-wiper ticked away against a faint drizzle.

"Well," he said, with loud cheerfulness, "we're nearly there."

"Yes," agreed Helen. "Nearly there."

The owner of the car, Miss Audrey Vane, was trying to lounge among suitcases in the cramped back seat.

"You two," Audrey complained, "are the most horribly depressing people I've ever met. I've been trying to entertain you with light conversation all the way from town. And you haven't heard a word of it. Now have you?"

"Yes," said Helen.

"No," said Kit. "I mean," he hastened to correct himself, "here we go."

The car roared through the gates on to gravel.

Helen's face was pale, and there were shadows under her eyes. She stared straight ahead, smoking a cigarette with the air of one unaccustomed to it. Either the car jolted, or her hand was unsteady, for she dropped the cigarette on the floor, and had to bend down and pick it up.

Kit Farrell never forgot any detail of her appearance then. She wore a grey mackintosh pulled closely round her. She held tightly to the cardboard box—he didn't know what was in that box, and didn't like to ask—she had carried for the whole journey. He noticed her tan stockings, and the scarlet and black patent-leather shoes that looked so incongruous in the country.

On their right was the lodge, a little octagon-shaped stone house with a window in each side. Firelight shone from the trellised windows. They could see the white shirt-sleeves and grizzled hair of the lodge-keeper, peering out with his hands cupped over his eyes. Then, as they swept past, they saw him dive for the telephone.

"Evidently," said Audrey, "they're not expecting us."

Helen woke up a little, throwing her cigarette out of the window.

"I told Benson not to expect me for another week. He'll be furious with me for not sending that telegram sooner." She turned her head and smiled. "Is it an awful bore for you, Kit ? Leaving your work to come down here ?"

(My God, he thought, if you only knew !)

"No," he said, with a sort of embarrassed gruffness. "No, that's all right."

He was conscious of Audrey's eyes, fixed on Helen and on himself with affectionate amusement. He hoped Audrey wouldn't pipe up with any facetious remarks.

"Poor Kit !" was what Audrey, actually said. "How's the legal business ? Any new briefs ?"

"I had a brief," said Kit, "two months ago. About a dog," he confessed gloomily. "It wasn't very interesting."

"Or profitable ?"

"Or profitable."

Audrey laughed.

Though she was only five or six years older than Helen, and certainly not as old as Kit, she affected great motherliness towards both of them. Audrey exuded the aura of Mayfair in the bright, sterile nineteen-thirties. A slim, dark-haired, dark-eyed girl, with a vivid make-up and clothes which even Kit recognized as being of exceptional smartness, she put a hand on the shoulder of both the persons sitting in front of her.   It was a light, soft touch.

"What I ought to do for you, Kit," she declared, "or maybe Helen should do it instead"—he caught her smile in the driving mirror, and glowered—"is commit a crime. Then you could lead for the defence and make a terrific name for yourself."

"You don't lead for the defence until you're a K.C."

"Oh.   And how long before you get to be a K.C. ?"

"About fifteen years, I should think."

Audrey was considerably damped.

"Well," she insisted, "couldn't you be junior to some big-wig and just steal his thunder ?   Make the poor old horse look absolutely silly ?   What'd happen then ?"

"I damn well never would get to be a K.C."

"You barristers aren't a very go-ahead lot," said Audrey. "And I still think . . ."

The sky went pale with lightning, making them all blink. Against it moved the tops of oak-trees, budding but not yet in full leaf, under which the broad drive curved. All of them fell silent, listening to the slur of wheels on gravel, until they at length emerged before the Hall.

In front of Severn Hall were big hedges and trees of box and evergreen, clipped into the shapes of animals and chess-men after the Italian style.   Beyond these and the turn of the drive, two shallow steps led up to a stone terrace.   And set back from the terrace, piled up in an immense splendour of eighteenth-century grandioseness, rose the Gothic citadel of which the first Countess of Severn had dreamed.

Ivy, nowadays known to be productive of vermin, had been trained to grow across its face.   There was a clock-tower, half lost in rain, from which bygone romantics could hear the hours ring dismally above their musings. The immense front door, under its pointed stone arch, was of oak bound with iron.   Pointed windows had an air of aloofness, even where lights gleamed inside them or sharpened the colours of stained glass.   Notable was the line of stained-glass windows just over the front door.

"At last !"   Helen said abruptly.

As though in that rain-sharp air she breathed a new atmosphere, Helen was shaken into life.   Opening the door of the car, she sprang out and faced her companions.

"I said I was going to do it," she cried. "and now I *am*."

Kit stared at her. "Do what?"

Helen was smiling, though her eyes looked strained. She opened the cardboard box.

This was the first time either Kit or Audrey had seen the bronze lamp. But no explanations were necessary. They knew what it was, as half the world knew. Helen threw the discarded box back into the car, and held the lamp in both hands. It looked very small, a withered toy incapable of harm, as a drop of rain struck its edge.

"This goes on the mantelpiece in my room," said Helen. "And then, Kit. . . ! *Then!* Excuse me."

And she turned round and ran quickly up the two steps, across the terrace.

"Helen! Look! Wait a minute!"

The shout was wrung from Kit Farrell; he never knew why. But Audrey spoke softly.

"Let her go, Kit."

Twisting the iron ring which served as a knob, Helen pushed open the big front door. For a brief second he saw her standing there—a small figure, intensely beloved, with the lights from the main hall shining golden on her hair—before she slipped inside and closed the door with a soft slam. Then there was only the faint spatter of the rain, running across stone terrace-flags and rustling among grotesque shapes of box and evergreen.

"Ah, well" muttered Kit Farrell. He began hauling suitcases out of the car, ranging them in a neat line beside the running-board.

Audrey drew a transparent waterpool over her short silver-fox cape. She slipped out over the up-ended front seat, as trim and *soignée* as though the waterproof were a kind of cellophane wrapping. He saw the twinkle of amusement in her eyes as he went towards the back of the car, where a cabin trunk and two more valises were fastened with straps to the luggage-grid.

"Kit."

"Uh?"

"You idiot," said Audrey. "Why don't you marry the girl?"

"Now look here, Audrey . . . ."

She followed him, and watched while he yanked violently at the nearest trunk-strap.

"You're so gone on Helen," she went on, "that you're practically a public danger. She suffers from the same complaint about you. And both of you show it. Then where's your enterprise, Kit? What on earth is the matter with you?"

Kit looked very hard at the trunk, giving another violent tug at the strap, before he raised his eyes.

"I'm no good," he stated flatly.

"Why not?"

"I don't make money."

"Well! Neither does Sandy Robertson. But that doesn't prevent him from . . ." Audrey's voice raised a little. "I saw your eyebrows come together, Kit Farrell! Were you going to make some remark about Sandy?"

"Lord, no," said Kit in surprise. "I envy him."

"Oh?"

"You can't imagine Sandy staying anywhere except at the best hotels. He's known in every West End bar and night club. No horse or dog track is complete without him. I wish," said Kit despondently, getting the first strap loose and attacking the second, "I wish I knew how the hell he does it. When I take somebody out to dinner at the Savoy or the Berkeley, I live off sardines and biscuits for the rest of the month."

Audrey threw back her head and laughed.

"Honest Kit, the People's Choice," she commented fondly. "That's because you insist on paying."

"Naturally I insist on paying! What's so very odd about that?"

"Besides, Sandy has a lot of luck with the dogs and the horses."

"That's no good to me, I'm afraid. I had a fling once because I liked the name of the horse, and at the end of the race they were still looking for him with a lantern."

"Then you won't do what you want to do," smiled Audrey, "simply because Helen is the daughter of the Earl of Severn with umpteen thousand a year? Isn't that rather old-fashioned of you?"

"Is it?" enquired Kit. With a sudden powerful heave, as though to find an outlet for his feelings, he lifted the heavy cabin trunk and brought it to the ground with a bang.

"All I know," he added simply, "is that it never works. I had a friend once who married a girl with money. The last time I saw him, she was handing him his bus fare and saying she hoped she could trust him with it. No, thanks, Audrey. No, thanks."

"Suppose something happened to Helen?"

"*What's that?*"

"I mean, suppose she married Sandy Robertson?"

Kit contemplated her for a moment. Then he swept up an armful of small luggage under his left hand, and picked up the biggest of the suitcases with his right.

"This rain isn't doing your fancy hat any good, Audrey. Come on."

They crossed the terrace without speaking. In response to Kit's nod, Audrey turned the iron ring and swung open the big door. With a pleasant sense of home-coming if not of well-being, Kit crossed the threshold after her. He had dropped the luggage on the floor, with its resultant echo from a lofty roof, before he realized that something was wrong.

Motionless in the middle of the main hall stood Benson and a woman whom he supposed to be the housekeeper. Kit Farrell was a great favourite of Benson's, and knew it. He expected the quietly beaming welcome, the inclination of the head, the bustling forward to take the luggage. Instead Benson merely stood and looked at him out of round light blue eyes.

"Hel-lo, Benson!" said Kit, obstinately cheerful. His voice sounded hollow under the groined roof. "Mind giving me a hand with all this stuff?"

"Mr. Kit, sir! Allow me!" Then Benson did move forward, instinctively. But he stopped half way. "Sir," he added, "may I ask where Lady Helen is?"

"Lady Helen?"

"Yes, sir."

"Haven't you seen her?"

"No, sir."

"But she came in here not three minutes ago! She was going straight upstairs! She wanted to put that infernal bronze lamp on the mantelpiece in her room!"

"I rather doubt, sir, whether her ladyship did that."

On the housekeeper's face there was an expression of something very much like horror. Benson, too, was behaving oddly. He kept his hands behind his back, as though he were hiding something. Kit's voice went up.

"Look here, Benson, what *is* all this?"

"Well, sir." The butler moistened his lips and took another step forward. Footsteps, as well as voices, had a hollow sound here. Benson's eyes moved sideways. "We ... I really do beg your pardon, sir! And yours too, Miss Audrey! This—this is Mrs. Pomfret."

"How do you do?" Kit said mechanically. "Well?"

"Mrs. Pomfret and I were in my pantry, sir. The lodge-keeper phoned to say the car was on its way up."

"Yes?"

"We came down the passage, sir, through the green-baize door there into the hall here. We did not see Lady Helen, Mr. Kit. But in the middle of the floor here we found these."

Benson took his hands from behind his back. In one hand he held Helen's grey mackintosh, with the raindrops still on it. In the other hand he held the bronze lamp.

Silence.

The electric lighting here was concealed, so that nowhere did you see any anachronistic bulb. It gave a bleak, bare radiance to a groined vault already bleak and bare enough. But there were two wide fireplaces, one on each side of the main hall; in each a big blaze of logs softened the harshness of stone. By the upper edge of one fireplace, and by the lower edge of the other opposite, stood a suit of Milanese armour, one black, the other inlaid with gilt. A steep staircase—even its balustrade of arabesque stone—curved up along the right-hand wall at the rear.

Again Benson moistened his lips.

"I suppose, sir," he held up the lamp, "this object is what I think it is? I've only seen pictures of it, of course."

Kit ignored this.

"Where did you find those things, Benson?"

"Thrown down in the middle of the floor, sir. Where I was standing a moment ago."

Kit inflated his lungs for a yell.

"Helen!" he bellowed. And his voice came back to him in an echo, but there was no reply.

"Steady, Kit," interposed Audrey. "This is absurd!"

40

"Of course it's absurd. Helen's here. We saw her go in. She's got to be here. *Helen!*"

"Probably," insisted Audrey, "she went upstairs after all."

They jerked up their heads, now, as they heard footsteps on the staircase. But in the first clump of those hobnailed boots Kit's hopes died. Down the stairs tramped a stocky, gnarled, elderly man with a truculent expression. He wore a stained coat above stained overalls, and carried a leather tool-bag. His appearance shocked Benson back into normal behaviour.

"Just one moment, sir," Benson implored Kit. He swung round towards the man on the staircase. "And who, may I ask, are you?"

The newcomer stopped short.

"Me?"

"Yes, you!"

An expression of unholy relish animated the man's face. He completed the descent, making an event of each step, before answering. Then he walked up to Benson.

"I'm the plumber, Duke," he said hoarsely. "That's 'oo I am. Bill Powers, Duke. Thirty-seven 'Igh Street."

"Didn't I tell you?" cried Mrs. Pomfret under her breath. "Insolence!"

"Don't you know better than to use the main staircase?" Mr. Powers welcomed this.

"Do you know wot I am, Duke?"

"I have not the slightest interest. . ."

"I'm a Socialist, see? A bloke," explained Mr. Powers, "that's as good as anybody else. Stairs is stairs, Duke. It's all one to me."

Kit brushed aside this discussion. "Never mind the politics, old man! Did you see the young lady?"

"Wot young lady?"

"The young lady who went up those stairs only a few minutes ago!"

"There's been nobody up these stairs, governor."

Kit exchanged a glance with Audrey, who shrugged her shoulders.

"Now wait a minute!" Kit persisted "Where were you?"

"In the bathroom opposite the 'ead of the stairs."

"With the door open?"

41

"Ah."

"Didn't you hear anybody come into the house?"

Mr. Powers's belligerency was gradually fading into real interest. He pushed his hat to the back of his head, ruffling his fingers into greyish black hair heavily brilliantined.

"Oh, ah!" he muttered. "Come to think of it, I did!"

"Well, then!"

Mr. Powers made a gesture, slowly.

"The front door opens and closes, see? And I 'ear a woman's voice—young, it was—say something I don't catch. Then there was some footsteps on this stone floor 'ere, and then . . ."

"Then what?"

"They stopped."

"What do you mean, stopped?"

"The footsteps stopped," replied Mr. Powers, staring at memory. "They didn't go nowhere."

Again silence, while only the firelight moved.

Benson, concealing whatever he felt beneath his dignity, held out the mackintosh and the lamp. Kit took them. About an article of clothing worn by a loved one, even a crumpled mackintosh, there is so intense and painful a reminder of absence that the loved one's image grows even more vivid. But the bronze lamp was different. Incredibly ancient, winking malevolently where the firelight caught it . . .

"Benson!"

"Sir?"

"I don't want you to think I'm scatty."

"No, sir."

"But this isn't exactly unexpected."

Benson quivered. "I beg your pardon, sir?"

"Something happened in London," said Kit, "that scared the ears off me. I want you to find Helen, Benson." He gestured fiercely, forestalling reply, and spoke to convince himself. "This *may* be perfectly all right, you understand. Nothing to be alarmed about. Nothing at all. But—find her, Benson! Do you hear me? Find her!"

6

Eight o'clock.

Someone, invisible, had late that afternoon finished repairing the clock in the tower. They heard the hour ring out, faintly and dismally, as they waited in one of the few rooms at Severn which had been fitted out in modern fashion—Helen's room up on the first floor.

It was long and spacious, a combination of bedroom and sitting-room, with a line of windows overlooking the front lawn just above the main hall. When the curtains were drawn against darkness, you might have imagined yourself anywhere but at Severn Hall.

Panels of light grey wood masked the stone walls. There was a fitted carpet on the floor. The easy-chairs had bright cretonne covers; lamplight shone on a white marble mantelpiece, with a modern etching above and a wink of brass and irons below. There were white painted book-shelves at waist level. And a door at one end led to a dressing-room similarly decorated.

When they had first come in here to wait, and wait, and wait still longer—they found a fire burning, and a bowl of fresh yellow flowers on the writing-table. Now Helen's luggage, including the cabin trunk, was piled eloquently at the foot of the bed. Kit's first action had been to put the bronze lamp in the centre of the mantelpiece.

He stared at it now out of a fog of cigarette smoke, and then threw his dozenth cigarette into the fire.

"Audrey. Suppose Helen's dead."

"Don't!" cried Audrey, and stirred uneasily. She was sitting with her knees drawn up beneath her on a sofa turned sideways to the fireplace. A tall girl, perhaps a little too tall. But her glossy black hair, her bright dark eyes with the sharply defined lashes, the vivid dark-red mouth, were softened and warmed by firelight.

"Don't talk like that!" she protested, moving her shoulders. "How can Helen be dead?"

"I don't know."

"It's absurd! Who would want to hurt her?"

"I don't know that either."

Kit resumed his pacing, his hands dug into the pockets of

a rather shabby coat. If anybody had asked Audrey Vane to write down the thoughts which crowded through her mind at that moment, she would wildly have scribbled something like this:

He *is* attractive, in a grey-eyed Irish way. Brown hair cut close. Vertical line between the eyebrows. Not attractive like Sandy Robertson, of course. When she thought of Sandy, that dirty dog, a rush of anguish went through her and stung behind the eyes. No, not like Sandy. But still attractive. Exactly suited to Helen; that's it. Oh, God, if anything *has* happened to Helen . . . !

"Kit. What are you thinking?"

Brooding, he stopped short.

"Do you remember the day we met Helen's plane at Croydon?"

"Yes."

"The plane," said Kit, "was thirty minutes late. Only delayed by fog, of course. But . . ."

"You started to worry?"

"It wasn't ten minutes late," replied Kit, "before I started wondering, suppose the plane's crashed? Suppose they ring up to tell us we'll never see Helen again? It got so blasted vivid that by the end of twenty minutes I was practically convinced the plane *had* crashed. I could see Helen all over the place; I could imagine every expression on her face; but she wasn't there. I wondered what it would be like if they came and told me she was dead mangled or some infernal thing.

"It's the same thing now, Audrey. We've got to stop scaring ourselves. Our common sense ought to tell us there's some simple explanation."

The door of the room softly opened, and Benson came in.

Behind him, obviously bubbling with suppressed excitement, came a lanky tow-haired young man in a chauffeur's uniform. Both Benson and the chauffeur had the look of being brushed and their hands new-washed, as though after a long and grimy job.

Audrey Vane started to get up from the sofa, but sat down again. It was a few seconds before Kit could trust himself to speak; and, even then, Benson got in first.

"According to your instructions, Mr. Kit," he nodded his head towards the chauffeur, as he might have nodded towards a dog, "Lewis and I have just made a search of the house."

"Well ?"

Benson's face in the mist of cigarette smoke had an ugly, evasive and perspiring look. He cleared his throat.

"First of all, sir, it's absolutely certain that Lady Helen did come into the house."

Kit stared at him.

"Of course she came into the house ! Didn't Miss Vane and I tell you so ?" He paused as Audrey started to laugh. "Wait a minute, Benson ! You didn't by any chance doubt *our* story ?"

Benson changed colour. "No, sir. Of course not. But . . ."

"But what ?"

"Will you hear the rest of it, sir ?"

"Sorry. Go on !"

"The under-gardener," pursued Benson, "was working on the front lawn. He saw Lady Helen go in, and you and Miss Audrey following with the luggage." Benson paused. "It's also established, sir, that her ladyship hasn't left the house since then."

Audrey Vane sat up straight.

"How can you be sure she hasn't left the house, Benson ?"

"We're putting the grounds in order, Miss Audrey !"

"Yes; well ?"

"We have employed," the butler explained, "about a dozen men, to go on until the work is finished. There were people working on every side of the Hall this afternoon. Every door, every window, was under observation. I want you to believe that, Mr. Kit, because all the temporary gardeners—they're well-known characters in Gloucester, and wouldn't lie—can confirm it. Unfortunately . . ."

"Go on !"

And now it came out in a rush, while Benson's fingers twitched at his sides.

"Unfortunately, sir. Lady Helen is not in the house either."

There was a brief silence.

"*What's that ?*"

"Lady Helen sir," Benson repeated stolidly, "is not in the house."

"Look here, Benson.   Are you clean daft?"

"No, sir."

"But . . ."

"You told me to search, sir."   The butler's voice was growing louder.   "And we did search, Lewis and I."   His glance indicated the goggle-eyed chauffeur, who hovered seething in the background.   "I've known Severn Hall ever since I was a boy.   And there's not an inch of it—take my word for that, Mr. Kit—we didn't search!   Lady Helen is not in the house."

What Kit Farrell felt during those first minutes was not so much fear or anxiety as a creepy and dazed kind of disbelief.

This wasn't happening.   It couldn't be happening.   If, for example, you are told by a sober and serious-looking informant that some friend of yours has got up from a chair and floated without support out of a third floor window, your first reaction is not apt to be anxiety in case the friend has fallen.   You feel instead that your wits have caught in a cog-wheel, that your brain is not working, and that at the same time you are being the victim of a solemn-faced practical joke.

But it wasn't a practical joke.

Kit glanced at Audrey, who was now kneeling bolt upright on the sofa, supporting herself with one hand on the edge of the mantelpiece, and looking at Benson with the same stunned incredulity.   Kit adopted a tone of dogged reasonableness.

"Listen, Benson.   This is rank lunacy."

"Yes, sir."

"You can't tell me that Helen, carrying a bronze lamp, walked into this house and then vanished like a soap bubble!"

"No, sir."

"It's impossible!"

"Yes, sir.   I also came to tell you," Benson added, "that dinner will be served in ten minutes."

"Dinner," said Kit.   "Dinner!"

"I'm very sorry, Mr. Kit."   Benson's own eyes, a guileless blue, also looked strained.   "It—it can be postponed, of course, if you prefer."   Then Benson, inflating his chest, swung round on the unfortunate chauffeur.   "Will you please explain, Lewis, why you are still here?" he demanded though Kit had not heard him order the chauffeur to go out. "It seems a pity, Lewis, a very great pity, if my instructions are to be continually disobeyed!"

But young Lewis, a gawky tall figure shifting from one foot to the other, could no longer be repressed.

"Sir," he appealed to Kit, "I seen a film once."

"Don't stop him!" urged Kit, as Benson's cold eyes turned once more towards the chauffeur. "If he's got anything to say, let him say it!"

"I seen a film once," explained Lewis, "where they hid the body in a mummy case."

"What body?" cried Audrey in horror.

Lewis was brought up with a bump.

It had honestly never occurred to him that he was scaring anybody. Like the others he was a new servant; to him Lady Helen Loring was only a fascinating name; his idea was murder, the bloody kind of murder he relished in the newspapers, and the expression on his listeners' faces brought him up, gasping, with something of a qualm in the stomach.

"What Lewis means," Benson spoke with crushing weight, "is that in his lordship's study downstairs there are two or three sarcophagi brought back from Egypt." He gave Kit a meaning glance. "The rest of the suggestion, Mr. Kit, you can guess."

"I see," said Kit. "Did you look inside the mummy cases?"

"Yes, sir."

"And did you find . . . ?"

"No, sir."

"But what I mean is," persisted the chauffeur, "that it gave me another idea. About a film, I mean. After all, sir, the young lady's got to be *somewhere*, now hasn't she? And in this other film they put the body in a secret hiding place in the wall that nobody could find." At a loss for words, Lewis made a gesture that seemed to embrace the whole house. "Look around at this place, sir! See what I mean?"

Kit Farrell caught at the hope.

"A secret hiding place," he declared, "is very definitely an idea. You hear that, Benson?"

"Yes, sir."

"What do you say to it?"

"It isn't feasible, Mr. Kit."

"Why not?"

With a murmured word of apology, Benson moved past Kit and approached the low bookshelves built under the line of windows. They watched him in dead silence, while the fire crackled and popped. Fitting on a pair of shell-rimmed spectacles, he bent down and selected a fat blue-bound book. When he turned round again, holding the book diffidently, the spectacles against his pink complexion gave him a homely clerical appearance.

"This, sir," Benson held up the book, "is Mr. Horace Linnell's great work."

"Well? What about it?"

"I am instructed to say, sir, that Mr. Linnell is the greatest living authority on secret passages and secret hiding places. May I take the liberty of reading you something from it?"

Kit felt a constriction at his collar.

"Are you going to tell us," he asked, "that there's no such thing as a secret hiding place at Severn Hall?"

Benson inclined his head.

"Yes, sir. With the permission of his lordship, Mr. Linnell spent a fortnight's investigation here. He states quite definitely, for architectural reasons I'm afraid I don't understand, that there isn't and couldn't be any kind of secret hiding place."

Opening the book, Benson, slowly turned over its pages. His finger stopped at the page he was looking for.

"*I say this with regret*," he read aloud, "*since I approached this investigation with considerable anticipation. Severn Hall was built according to the wishes of Augusta, first Countess of Severn, whose collection of Gothic romances is still to be seen in the library. It seemed reasonable to imagine that a house of this sort could not fail to have some device of the nature. But . . .*"

"But it's got to be!" said Kit, as Benson significantly paused. "Otherwise, where is Helen?"

"I don't know, sir."

"As Lewis says, she's got to be somewhere! You can't get me to believe that . . . that . . ."

And instinctively they all turned to look at the bronze lamp.

There it stood on the mantelpiece, with its thin stiff-drawn figures engraved round the bowl. It had begun, if only from the effect of their imaginations, to emanate a poison that infected the air around it. It touched on the deepest superstitions of human nature. It flowed into their minds, showing them Professor Gilray dead and black and bloated in a Cairo nursing-home. And Helen?

" 'Blown to dust', " murmured Audrey, " 'as though she had never existed'. "

Then, catching Kit's eye, Audrey woke up. She got up from the sofa and hurried across to him.

"I don't really believe it, old boy," she assured him with a passion of earnestness. "As a matter of fact," her dark eyes searched his face, "I'll bet I believe it less than you do. You've been half expecting this to happen, and I haven't." She hesitated. "Kit. Why were you expecting it to happen?"

"Because of . . ."

"Because of something that happened in London. I know ! You told us that. But what happened in London ?" Suddenly her mood changed. "No ! Wait ! Don't tell me ! I don't want to know !"

"Take it easy, Audrey."

"I'm scared, Kit. Oh, God, I'm scared ! If you ask me what I'm scared of, I can't tell you. But do you realize we've got to sleep here, Kit ? And I wonder where Helen is sleeping to-night ?"

He took her arm and pressed it reassuringly, though the picture she conjured up was too ugly to be faced.

"Besides," continued the badly frightened girl. "what on earth are we going to do about it ?"

"I'm going to have another search of the house. Not that I doubt you, Benson," he turned to that ancient rock, whom he had known and liked since boyhood. "but I want to see for myself."

"You wont' find her, Kit." Audrey spoke positively. "There's something funny and queer and horrible in this, and I *know* you wo n't find her. What happens then ? Do we call in the police ?"

"No ! We can't do that !"

"Why not ?"

"Helen's father."

"Yes," admitted Audrey. "Yes. There is that."

"Whatever happens," said Kit with some violence, "this story mustn't get into the press." A vision of Lord Severn, elderly and stoop-shouldered, with his mouse-coloured hair

49

and the deep furrows down his cheeks, rose in Kit's mind. "The old man hasn't been well for a long time. His wife, if you remember, died of blood poisoning when Helen was a kid."

It was something Audrey hadn't known, since her acquaintance with Helen went back only five or six years. She stared at Kit.

"Blood poisoning ? Helen's mother ?"

"Yes. And now Helen tells me there's something wrong with his heart. News like this, coming on top of Professor Gilray's death, would probably kill him. Don't you agree, Benson ?"

"Yes, sir," answered Benson. Abruptly Benson turned and bent down to replace the blue-bound book on its shelf, at the same moment that Mrs. Pomfret the housekeeper came into the room. Mrs Pomfret cast merely a glance at the uneasy Lewis, but it was sufficient to send that young man hurrying out. Whereupon Mrs. Pomfret gave her bust a settling shake. She had evidently mounted the steep staircase in something of a hurry herself.

"If you'll excuse the intrusion, sir," Mrs. Pomfret addressed Kit, while casting a professional eye round the room. "I thought I had better tell you about the new unpleasantness. Somebody has telephoned the press about her ladyship's disappearance."

"Telephoned the press ?" echoed Audrey, and swung around to Kit with a glazed and uncertain look in her eyes.

"Yes, miss." Mrs. Pomfret breathed hard. "Telephoned the press, and the police too. There are three reporters, and the local superintendent of police, down at the lodge-gates now."

"*Who* telephoned the press ?" demanded Kit.

"That's just it, sir. They don't know. It was a man who wouldn't give his name. A deep voice, speaking a bit foreign. They say he gave a nasty kind of laugh, and said . . ." Here Mrs. Pomfret, whose gaze had been wandering about the room, saw what was on the mantelpiece. She took a quick step backwards.

"And said " she continued, "that the bronze lamp had got Lady Helen Loring. Those were the exact words, sir, 'got' Lady Helen Loring. And if they didn't believe it, this person said, they could go to Severn Hall and see."

"So !" muttered Kit Farrell.

He put his hands to his temples, pressing hard. To gain time for thought he walked to the centre table, on which were magazines, and the china bowl of yellow daffodils, and a cigarette-box with a scarab set into the lid. Kit opened the box, took out a cigarette, and lit it unsteadily with a pocket lighter. Mrs. Pomfret spoke to him reproachfully.

"I should like some instructions, sir. I spoke to Leonard on the phone, and told him to close the gates. But with all these things happening, and those people making such a noise and all . . ."

"We can't let the press in here, Mrs. Pomfret."

The housekeeper raised one shoulder.

"I'm sure it's none of my affair, sir. But I don't very well see how we can keep the police out."

Kit Farrell was himself again, a cool and dogged young man with a practical problem to handle.

"On the contrary," he said dryly, "that's exactly what we can do. After all, there hasn't been any crime committed here."

"Hasn't there?" murmured Audrey.

The veins stood out in Kit's forehead. "So far as we know, there hasn't been any crime committed. We can tell the whole police force to go to blazes, if we want to keep 'em out. Don't you understand, Mrs. Pomfret, that the main thing is to keep this business from Lord Severn as long as possible?"

"Oh!" said Mrs. Pomfret suddenly. She put one hand over her mouth in consternation. "I'm sorry! I *am* sorry! But really! There have been so many dreadful things! The cablegram from Cairo!"

Kit took the cigarette out of his mouth.

"What cablegram from Cairo?"

"From his lordship, sir. Mr. Golding at the post office phoned it just before six o'clock, when the post office closed. It was addressed to," she nodded towards Benson, "but he was interviewing gardeners like a detective, and talking to every-body, and searching the house. He said he didn't want to be disturbed. So I wrote it down, and I'm afraid I simply . . ."

As she spoke, Mrs. Pomfret was fumbling in the girdle of her pleated dark skirt, with a distracted hitch of the shoulder rather as though she were undressing. She produced a slip from a memorandum pad, which she unfolded and smoothed out.

"Allow me, sir," Benson intervened smoothly.

He came sailing forward, his hand extended. But Kit, with regrettable manners, took the paper from Mrs. Pomfret. What he saw there destroyed, with a crash, every plan he had been preparing.

IS HELEN ALL RIGHT ? ALIM BEY HAS MADE NEW PROPHECY. NOT DISTURBED BUT SHOULD LIKE TO BE REASSURED. PLEASE TELEPHONE ME CONTINENTAL-SAVOY HOTEL CAIRO NINE O'CLOCK TONIGHT YOUR TIME.

SEVERN.

"That's torn it," breathed Audrey, who was reading the words past Kit's shoulder. "We can't help ourselves, Kit. We've got to get in touch with him now."

"Yes, I'm afraid so."

"If we don't," said Audrey, "he'll only ring us and be convinced there's something wrong no matter what we tell him. Kit, this is awful ! Somebody's been . . ."

"Upsetting the apple cart. Yes, I've noticed it."

"If you will allow *me*, Mrs. Pomfret," interposed Benson, moving the housekeeper to one side with a kind of dignified backwash, and drawing himself up, "*I* will deal with this matter of the press and the police. Do I understand, Mr. Kit, that nobody is to be admitted here ?"

"Nobody," said Kit, "is even to be admitted to the grounds until we decide what we're going to do. If you've got any dogs, turn 'em loose."

"Excuse me, sir," said Mrs. Pomfret, and blandly hurled another bombshell, "but that can't apply to the gentleman who's already here. The gentleman," she explained in a louder voice, as three persons swung towards her, "who got here before the reporters. He simply drove in, Mr. Benson ! The front gates are never closed ! He's down in the library now, looking at the books. But he says . ."

It was unnecessary to complete this sentence.

They had not heard the clumping footsteps outside the door. But they heard a heavy hand turn the knob. In the doorway filling its breadth, stood an apparition which at first glance made Audrey Vane shy back.

"I'm a patient man," declared the apparition, giving each of them an evil glance in turn, "but burn me if I'm goin' to sit in that mausoleum down there till the ghosty bell tolls midnight. Do you always keep guests waitin' like that? Or is it just a liking for persecutin' me?"

Mrs. Pomfret stood to one side.

"Sir Henry Merrivale," she said.

7

It may have been a bad beginning. But afterwards nobody —not even H. M. himself—could have complained about the warmth of his welcome.

His name was well known both to Kit Farrell and to Audrey Vane, though for different reasons. To Audrey he represented the grousing figure who had provided Helen with so much amusement in Cairo. But to Kit Farrell, barrister-at-law, he represented something else altogether.

For this was the Old Maestro, the crafty old devil from the War Office, the one man who, if he had been able to choose, Kit would have whistled out of nowhere for their assistance. Though he had never met Sir Henry Merrivale, he was very familiar with that gentleman's exploits. Kit breathed an inner prayer of relief which was something like a shout.

The crafty old devil stood now in the doorway, peering round suspiciously. The weather, it must be recorded, was not bitterly cold. Yet H. M., in addition to his overcoat, was wearing an arctic fur cap with ear-flaps—a sight so horrible, as it framed his broad face and spectacles pulled down on the blunt nose, that Mr. Benson stepped back in astonishment.

"Sir," said Kit Farrell, "we're very glad to see you."

"Awfully!" agreed the girl. "Do sit down and have a drink and get warm!"

They set on him like dogs on an arctic explorer. They hurried him across to the sofa by the fire, where they sat him down. Audrey removed his fur cap, at which he snatched vainly as she bore it up to place it on the mantelpiece beside the bronze lamp. Kit poured more coal on the fire, which promptly emitted a gush of smoke into the great man's face. Out of this emerged gleaming spectacles, an even more malignant mouth, and a polished bald head.

"But how on earth," continued Audrey, "did you happen to turn up here ? I suppose Helen asked you to come ?"

H. M.'s big face smoothed itself out.

"Well, no," he admitted. "To tell you the truth, I don't expect she'll be very pleased to see me."

"Then how did you happen to come ?"

"I got a conscience," H. M. said querulously. He sniffed. "For days it's been bothering me like blazes. I had an idea, d'ye see ?" He raised almost invisible eyebrows to emphasize this. "If my idea was right, then things were all right. But if my idea was wrong . . . oh, lord love a duck !" Here he broke off to look at Audrey, noting with sour approval the tall, slim figure in the dark-green frock. "I expect you're Audrey Vane ?"

"That's right. And this is Kit Farrell."

"I sort of suspected that, too," grunted H. M., eyeing Kit up and down.

"You were saying, Sir Henry ?"

"I was talkin' about my conscience," roared H. M. "This afternoon, just to make me feel easier, I rang the Semiramis Hotel. They said she'd gone off to Severn Hall. And so . . . well, here I am. But I see the gal got here safely after all." He nodded towards the bronze lamp on the mantelpiece. "Where is she now ?"

"She isn't here," Kit answered clearly. "Helen disappeared practically under our eyes, and left that lamp on the floor down in the main hall."

For the space of about ten seconds H. M. looked back at him. Not a muscle moved in his face, and poker players at the Diogenes Club have found any attempt to read H.M.'s expression a highly unprofitable proceeding.

But this imperturbability did not last. As Kit went on to explain the situation, tersely but clearly, ending with mention of the extract from Mr. Linnell's book on secret hiding places, H. M.'s look slowly changed. His mouth fell open in genuine consternation.

"Oh, lord love a duck !" he breathed. "Is this," he added with violence, "strictly on the level ? Are all of you tellin' me the truth ?"

Four voices spoke out and affirmed it.

For a moment H. M. remained silent, staring at the fire. Then he got to his feet.

"This sounds bad," he said. "This sounds about as bad as it can be."

"Do *you* think anything's happened to Helen?" asked Audrey.

"I dunno, my wench. It could be. Even the old man" —his next statement, an astounding one, showed the depths of H. M.'s worry—"even the old man," he said, "can be wrong sometimes. Got anything else to tell me?"

"Only," responded Kit, "that somebody's tipped off the press. And Lord Severn's cabled, asking us to ring him in Cairo at nine o'clock." He gave the details. "The point is, sir, what are we to do?"

There was a long silence.

H. M., sunk deep in brooding thought, seemed vaguely and irritably conscious that he was still wearing an overcoat in a too hot atmosphere. Benson stepped forward, removing the overcoat so deftly and smoothly, like a pickpocket lifting a watch, that H. M. never noticed it.

Again H. M. sat down on the sofa. His expression had now grown hideous to behold. Taking a leather case out of his pocket, he extracted a vile black cigar, sniffed at it with ghoulish voluptuousness, stuck it into his mouth— while Benson held a light for it across his shoulder—and smoked for aching moments while they watched him.

"Do?" he said, abruptly waking up. "You want to know what to do?"

"Very much so."

"The most important thing," said H. M., blowing out smoke deliberately, "is to put through that call to Lord Severn and tell him the whole business straight out."

"*What's that?*"

"You ask me," said H. M. "I'm tellin' you."

"But Lord Severn . . . !"

"Sure, sure. He's not well. But how long do you think you can keep it from him, with a howlin' mob of reporters on your doorstep?"

"We haven't seen the reporters. They don't know anything for certain."

"Oh, my son!" said H. M. dismally. "Any newspaperman worth his salt won't need to know for certain. He'll twig it dead-sure just as soon as you don't deny it; he'll run for his news editor and Bob's-your-uncle. Y'see," H. M. scowled meditatively at the tip of the cigar,

"I got an awful yearning to have a few words with Lord Severn myself."

"Lord Severn ? Why ?"

"Never you mind why," said H. M. with austere majesty. "You just trust the old man. And it must be goin' on for nine o'clock now. Where's your telephone ?"

Benson coughed to attract attention.

"There are two outside phones, sir," he answered. "One in the library, and one in my pantry. And Mr. Kit, may I ask you what time you would like to have dinner served ?"

For the second time that night Kit Farrell opened his mouth to heap fiery curses on the name of dinner. But he caught sight of Audrey's tired face, with the faint lines now etched at the corners of the mouth and eyes. He was conscious of his own weariness and light-headedness, scratching at the nerves.

"Benson !"

"Sir ?"

"I suppose, in Lady Helen's absence, we can consider ourselves as hosts ?"

"Naturally, Mr. Kit !" smiled Benson.

"Go down to the library," Kit instructed him, "and ask for a personal call to Lord Severn at the Continental-Savoy Hotel in Cairo. They'll probably take a long time to connect you . . ."

"Wouldn't it be better," suddenly interposed Audrey Vane, "wouldn't it be better, Kit, if we made the personal call to Sandy Robertson ? That is, if Sir Henry has no objection ?"

"Me, my wench ? I got no objection."

"Then Sandy could sort of—well ! break it gently. And Sir Henry could talk to the old boy afterwards." Audrey's manner was all bright casualness and unconcern. "Maybe," she added, "I could have a word with Sandy myself ?"

Kit nodded.

"Make it," he told Benson, "a personal call to Mr. Robertson at the same hotel. And, incidentally, Benson, Sir Henry Merrivale will be staying to dinner, and also staying the night. You are staying," Kit said grimly to H. M., "if I have to wallop you over the head with a life-preserver."

"Thank'e kindly," said H. M., "for the hospitality. I was goin' on to The Bell at Gloucester. But I don't mind if I do bunk here. Because I'm expectin' developments in this business."

"Developments?" cried Audrey.

"Uh-huh."

With difficulty, Kit forced his attention back to Benson. For H. M., with the cigar exactly in the centre of his mouth like a peppermint stick, was slowly looking round Helen's room, and something on the centre table appeared to interest him very much.

"Put Sir Henry," Kit went on, "in the Black Room, otherwise known as the Haunted Room. You can serve dinner as soon as we've finished the phone-call. And keep out reporters."

"Very good, sir."

"That's all, thanks."

H. M. took the cigar out of his mouth.

"Just a minute, Benson," he said softly.

It was as though a small sharp dart had jabbed into Benson's back. He had turned towards the door, unobtrusively motioning Mrs. Pomfret to precede him, when H. M. spoke. It seemed to Kit Farrell that Benson's half-smiling poise was wearing a trifle thin. But he inclined his head in patient deference.

"You're Benson, hey? And you're Mrs. Pomfret? Yes. I'd like to speak to you," said H. M. apologetically, "about a few things in this miracle."

"Meaning, sir. . . ?"

"A gal," said H. M., "who walks into a house and then vanishes like a soap bubble under the eyes of witnesses."

Benson came very near to bursting out: "I can't help it, sir! It's true! Every single word of it is true!"

"Sure, son, sure." H. M. was reassuring. "I don't doubt it. All I want is a little bit of information." He remained silent for a moment. "You knew, a' course, that Lady Helen Loring had got back to England from Egypt?"

Benson's eyes opened wide.

"Certainly, sir. In fact, I went up to London to see her."

"Oh, ah? At the hotel?"

"Yes, sir. The Semiramis Hotel."

"And you'd heard, naturally," H. M. pointed with his cigar to the bronze lamp on the mantelpiece, "you'd heard all about that?"

"Considering, sir," smiled Benson, "that for the past two years I have done little but paste items relating to the archæological expedition into a series of scrapbooks . . ."

H. M. was galvanized. "You keep a scrapbook ?"

"About the family ? Yes, sir. I have done so for years."

"That's very encouragin', son, " declared H. M. nodding with extraordinary vigour. "So do I. I got a beautiful scrapbook with me. It's downstairs in my car now." He pondered this, and reluctantly discarded the subject. "Never mind, son ! That can wait." Abruptly he added: "Were you expectin' Lady Helen here to-day ?"

"Good heavens, no, sir ! I didn't really expect her ladyship for another week at least."

H. M. closed his eyes, and opened them again.

"You, Mrs. Pomfret ?"

"All decisions," replied Mrs. Pomfret, her voice rising into a strange key after the effect of long silence, "all decisions and expectations are made by Mr. Benson, sir. I did not expect her ladyship."

"So it sort of caught you on the hop. Is that it ?"

"Yes, sir."

"With your pants down ?"

Benson coughed. "One *could* phrase it like that, sir."

"As I understand it, you were both in the butler's pantry when the lodge-keeper rang up to say the party was on its way up ? Yes. And from the butler's pantry you went straight to the main hall ? Yes. How long did it take you to get to the main hall ?"

"Well, sir. Say two minutes or perhaps a little more."

"Two minutes ?" repeated H. M. sharply. "Or even more ? That's rather a long time, ain't it, just to walk from the front of the house to the back ?"

"Mrs. Pomfret and I exchanged some conversation, sir. We were—somewhat upset."

Was it his imagination, Kit Farrell thought, or did Mrs. Pomfret partly open her mouth to make some comment ? And did Benson's arm, as though by the merest accident, brush against hers ?

Kit could not be sure. H. M. certainly couldn't be suspecting Benson or the housekeeper of any complicity in this ? The idea of Benson being connected in any shady business was so grotesque as to be almost comic. And yet the whole weird, unnatural atmosphere of that afternoon was closing in again—the rustle of rain in evergreens, the brush of lightning, the disappearance of Helen Loring into nothingness.

"What I'm gettin' at is this," persisted H. M. patiently. "Did anything happen to delay you in gettin' to the main hall? Anything at all?"

Again Kit could have sworn Mrs. Pomfret was on the verge of blurting out something.

"No, sir," Benson returned firmly.

"Were you and Mrs. Pomfret together the whole time?"

"Yes, sir!" Sheer relief, a tensing of muscles, poured out of the butler's reply. "We were never out of each other's sight from the time we received the lodge-keeper's message until the time we found the mackintosh and the bronze lamp lying on the floor in the main hall. Mrs. Pomfret can confirm that."

"According to young Farrell's evidence, a plumber named Powers heard Lady Helen come in."

"Yes, sir."

"He heard the front door open and close. He heard a gal's voice say something. He heard footsteps, and the footsteps stopped. Oh, my eye! They stopped." An expression of awe overspread H. M.'s face. "Did *you* hear any of this?"

"No, sir," replied Benson, and Mrs. Pomfret vigorously agreed.

"How do you account for that?"

"Well, sir, my pantry is at the end of a passage. At the front of the passage there is a heavy green-baize door. It is not likely we should have heard any noise unless the noise happened to be inordinately loud."

H. M. balanced his cigar on the edge of a standing ash-tray and leaned forward.

"But looky here, son! With a house full of people, didn't anybody hear or see anything, except that plumber? What about the servants?"

"They were having their tea together in the servants' hall, sir; all except the between-maid, but she had the day off. The only other persons working inside were the plumber, Powers, and a man who was repairing the clock in the tower."

As though to emphasize this, the heavy old clock far up

in the tower faintly jarred and clanged out with the first stroke of nine.

"Mrs. Pomfret and I," said Benson, "went into the main hall. And I'm afraid that's all I can tell you, sir."

"But burn it all, son . . . !"

"The lamp was there," said Benson. "The mackintosh was there. But her ladyship had gone."

The last stroke of nine vibrated away in the pause that followed. It had begun to rain again, too; they heard a few drops sting against the window-panes behind drawn grey and gold curtains, adding a new loneliness to the night that pressed round Severn Hall. Audrey Vane, curled up in a chair across the fireplace from H. M., shivered and glanced towards the windows.

"That's all, son," H. M. said dully. "Cut along and put through that telephone call."

Taking up H. M.'s overcoat from the back of a chair, and the unmentionable fur cap from the top of the mantelpiece, Benson bowed slightly before he followed Mrs. Pomfret out of the room. The door closed with a soft, decisive click. H. M. picked up his cigar and sat back.

"Alive or dead?" said Kit Farrell. "Alive or dead? I stick by the old contention, sir, that Helen has got to be somewhere."

"Uh-huh. It'd seem so, wouldn't it?"

"Do you see any clue? Any clue at all?"

H. M. ruffled his hands across his big bald head.

"Well now. Not much of a clue, no." He looked up. "Unless you can supply one."

"He wants to know, Kit," said Audrey, folding her arms, "why you more or less expected this to happen."

"I wasn't exactly expecting it," retorted Kit, "except in what the psychologists would call—well! a subconscious way. Because I was afraid of it." He considered, groping for words. "Audrey and I," he went on, "met Helen's plane at Croydon when she got back from Egypt."

"Uh-huh, son?"

"You were there too," said Kit, suddenly realizing. "You must have been there, because Helen said she'd travelled back with you. But I don't remember seeing you."

"You didn't, son. I broke the last lap of the trip in Paris. Go on, go on, go on!"

How to explain what he felt? To Kit it came back in a series of voiceless pictures. The big silver shape of the airliner, against a misty April sky. The last explosive chug as it wheeled around and taxied in. Attendants hurrying with the portable steps for the plane door. Reporters waiting behind the barrier, waiting for the series of small wind-blown passengers to emerge from that door. . . .

His first sight of Helen hurrying towards them, with the wind moulding her frock against her body. Audrey kissing Helen—and he (big gawk) doing nothing of the kind, though he had instinctively put out his hands, and she had done the same, and then they both stopped. The lift of Helen's brown eyes, her uncertain smile, the touch of her hand.

Then the big airport bus that carried them away. Everyone in the bus talking, a soundless babble as he remembered it now. The Semiramis Hotel, noisy and glaring, overlooking the lamps of the Embankment in the twilight. And, through everything, the image of Helen's face.

"I saw her," Kit explained, "every day afterwards. She was worried about that prophecy of Alim Bey's. She pretended not to be. But she was. You've probably noticed how—what the devil do I want to say? How intense Helen can be?"

H. M. nodded.

"Yes, son, I've noticed it. Well?"

"I think she'd have done anything, anything, to prove the curse was all rubbish. And yet at the same time she was afraid of it. It's been a good deal on my mind, you see, because . . . this isn't the first time she's disappeared."

H. M.'s little eyes, magnified behind their spectacles, glanced with quick new interest. Audrey sat up straight.

"No, wait!" said Kit. "There was nothing supernatural about the first time, if that's what you're thinking."

"You never," cried Audrey, "you never told me anything about this!"

"No."

"Why not?"

"Because Helen asked me not to."

"Go on, son," said H. M., woodenly.

"I supposed," Kit said to Audrey, "she would tell you herself. It wasn't that she didn't trust you, or anything like that. But—what day of the week is this?"

61

"Thursday, son."

"I'd been trying to take Helen's mind off things. My God, I'd have done a high-dive off the roof of the hotel if that would have amused her. She wouldn't talk about Egypt. Anything but Egypt, though I could see she was thinking about it. Then, when I went round to the Semiramis on Monday, I found she'd gone."

"Gone," muttered Audrey Vane.

"According to the hall porter. she took no luggage and left no address. But she did leave a note addressed to me. The note said I wasn't to worry. It said I was to ask or answer no questions of anybody, to pretend she was still at the hotel, and to keep away visitors, especially reporters, if any came round. She even left a key so that I could keep guard on the hotel suite."

Kit wrinkled up his forehead. He tried to grin, showing strong teeth, but the grin was a failure.

"Bit of a change for me," he said. "Sitting at the Semiramis like a poor relation and watching the waiters' eyebrows lift. But I did it. And I kept out the visitors all right, though it was a near thing when an American named Beaumont tried to get it. Then, this morning, Helen turned up again. I walked in early, and found her sitting in a chair in the bedroom—white as death, wearing a lace négligé, and refusing to say where she'd been. That's all."

The shorn words conjured up an image of intolerable vividness.

"Then that," said Audrey, "is why you two have been behaving so oddly all day ? Didn't you ask her where she'd been ?"

"Naturally."

"But she still wouldn't say anything ?"

"Not a word. She—well, she started to cry."

"Idiot," said Audrey pityingly. "That's where you should have put your arms round her and . . ."

Seeing the expression on his face, she broke off. Kit went forward and kicked with some viciousness at the fire, which emitted a gush of sparks.

"But, Kit !" persisted Audrey, tastening her scarlet-nailed fingers round the arms of the chair. "If you had to behave like such an asininely perfect gentleman, what did you imagine was wrong ? What did you *think* ?"

"Oh, that it was some man or other."

"Ass! You know perfectly well ... !"

"At least, that's what I thought at first. Later I wasn't sure. Anyway, it doesn't matter." Kit turned to H. M. "That's the story, sir, for what it's worth. Do you make anything of it?"

H. M.'s cigar had gone out. Piled into one corner of the sofa, gloomily contemplating his big shoes, he became conscious that the cigar was out. Twice he opened his mouth to make some profound remark, and twice, scowling, he refrained. From his inside pocket he took out an old letter, tore a long strip from it, and thrust the end into the fire to get a light. As the paper flared up wildly, its flame threw on the wall above the mantelpiece a big unsteady shadow of the bronze lamp.

That was what they saw as Benson opened the door.

"Your telephone call, sir," the butler said.

8

HALF a world away from them, in the yellow drawing-room at the Continental-Savoy in Cairo, Sandy Robertson stood clutching the telephone.

"Yes," he was saying. "Yes, we're expecting the call. From a man named Benson, at Severn Hall in Gloucestershire. Yes! What?"

Nine o'clock by Greenwich time is eleven in Egypt. Outside the long windows of the drawing-room showed a deep violet sky so crowded with stars that it seemed to shimmer and ripple in the warm air that stirred through. Lord Severn, his hands in his pockets, stared out of a window with his back to the room.

"Here's Benson, sir," called Sandy. "Don't you want to talk to him?"

"No," said Lord Severn.

"You don't want to talk to him?"

"Not," responded the tired voice, "for just a moment."

Sandy, in a white tropical dinner-jacket, leaned one elbow against the grand piano while he shouted at the phone. His face, that face of humorous ugliness with the dark clever eyes and the faintly lined forehead, already looked distracted enough.   Lord Severn nearly completed his demoralization.

Somewhere along the line, an operator was shifting gears. A series of piercing clicks, assaulting the ear-drum, made Sandy yank the phone away from his ear. Those same clicks, across a thousand miles of space, were clearly heard by the persons in the library at Severn Hall.

In the library at Severn, a gloomy vault where the shifting glare of firelight poured out of an immense chimney-piece, Audrey Vane sat at the telephone table under stained-glass windows.   Sir Henry Merrivale was at her elbow, with Kit Farrell in full firelight not far away.

Audrey no longer troubled to conceal her eagerness as she waited for Sandy's voice. It was difficult, under these gaunt walls of books, with rain slashing the windows and draughts lifting the carpets, to picture any other climate. But it was very easy to picture Sandy.

"For Christ's sake, Benson, what's going on at home?"

Thin and frantic, raw as an exposed nerve, that voice could be heard by all of them.

"Listen, Sandy dear ! It's . . ."

"Who is that speaking ? You're not Benson ! Who are you ?"

"Benson isn't here, Sandy.   It's me !   Audrey Vane."

"So it's you, is it ?" said Sandy coolly. "Get off the line, can't you ? And let me talk to somebody who knows something."

The sheer, unintentional cruelty of that remark brought a sick expression to Audrey's mouth and eyes.

"Nice feller, your friend Robertson," observed H. M.

"He doesn't mean it !" cried Audrey, putting her hand over the mouthpiece of the phone. She seemed desperately anxious to convince them that he didn't mean it. "It's simply . . . his way. We all pretend to be like that. Kit ! Here !   You talk to him."

And she ran away from the telephone.

"Kit Farrell, eh ?" repeated Sandy, as Kit introduced himself. "I might have known it would be. Just tell me this, yes or no: is it true that Helen's been blown to pieces ?"

"Blown to pieces ?"

"Destroyed !   Killed !   Wiped off the map somehow !"

Kit exchanged a glance with H. M. who was still drawing at a dead cigar.

"What makes you think anything's happened to her, Sandy?"

"A pal of mine in Mutual Press rang up from London not half an hour ago. He said they'd got a straight tip from their Bristol correspondent that something damned unpleasant had happened to Helen, and confirmed it because nobody would answer questions."

"So!" said Sir Henry Merrivale.

"Earlier in the afternoon, Alim Bey was here at the hotel. In the presence of Lord Severn and two reporters and your obedient servant, he calmly said something *had* happened to Helen. That was why we sent the cable. He also said Lord Severn would be the next to go."

The next to go!

It was perhaps the first time those words had ever been used, though they were to be heard many times, with heightening terror, in the days that followed.

"But never mind that," the thin voice bawled. It shouted at Kit; it even pleaded with him. "It's all a lot of rubbish, isn't it? Just tell me it's all a lot of rubbish! Helen's not . . . ?"

And Kit told him.

"I don't believe it!" said the voice.

"Then hang it all, Sandy, why ask me? I tell you it's true!"

He heard Sandy Robertson curse just once, with such intense and despairing anguish that Kit wanted to hang up to get the sound out of his ears. Kit's own throat felt dry and shaky. He couldn't stand much of this; it was what he felt himself. The man in Cairo, the little man with all the charm of manner, was having his own heart wrung and devilled as he had wrung and devilled Audrey Vane's. Kit would have pitied Sandy if he had not seen Audrey standing motionless in the firelight, after which his sympathies grew all mixed up again.

"Listen. son." Sir Henry Merrivale touched him on the shoulder. "Ask him how Lord Severn behaved when he first heard about this. Ask him what Severn's doin' now. Ask him whether I can have a word with the old boy." H. M.'s voice was furiously insistent. "Ask him!"

"Sandy, listen. How's the old man taking this?"

No reply.

"*Sandy!*"

"Hello. Christopher," spoke the mild voice of Lord Severn.

In that yellow drawing-room in Cairo, Sandy Robertson was now sitting in front of the grand piano and raving like a maniac. Lord Severn—one hand holding the phone, and the other inside his coat, feeling his heart—kept an absent-minded eye fixed on a corner of the ceiling as he talked. The listeners could not see his sun-leathered face, or the tired weighted look of his forehead. But the cheerful tone of his voice raised Kit Farrell's hair.

"How are you, my boy? Quite well, I hope? Mr. Robertson,"—in his voice was now a faint, curious note of contempt—"is upset. I can't understand what's happened to Helen; but don't worry. I'm not worried unduly. In fact, I propose to come to England and try to clear the mystery up. I have also some unpleasant business at home."

"But, sir! Your health . . ."

"Tut, tut!" The voice was mildly annoyed. "Nonsense! Not as bad as all that. I've chartered a special plane for to-morrow morning. Mr. Robertson and I will be with you in a very few days. Professor Gilray—dead. Helen—gone. And I am supposed to be the next victim."

Suddenly Lord Severn laughed, an inoffensive modest laugh.

"Good night, Christopher," he added. "Give my regards to everyone." There was a click, and the line went dead.

"Lord Severn, wait! Sir Henry Merrivale wants to . . ."

In vain Kit jiggled the receiver. The fragile communication was snapped; a wall closed, leaving its tantalizing puzzles. Kit left off speaking to unresponsive carbon only when H. M. touched him on the shoulder.

"It's all right, son," H. M. told him. "Don't chivvy the Exchange. I heard what I wanted to hear. Or, if we got to be exact, I didn't hear what I didn't want to hear." For a moment he scowled, jingling coins in his pocket. "This feller's supposed to be very fond of his daughter, isn't he?"

"Supposed?" cried Audrey. "He *is* fond of her. And Helen idolizes him! He's the only one who'll treat her with complete seriousness when she goes all scholarly."

"Uh-huh. That's what I understood from the gal herself —scholarly," repeated H. M., and slowly turned round from the telephone table.

His sour eyes ran over the vault of books, with its little iron gallery halfway up. So bright was the yellow-red blaze of logs, pouring in a tunnel from the arch of the chimney-piece, that it lighted the room fairly well. A withered leather settee had been drawn up to the fire. Half a dozen books, taken down from the shelves by H. M. himself when he had waited in here an hour ago, lay scattered on a table by the settee. H. M. contemplated these books.

"We got a problem," he announced.

"You amaze me," said Kit.

After giving Kit a dark, evil glance of suspicion, H. M. lumbered over with his corporation preceding him in splendour, and plumped down on the settee.

"While you were keeping me waitin'," he continued in an aggrieved tone, "I thought it might be interestin' to have a look around here." He waved his hand. "Lot of stuff. Including items from the famous collection of Gothic romances. Yes."

Flipping his dead cigar into the fire, he picked up the books in turn. An expression of glee stole over his face.

"*The Mysteries of Udolpho*," said H. M., "featurin' the sinister Count Montoni and little Emily. She had a high old time, she did. *The Old English Baron*, where the rightful owner of the castle gets murdered and stuck under the floor. *The Vampyre, a Tale by Lord Byron*. It wasn't by Byron, incidentally; it was by a doctor named Polidori."

"Very, very nice," said Audrey uncertainly, and looked at him in perplexity.

"You think so too, hey?"

"But what on earth has it got to do with us?"

"Maybe a whole lot, my wench," said H. M. seriously. He picked up another book. "Oh, my eye! You can almost smell the eighteenth century! What they thought, what they felt, what they dreamed about. Look at this house." He nodded towards a door at the rear of the library. "Where does that door lead to, for instance?"

Audrey followed the direction of his glance.

"Lord Severn's study. Mummies and things. The chauffeur," Audrey turned rather white, "thought Helen was shut up in one."

"And the door opposite, towards the front?"

"Picture gallery."

H. M. laboriously craned his neck round, towards the big doors giving on the main hall behind him.

"And across the hall out there ?"

"A drawing-room, and a music-room, and a big dining-hall, and oh, miles of rooms ! Why do you ask ?"

"All built up," grunted H. M. making a hideous face of emphasis, "because a romantic woman dreams about an ivied castle loaded with hootin' owls and secret sorrows." He opened the book and inspected its book-plate. "Augusta. Countess of Severn. Interestin' yes. I wonder what that gal was really like ?"

"Wait a minute !" Kit Farrell said sharply. His footsteps rang on the stone floor as he went to join them by the fire-place. "I can't tell you what the famous Augusta was like. But I can tell you she *looked* like. She looked exactly like Helen."

"So !" breathed H. M., and closed the book with a snap. "Maybe the idea I got isn't so wool-gatherin' after all. Or is this only another romantic tradition ?"

"It's not a tradition at all. It's a fact."

"So !"

"If you don't believe me," said Kit, "you can see for yourself. There's a portrait of Augusta here. It used to hang in the picture gallery, but it was done by a rotten bad painter, so they chucked it out and relegated it to . . ."

A new voice said:

"That was the picture. *That was the picture !*" And Mrs. Pomfret, with a surprisingly light tread, came hurrying in from the main hall.

So unpredictable were the acoustics of this library, perhaps designedly so, that the voice seemed to spring out beside them like the effect of a whispering gallery. It caused H. M. to give a convulsive jump, and nearly strangle himself in his collar when he craned around.

"I should have told you, sir," continued Mrs. Pomfret, casting a quick glance over her shoulder. "And I meant to tell you, when Mr. Benson said nothing delayed us. Well ! Perhaps it didn't 'delay' us, if you know what I mean. But the lightning came through the glass door, and it wasn't there !"

H. M. passed a hand across his forehead.

"Looky here, Ma'am. What exactly are you talking about ?"

"That picture, sir !"

"What about it ?"

"It's gone," said Mrs. Pomfret simply. "I never properly noticed the face, sir. But I do remember the little name plate, with 'Augusta, Countess of Severn', and a date. It used to hang in the passage near Mr. Benson's pantry. I am willing to testify, sir, it was there at lunch time to-day. But at five o'clock it was gone."

"Gone, hey ? Who took it ?"

"Much as I wish to be helpful," replied Mrs. Pomfret, "I cant' tell you. Or why it was taken. Mr. Benson says . . ."

This was the point at which Benson, coming in to announce dinner, appeared in the doorway and stopped short. He had changed into evening kit, a formality the others had been given no time to imitate.

"Dinner is served," he said. In exactly the same tone he added: "And I fear, Mr. Kit, it will be impossible to keep the police out now."

When one tennis ball or one new idea is driven at you, it is easy to set yourself for the return stroke. When two tennis balls or two new ideas appear suddenly under your nose, you are apt to swipe wildly and miss both. H. M., however, was not disturbed.

"Just a minute about the police, son," he suggested gently. "Let's take this business of the picture first. Did you hear what we were talkin' about ?"

"Yes, sir."

"Well ? What happened to the picture ?"

"I cannot say, Sir Henry." Benson faced the other's scrutiny with a clear eye. "I have made inquiries, but no one professes to know anything of the matter With regard, however, to the police officer . . "

"Look here, what about the police ?" Kit demanded heatedly. "That Superintendent isn't still here, is he ?"

"No, Mr. Kit. This man " Benson swallowed "is from Scotland Yard."

"Scotland Yard ?" exclaimed Sir Henry Merrivale.

Benson inclined his head.

"And the matter, sir, would appear to be very serious. I have talked to this man. He states that he has been sent here by his office at the request of the Egyptian Government."

"Why ?"

"It seems, sir, that a gold dagger and a gold perfume box, both found in the tomb-chamber of the Priest-King Herihor, are missing from the exhibits which should have been conveyed to the Cairo Museum. Their combined value would amount to ten or twelve thousand pounds, but the main point is the serious view taken of such offences by the government."

Benson was either furiously angry or furiously afraid; Kit, who knew him well, could feel that as palpably as the heat of the fire.

"They have reason to think," Benson added, "that these articles were smuggled out of the country. Her ladyship," he emphasized the term with bitter contempt for the authorities. "helped to open the tomb. Her ladyship dealt much with these objects. Her ladyship is the only one of the party who has returned to England. They wish to question her about it."

H. M. had clearly not expected this. Mention of a gold dagger and a gold perfume box upset some edifice he was building with such care. H. M. was stumped; the old Maestro was well and truly stumped; and had his friend Chief Inspector Masters been there, Kit reflected, Masters would have commented on the fact with pleasure. H. M. pondered for a long time before he raised his head.

"Scotland Yard, hey ?" he replied. And then, quickly: "What's the name of the feller they've sent ?"

"Masters, sir. Chief Inspector Masters."

H. M. closed his eyes.

"I might 'a' known it," he said. "That reptile is followin' in my tracks as surely as . . . Stop a bit, though !" His roarings subsided, to be slowly replaced by a patient. unholy glee.

"This might be a whole lot worse," said H. M., rubbing his hands together. "Disappearance ! Miracle ! The thing that couldn't happen ! You watch Masters have a fit on the hearth-rug when I tell him. This time the blighter's goin' to get just exactly what he deserves. Send him up here, son, while we get some grub."

"Very good, sir."

"And Benson are those newspapermen still here ?"

"Yes, sir."

"Send 'em along too."

Kit's frantic protest was cut short by H. M.'s lordly gesture.

"I know what I'm doin', son," he declared. "I may be a cloth-headed old goop, and everybody enjoys kicking me in the pants. That's my destiny. But send 'em all up, Benson! I'll risk it. Send 'em all up!"

9

It was three days later, early on the morning of Sunday, April thirtieth, that Sir Henry Merrivale and Chief Inspector Masters stood on the flat roof of the clock-tower.

Time to establish, under Masters's patient questioning of every witness, that there was apparently no flaw in the evidence, that Helen Loring had been wiped from the earth and the very scheme of things. Time for every fact to be tested, every statement proved true. Time for the press of three continents to erupt in a sensation without parallel.

But not time enough, not nearly time enough, for hurts to heal.

Sunday, April thirtieth, was one of those warm, moist spring days which carry the breath of summer. One of those days both stirring and enervating, breeze and cloud mixed with sun. From the roof of the big, square, solidly built tower—its battlements built waist-high—you could look down over a countryside deepening into green. To the west lay the River Severn, a grey glitter. In the distance, north-east, were the roofs of Gloucester, and the stately square tower of Gloucester Cathedral, with its four corner-pinnacles, rising up against blue sky and motionless white cloud.

Nearer at hand, you looked down steeply on the domain of Severn Hall: curved roof-slates, weather and smoke darkened, ridges, chimney-stacks, gable-ends, old peering windows, dead dust in the sky. Behind lay the garages, once a line of stables. The chauffeur, a tiny figure, was polishing a car in the stable-yard. Two gardeners argued over a rose-tree. The between-maid, that curious drudge who is servant to the servants, padded out on slippered feet with a bucket of swill. Distantly, somebody was ploughing a brown field.

So Sir Henry Merrivale and Chief Inspector Masters stood on the roof of the clock-tower, taking the air after an early breakfast. But they were not looking at any of these things. Instead they were going on in a fashion which would have been familiar to any acquaintance of theirs.

"Now, now, Masters! For the love of Esau, keep your shirt on!"

"It's all very well to say that, sir. But do *you* see any explanation?"

"No, son. And if I did . . ."

"You wouldn't tell me? Oh, ah! I know!"

Masters, large and urbane, bland as a card-sharper, was buttoned up in his usual blue serge. A bowler hat concealed grizzled hair, carefully brushed to hide the bald spot. But his boiled blue eyes did not look urbane now.

"I oughtn't," he declared, "to be staying at this posh place. I ought to be staying at a pub. But can I do it? Oh, no! Not ruddy likely, with your friends the reporters all over the place! I oughtn't to be on this disappearance case, even. But when the Commissioner himself gives the orders . . . Lummy!"

"You lead a dog's life, Masters. It's awful."

Suddenly Masters drew a deep breath and lowered his defences.

"To tell you the truth, sir," he said, "I'm not keen on any of this. Any of the set-up, as you might say. This young fellow, Mr. Farrell," Masters hesitated. "I like him."

"Uh-huh." H. M. seemed uncomfortable. "So do I."

"That chap's headed for a smash," Masters said critically. "Pacing the floor, night after night! Up and down! Up and down! Lummy! It'd do him good if he did blow up!"

"He won't, Masters. Not just yet."

"How do you mean?"

"That's the Irish gentleman, son. About ten times more reserved than the English. But when a feller like that does blow up . . ."

"Just so," agreed the chief inspector, and rubbed a square chin.

They were finding the air of the roof not quite so exhilarating, when a veer of the breeze carried chimney smoke across to them. That breeze smoothed down H. M.'s unspeakable fur cap, with the ear-flaps. Under their feet jarred the ticking of the Hall clock, a ponderous mechanism. Masters took a turn up and down the roof, with measured angry steps.

"Not," he added, "that I blame the young fellow much. When I first got here, sir, I tell you straight I didn't believe one word of this business. But look at what we've got now !"

"For the love of Esau, Masters, put away that notebook !"

"Just look," repeated Masters, tapping the notebook, "at what we've got now. This young lady really did go into the house. We agree on that ?"

"Yes. Without a struggle."

"And she didn't leave it. It's taken three days to make me admit that, sir; but I can't help admitting it ! This place wasn't merely watched on the outside. It was surrounded."

Masters's eye looked wicked.

"Gardeners !" he said. "Even granting a rush-job on the grounds, I never saw so many odd-jobs men in all my born days. There were at least two of 'em on every side of the house. You can see for yourself," he swept an arm around, indicating the ground below like a map, "there aren't any trees or obstructions near the house. All of these chaps swear that nobody left the place, by a door or a window or any other way. And I'm bound to accept that.

"All right, then," pursued Masters, making mesmeric passes to keep H. M. silent, "where *did* the young lady go ?

"She didn't go down to the cellars, because the only entrance to the cellars is through the servants' hall, and eight witnesses were having tea there. She didn't come up to the roof here, because the only way up to the roof is through this clock-tower, and a man who was repairing the clock swears nobody came up. Lummy," muttered the chief inspector, rubbing his chin again. "It's almost as though somebody's posted a lot of people, inside the house and out, to make *sure* the young lady couldn't get away !"

"So," said H. M. in a very odd tone. "I had an idea about that, Masters, on Thursday night. But the idea was wrong. It couldn't be right !"

"All we know for certain-sure." said Masters, "is that she got as far as the main hall. And then—bang ! The footsteps stop. So does the evidence ! So does every ruddy thing ! Can you think of a single solitary lead ?"

"Well, now," said H. M., "what about the painting ?"

"Painting ?"

"A big painting of the gal who designed this house in the eighteenth century was hangin' on the wall at lunch time. Four hours later it was gone. Did you find any trace of it, son, when *you* searched the house ?"

"No. But what if I didn't ?"

"Oh, my son !" said H. M. dismally. "That means it wasn't just shoved away by accident, or because it gave somebody æsthetic agony. It's got a meaning—burn me, it's got to have a meaning !—in the pattern of Dirty Work. I got a hunch we might be in sight of the truth if we could find out what happened to that picture."

Shaking his head, H. M. stumped over to the parapet and stood glowering out across the battlements towards the cathedral tower in the distance.

"I could also bear to know," he added, "what to make of a missing gold dagger and missing gold perfume box. And just exactly what they have to do with the whole mess anyway."

Masters slapped the notebook.

"I keep telling you, sir." he retorted, "that I don't know any more than you do ! The Egyptian police make a complaint to us, that's all. The cable says that on information received, and a complaint made to them, they've got reason to believe the dagger and the snuff box were smuggled out of the country."

"Information received from whom ? Who made the complaint ?"

"Lord Severn himself."

"But looky here, Masters ! The old man surely isn't accusing his own daughter of pinching the stuff ?"

"So help me, sir, I still don't know ! My instructions were to come down here and question the young lady about it. That's all I can tell you. But you ought to get an answer pretty soon."

From his pocket Masters dragged a folded newspaper. It was Saturday evening's late night final of the *Daily Floodlight*. Masters tried to open it against the wind, which promptly flattened it against his face and exposed the staring black headline, CAN A CURSE KILL ?

"Lord Severn's expected in England to-day," said Masters, tearing the paper loose from his face. "You can ask him yourself. And if a dagger and a perfume box have any connection with this disappearance. But did you ever," he held up the paper, "did you ever see anything like the way they're carrying on ? It's all eyewash. Oh, ah ! I know that ! All the same . . ."

H. M. craned his neck to peer round.

"You're wonderin'," he asked, "whether there might be something in it after all ?"

"I'm not," the chief inspector retorted with dignity, "but I tell you straight, sir, a devil of a lot of people are. Remember ten years ago ? Lord Carnarvon and King Tut ?"

"And all they had to go on there," observed H. M., "was a little bit of a mosquito bite." A ghoulish smile flickered across his face. "I say, son. Suppose old Severn comes down here to-day, and he disappears. You'll be in the soup for fair then, won't you ?"

"Listen . . . !" began Chief Inspector Masters.

Inflating his lungs for a powerful oratorical flourish, Masters changed his mind at the last moment. Instead he merely pulled his bowler hat down on his head as though to cork himself. Almost with leisureliness he crumpled up the newspaper and flung it over the parapet, where the breeze caught it and carried it away with high sailing grace.

"I won't say," Masters declared, with powerful restraint, "what I was going to say. No. I won't even ask why it's always got to be ME who gets involved in these ruddy cases. I'll merely say, Sir Henry," his voice grew desperate, "will you in lum's name try to be practical and make a practical suggestion ?"

"All right," growled H. M. "Beaumont."

"What's that ?"

"Bloke called Beaumont. First name unknown."

"What about him ? Who is he ?"

"An American," returned H. M., "who turned up at our party's digging in Egypt and offered sixty thousand dollars for the gold mask worn by Herihor's mummy. Failin' that, he offered very big prices for—are you following me ?—a gold dagger and a gold perfume box. Still no sale."

Masters, himself again, whistled on a very significant note and was all attention.

"Wait a minute, now !" urged H. M. "Don't go runnin' away with the idea before we know what's in it. The gal herself . ."

"Lady Helen ?"

"Sure. Who else would I mean? The gal herself told me about him when we were on the train between Cairo and Alexandria. The only reason I remembered the name, d'ye see, was because on Thursday night it popped up again."

"How so?"

"Oh, Masters? You remember Farrell's story about how he guarded the girl's hotel suite in London during her very rummy three-day absence? Well. During that time, he said, an American named Beaumont came along and tried to see the gal. So I was just wonderin'..." H. M. paused.

The heavy square trap-door in the roof, communicating by means of a ladder with the clock-room beneath, was pushed up and back. Kit Farrell, in grey flannels and an old sports coat, the knot of his tie demonstrating that he hadn't been before a mirror when he tied it, climbed up to join them.

Kit's face looked heavy and dazed. The grey eyes were so smarted from lack of sleep that he had to close them, momentarily, against the wind. His shoulders were a little hunched up, as though he were ready on a hair-spring to lash his fist out against the world. Nerves! Nerves! Nerves! For a moment, before Kit closed the trap-door with a soft bang, they could all hear the heavy, deathly ticking of the big clock.

" 'Morning, son," grunted H. M., carefully avoiding Kit's eye. "Had your breakfast?"

"Yes," answered Kit. "They said you were up here. I thought you'd better have a look at this."

He held out to H. M. a folded sheet of notepaper. Then he went to the side of the tower facing front, turned his back to them, and began, very slowly and deliberately. to hammer his fist on the top of one battlement. Nerves! the beat of that fist seemed to say. Nerves! Nerves! Nerves! But H. M., who was not looking at him, uttered an exclamation.

For the note, in neat if shaky writing, said:

Sir:

Respectfully suggest, regarding missing portrait of first Lady Severn, you look in antique shop of J. Mansfield, 12 College Street, Gloucester. Saw it there yesterday, on floor with other pictures, while shopping.

Am not well and have taken to my bed, otherwise
would have told you last night.

> Yours sincerely,
>
> E. POMFRET.

H. M. handed the note to Masters and spoke sharply.
"Where'd you get this, son?"

"It was brought up to my room a while ago," returned
Kit without turning round. "I thought you'd better see
it."

"No, Masters," H. M. forestalled the chief inspector's
question sharply, "I haven't got the foggiest notion what
this means. But, oh, my eye!" He breathed with evil
satisfaction. "I very much want a word with this J.
Mansfield. J. Mansfield, hey? J. Mansfield?" He ruminated, and then raised his voice. "Do you happen to
know anything about him, son?"

"It's a her," said Kit. "Julia Mansfield. Keeps an
arty antique shop near the Cathedrals. Does picture restoring too."

"Picture restoring," repeated H. M., screwing up his face
even more. "If you ask me, Masters, I say we'd better cut
along there straight away."

"But it's Sunday, sir! The shop will be closed!"

"No, that's all right," Kit told them. "She lives at the
back of the shop. You can probably rout her out. But . . ."

Kit swung round. They saw the muscles tighten along
his jaws as he clenched his teeth. Yet he lounged there
with apparent calm, with unnatural calm, leaning one elbow
on the battlement. This tower, Chief Inspector Masters
reflected, was sixty feet high. And heights did queer
things to people's heads, when the sky seems to go round
like a wheel and even the bones feel lighter than air. Of
course, it wasn't possible this young man would . . .

"Sir Henry," said Kit, "what about the sitting and
thinking?"

H. M. started. "What's that, son?"

"I can't tell where it's got you," said Kit. "But *I've* been
doing a lot of thinking. A hell of a lot of thinking. About
Helen."

"Oh? With what result?"

"Audrey," said Kit, "thinks she's dead."

"*Easy, son!*"

77

"That's all right," Kit assured them, and laughed heartily. He wished to impress on them the fact that he had never been more cool-headed in his life. "I can't tell you," he went on, "whether she's alive or dead. But I can tell you this. We're not the victims of any Egyptian magic. Helen's been abducted."

Masters stroked his chin. He was all catlike benevolence now.

"Well, sir," Masters said in his comfortable, reassuring way, "I won't say but what that same idea hadn't occurred to me too. Among other ideas. What makes you think so ?"

"Hang it, man, look at the evidence !"

"Well, sir ?"

"Within an hour of Helen's disappearance, somebody rings up the police and the press and tells 'em she's gone. Does that sound like magical hocus-pocus ? No. It sounds like kidnapping made-on-earth. Have you traced those phone calls, by the way ?"

"No, sir, I can't say we have." Masters had the air of making a handsome concession. "Plenty of time, plenty of time !"

"And the person who rang up," Kit went on, "was a man with a heavy voice and a foreign accent. According to the descriptions of him, that would just about fit this fellow Alim Bey."

Kit pointed his finger, quickly forestalling reply.

"Alim Bey describes himself as a scholar. But, if we can believe the newspapers, he's actually a kind of glorified fortune teller. He makes his living by prophesying the future according to what he calls ancient Egyptian magic. All right ! Wouldn't it boost his stock sky-high, wouldn't it make him the most celebrated seer on earth, if he prophesied a thing like this and then *made* it come true ?"

"By abducting Lady Helen ?"

"Yes !"

"The trouble is," said Masters, "that there's an objection to it."

"I know that, Chief Inspector ! But . . ."

"Mr. Alim Bey," Masters smoothly crushed opposition, "was in Cairo on the day the young lady disappeared. You heard about it yourself. He was making more prophecies in front of Lord Severn and Mr. Robertson and two reporters. Oh, ah ! And that's not the biggest objection to the kidnapping theory, either."

Masters shook his head with a sort of sad indulgence. Himself almost at his wits' end, he found it something of a relief to pile his troubles elsewhere. Opening his notebook, he squared himself to preach from it.

"Now, sir, within a few minutes of the young lady's disappearance you ordered this fellow Benson to search the house, eh ?"

"Yes ! But . . ."

"Just so. And he did search, together with young Lewis the chauffeur, and," Masters ran his finger down a page of the notebook, "Mrs. Handyside the cook. While they were searching, he told all the other outside witnesses to stay at their posts and make sure nobody slipped out. Eh ?"

"I don't doubt that, Chief Inspector ! But . . ."

Masters raised a hand hypnotically.

"Just so. Which they did. Cellar's down there," he pointed, "and roof up here," he pointed again, "are both ruled out by witnesses. Benson, Lewis, and Mrs. Handyside all testify there wasn't an inch they didn't search, while the others swear nobody slipped out or away or anywhere else. Now, sir !"

Here Masters's smooth voice rose plaintively.

"Suppose," he concluded, "the young lady was kidnapped by Mr. Alim Bey. Eh ? Suppose she was kidnapped by Herihor or Mussolini or King Tut or anybody else. Never mind *who* it was ! Will you just tell how in lum's name the abductor managed to get her out of the house—and himself out as well ?"

H. M. spoke softly.

"Take it easy, Masters," he said.

With a preparatory whir and grind of great weights, with the slow stirring-back of a hammer taut as a bowstring, the big clock underneath vibrated like a metallic dragon on the stroke of the hour. That reverberating clang, when it did come, was a shock of sound which would have been startling even to a person of steady nerves and in his right senses.

And Kit Farrell, momentarily at least, was not quite in his right senses.

How it happened they never quite understood, even afterwards. Perhaps they had underestimated the danger and

79

dizziness of heights. Perhaps the young man before them loved Helen Loring a little too much.

As the heavy clock hammer banged out the first note of nine, as birds shot whirring and fluttering out of the window slits in the grey stone tower, Kit Farrell took a step backward. His sinewy left hand fastened on the top of the parapet. They saw his face, and the sudden wild tensing of muscles for the spring that would carry him head downward over the parapet—to crash, skull-first, on the stones of the terrace sixty feet below.

"*Look out !*" yelled Masters.

But it was H. M. who covered that distance. He had Kit by both shoulders, gripping tightly, while the clock banged out nine.

"Easy, son," H. M. said gently. "Easy, now !" And they stood in that manner while the echoes died away, and the split-second madness, such as might happen to anybody, faded out of Kit's eyes.

"Funny !" said Kit. He quite seriously believed what he was saying. "I got faint all of a sudden. Can't think what happened to me. Almost fell."

"Sure you did, son," agreed H. M., turning him round and impelling him firmly towards the trap-door. "But never mind that now. We're goin' off to this antique shop and find out who took the picture there. Down you go, now !"

"Yes," said Kit. "Yes. Quite. Funny."

So the tall grey-eyed young man, still shaking his head, descended the ladder with a puzzled look around his forehead and an inexplicable cold chill at his heart. H. M., fists on hips, stood blinking after him. Masters's ruddy face was far from ruddy now.

"That," the chief inspector muttered, "was a near thing."

"Cor !" said H. M... "So you've discovered that, have you ? Masters, you flamin' fathead."

"All right, all right ! Maybe I shouldn't have talked like that in front of the chap. Set him off, like."

"And why did you want to tell him the police hadn't traced those phone calls ? You know smackin' well one of 'em was a toll call, and . . ."

Masters brooded.

"Benson, Benson, Benson !" he said cryptically. "If I could find any real evidence against that gentleman ! But

Mr. Farrell, now. Do you think he's all right in the head?"

"Oh, my son! He's just slowly goin' to pieces because we can't find Helen Loring. There. but for the grace of God . . ."

"Well," ruminated Masters, exploring his jaw as though wondering whether he needed a shave, "I can't say I'd have taken it like that if something had happened to *my* old woman, even in the days when I was courting. Still, there you are. For the last time, Sir Henry, can't you even guess what might have happened?"

"For the last time," said H. M., "no. I did think of a possibility on Thursday night—beautiful burnin' splendid notion too. The only trouble is, it won't work. There's only one thing I can tell you, Masters, we've got to find that gal somehow! We've got to find her!"

10

THE antique shop of Miss Julia Mansfield, at Number Twelve College Street off Westgate Street, slept in a Sunday hush.

It was barely ten o'clock when H. M.'s car, with Masters at the wheel, H. M. beside him, and Kit in the back seat, drew up before the shop. No members of the press were as yet astir to molest them. Not even a clangour of church bells, that hollow lethargic sound, awoke the somnolence of the old town of half-timbered houses mellow with spring sunshine.

College Street proved to be a tiny short thoroughfare leading into the very shadow of Gloucester Cathedral. The Cathedral, behind green trees, and a green open space, towered above the little houses as it towered above human motives; dark, austere, gaunt-ribbed, making the trees seem a pleasant futility. Nearly a thousand years had run out since its first stone was laid; it snared imaginations into the web of the Middle Ages, the dark true fathomless Gothic. All three visitors were instinctively silent when they saw it.

"Hurrum!" said Masters, breaking the spell by clearing his throat and slamming the car door as he got out. "But so help me," he turned to H. M. with a deep grievance, "there's one thing you're going to do before we as much as set foot inside that shop!"

"Oh, son? And what's that?"

"You're going," said Masters, "to take off that infernal fur cap."

"You keep away," howled H. M. clutching the cap. "I got delicate ears!"

"Horse-radish," said the chief inspector.

"I got delicate ears," said H. M. "And I've just come from a month in Egypt into a climate that'd give shriekin' rheumatics to a rubber man. What's the matter with this hat, anyway?"

"If you can't see for yourself," said Masters, "there's nothing I can tell you. Sir, haven't you got any sense of dignity?"

"Me?" breathed H. M. It was as though you had asked Napoleon Bonaparte if he ever saw a battle. "Dignity?"

"All right!" snapped the chief inspector. "Suit yourself. But we're going to question a very important witness. Don't blame me if she laughs in your face." Darkly Masters surveyed the street. "And I don't like this either. According to Mrs. Pomfret's note," he fished it out of his waistcoat pocket, "she saw the picture in the antique shop when she was out shopping yesterday. Did she go shopping for antiques, or what?"

"Look here!" Kit Farrell called sharply.

Above the bow-window of the shop, a long shallow curve, were painted the words, *J. Mansfield, Antiques*. Many panes in this bow-window were of wavy bottle glass, so that you saw objects inside like images in water. The outside was white-painted, scrubbed, spick and span. To the left of the broad window they saw a door with a glass panel, and a polished brass bell-push beside it.

Kit was standing in front of the window, his hands cupped over his eyes, peering into the dim interior. The others joined him in something of a hurry.

"There you are," said Kit, and pointed.

The display ledge inside, of light oak scrubbed spotlessly clean, at first glance seemed to contain nothing but a chaste tea set of Wedgwood china and a heavy cavalry sabre, *circa* 1815, in a brass and black leather scabbard. Then you looked obliquely to the right. Leaning against the side wall, as though stacked inside the display ledge to get them out of the way, were three or four large canvases without frames.

And the face of Augusta, first Lady Severn, smiled back at them obliquely through the wavy glass.

"So !" muttered Sir Henry Merrivale.

Despite time-darkened and faint cracks, despite the brush of a bad painter, there could be no mistaking the extra-ordinary likeness to Helen Loring.

The woman in the portrait might have been twenty-five, Helen's own age. It was a half length, showing her in one of those high-waisted gowns, imitating the Roman style, which were fashionable at the close of the eighteenth century; and her yellow hair done into short ringlets.

But the brown eyes were Helen's. The forehead was Helen's. The short nose and rather broad mouth were both Helen's. Struggling through dirt and grime on the canvas, the face peered back at them blankly, with a dead absence of expression, through the wavy glass.

"Stop a bit !" said Masters, who was pinching at his under lip. "I've seen that face somewhere before !"

"Sure you have, son," agreed H. M. sourly. "In about umpteen dozen newspaper photographs." He turned to Kit. "You say this Julia Mansfield lives at the back of the shop ?"

"Yes," said Kit, who could not take his eyes off the picture.

"Oi ! Son ! Wake up ! Are you acquainted with her ?"

"With whom ?"

"The Mansfield gal, dammit !"

"I've seen her, yes. Never met her formally. She probably wouldn't know me. Try pressing the bell beside the door."

"If," growled H. M. with powerful pessimism, "she answers the door at all. Burn me, Masters, I could make progress like billy-o if only," he pointed malevolently, "if only I knew what that picture's doing here, and how it got spirited out of the house ! It seems too much to hope we'll get a bit of luck now."

But it was not too much to hope.

He had barely touched the electric bell, which they could hear ringing far away, when a door opened at the back of the darkened shop, emitting electric light. Someone ran lightly and quickly towards the front door. It was a response so instantaneous that Masters, still scrutinizing the picture as though vaguely dissatisfied, jerked up his head.

A key turned in the lock, a bolt was drawn, and the door opened with a ping of the shop bell above it.

"I'm most awfully sorry!" a contralto voice began. "But I've been laid up in bed with a dreadful cold, and . . ."

Seeing H. M., she stopped.

It was several years since Kit had seen Miss Mansfield; since, in fact, Lord Severn had closed the Hall to winter in Egypt and summer in the south of France. But Miss Mansfield had changed only in growing more sturdy, more self-reliant, more businesslike; and at the same time, one felt, she was more deeply dissatisfied.

Miss Mansfield was in her middle or later thirties, though she looked younger. She was pretty in a solid undistinguished way, with blue eyes setting off a good complexion, and soft light-brown hair rather severely dressed. She had a sturdy figure, a pleasant laugh, a passion for cleanliness, and, just at the moment, a bad cold.

This cold thickened her speech and made pink the tip of her nose, though without much discomposing her. In addition to a heavy brown skirt and wool jumper, Miss Mansfield was wearing a light-yellow jacket of soft leather, with a Russian scarf wound round her throat and its ends tucked into the opening of the jacket. Pressing the fingers of one hand against her throat—a defence against colds—she looked from one to the other of her visitors.

"Yes?" she said tentatively, and coughed.

. It was Masters, at his blandest and most smarmy, who sailed into action then.

"Morning, miss!" he said heartily. "Sorry to disturb you on a Sunday. Very sorry! You're Miss Julia Mansfield?"

"Yes?" It was both an answer and a prompting.

"I'm a police officer, miss. I wonder whether you'd do me the favour of answering one or two questions."

Brief silence.

The expression which pinched in Miss Mansfield's eyebrows was not in the least alarm, merely wonder. Then she gave a little laugh, and the faint discontented lines vanished from the corners of her mouth.

"Police officer! Really! What have I been doing now?"

Masters joined in her laugh.

"Nothing, miss!" he assured her. "Nothing, at least, that need worry you at all. Mind if we come in?"

"Please do."

She turned, and walked with quick vigorous strides towards the back of the show room.

Most of us expect antique shops to be crowded and dingy, smelling of old clothes, full of objects that have a rusty rime to the touch. This one was clearly nothing of the kind. Little light penetrated its duskiness from the street; few details could be seen; but the word 'arty' re-occurred to Kit Farrell.

Miss Mansfield took up her position behind the only thing in the room which savoured of the commercial, a small glass display case, with glass shelves and tiny electric lights inside. Miss Mansfield switched on these lights, the only illumination for their conversation in a core of gloom.

"Yes?" she prompted, straightening up again. "What did you wish to question me about?"

"As a matter of fact, miss, I'm not the one who's most interested. The one who's most interested is my friend here—Sir Henry Merrivale."

"Oh?" said Miss Mansfield, her interest quickening at the mention of a title, any title. She smiled brightly from behind the lighted show-case.

"He's interested," pursued Masters, "in a painting you've got in your window over there."

"Painting?"

Masters walked leisurely to the front of the shop, hoisted the picture over the oak rail, and returned with it.

"This one, miss."

"Oh, Lord!" cried Julia Mansfield. "How stupid of me!" Her forehead was pitted with little wrinkles, and her half-smiling mouth wry with apology. She coughed again, pressing the scarf closer to her throat. "How very stupidly careless of me to put it there! But I had a racking headache, with 'flu coming on, and I simply . . ." She broke off. "My dear man! That picture isn't for sale!"

"Oh, ah. We guessed that, miss. What we want to know is, how did it come to be here?"

"How did it come to be here?"

"Yes, miss."

"But, my good man! It was brought here! It was brought here to be restored. I've often done work like that for Lord Severn."

"Do you remember when the picture was brought here, miss?"

"Of course I remember. It was on Thursday evening."

"Wow!" said Sir Henry Merrivale.

He did not say this aloud. But he thought it so strongly that the emotional temperature of the room shot up several degrees. Miss Mansfield felt this too, though apparently she did not understand it. Her blue eyes—perhaps not highly intelligent eyes, though Miss Mansfield believed herself intelligent and wished passionately to be thought so —looked back at Masters with perplexity.

"*Thursday* evening, miss? You're quite sure of that?"

"Of course I'm sure. It was the rainy night with all the lightning."

"Just so. What time on Thursday evening would this be, miss?"

"Just before six o'clock," replied Miss Mansfield promptly. "I close at six, you see. And I was looking forward to it. My cold was coming on horribly, I felt like nothing on earth, and . . ."

"Just so. And who brought the picture here, miss?"

"That's very easy to answer," replied Julia Mansfield, patting the scarf at her throat. "It was Lady Helen Loring."

Silence.

So thick and eerie a silence, in fact, that a clock could be heard ticking through the partly open door to the living quarters at the back. But that was not all. Miss Mansfield might have been justified in thinking that she was looking at three men bereft of their wits. Then the hush shattered to bits.

"She's alive," said Kit Farrell. "*By God, she's alive!*"

It wasn't a statement, it was a shout that rang powerfully in the decorous show room, seeming to draw a vibration from the glass case. He took a step forward, and Miss Mansfield took a step back. Sir Henry Merrivale's hand clapped down on his shoulder.

"Easy, son!" urged H. M. "Easy, now!"

Julia Mansfield's colour went up, to match her pink nose.

"Has this young man," she asked, "been drinking?" And then, frowning at Kit: "Haven't I seen you somewhere before?"

With careful hands Chief Inspector Masters put down the painting, propping it against the glass case.

"Listen, miss!" he said, with strangled earnestness. "You're quite sure you know what you're saying?"

Miss Mansfield was so angry that it set her off coughing.

"Of c-course I know what I'm saying!"

"Tell me, miss. Where have you been for the past two days? Haven't you talked to anybody in this town? Haven't you seen a newspaper, even?"

"For the past two days," retorted Miss Mansfield with spirit, "I've been sick as a dog with 'flu. I haven't so much as tottered out of my bedroom. Not that any of my *friends* cared." The lines of self-pity, of discontent, were back round her mouth. "And I haven't so much as glanced at a newspaper, either. What is all this, please?"

"At a few minutes past five on Thursday, miss, Lady Helen disappeared from Severn Hall. A whole string of witnesses are willing to swear she didn't and couldn't have left the Hall in any way. Yet you say you saw her here at shortly before six?"

"Yes."

"You couldn't... hurrum!... you couldn't be mistaken, now? You knew her pretty well?"

A curious haughtiness invaded Miss Mansfield's stolid demeanour.

"I have never had the pleasure of meeting Lady Helen. I am quite sure," she seemed very positive about this, "Lady Helen is unaware of my existence as a person. *I* dealt with Lord Severn. But I am quite familiar, thank you, with Lady Helen's appearance. Now please be good enough to tell me what you mean about a disappearance?"

"Blown to dust. Phoo!" said Masters. "The young lady took a bronze lamp out of Herihor's tomb in Egypt. And old Herihor got her, just like he gets all bad boys and girls."

Masters's heavy sarcasm was completely lost on Miss Mansfield.

In a detached way, Kit Farrell found himself staring at the glass case. Its yellow light half hypnotized him. He was not thinking of the articles he saw on the glass shelves

—on the contrary, he was thinking of Helen—yet these things registered after the fashion in which the mind will seize on trifles.

A set of ivory chessmen, red and white, on a wooden board with thin metal squares. Painted miniatures, gold-bound. A string of colourless glass beads. Two or three snuff boxes. And on a shelf lower down...

Surely those rings, with the dull stones and wavering designs cut into them, were Egyptian scarab rings? And that greenish lump, which might be of clay or metal, was a lamp in the form of another famous lamp? Well, why not? This was an antique shop, wasn't it?

A cold voice struck at him.

"May I ask," inquired Miss Mansfield, "what you're looking at?"

Chief Inspector Masters swept this aside.

"Never mind what Mr. Farrell's looking at, miss! Just tell me..."

"Farrell!" exclaimed Miss Mansfield. "Farrell! Of course!"

"Just tell me this," said Masters, getting out his note-book. "Will you swear you saw Lady Helen here at shortly before six on Thursday evening?"

"Yes. I will."

"Mind telling me what happened, miss?"

"But there's nothing to tell! It had been a horrible day, nothing but rain. And now there was lightning. And my 'flu was coming on. When I heard the shop-bell ring, I almost felt I couldn't go and answer it. But I came out into the shop here, feeling dreadfully ill. And there was a big flash of lightning through the window, and I saw her standing in the middle of the floor looking at me."

Masters glanced at H. M., whose expression was too wooden to be human. Then the chief inspector spoke sharply.

"Half a minute, miss! How was she dressed?"

Miss Mansfield cast up her eyes.

"Long grey cape, with a peaked hood. Hood drawn up and around as though"—the woman frowned—"as though to hide her face. She looked... rather furtive."

"But you definitely recognized Lady Helen Loring?"

"Yes."

Still the emotional temperature rose. Her three visitors

88

were concentrated on her so intensely that it might have shaken the nerves of anyone less self-possessed than Miss Mansfield.

"I see," said Masters, clearing his throat. "Any other details of dress besides the long cape?"

"No. I couldn't see anything else."

"Shoes, for instance?"

"I'm afraid I didn't notice."

That curious haughtiness—a turn of the head and an air of intense aloofness—returned to Miss Mansfield whenever she was asked for details about Helen. Miss Mansfield spread out her fingers on the display case, like a priestess over those genteel trinkets. The light, shining upward on her rounded chin, threw her shadow on the white-painted wall behind. Masters frowned.

"Did it surprise you to see her, miss?"

"Not at all. Why should it? Lady Helen's return from Egypt had been widely enough chronicled in the papers." The bitterness of her tone did not escape anyone.

"Go on, miss! What happened?"

"Oddly enough, it was the first time I had ever heard Lady Helen's voice. She had rather a common voice, I thought. She said: 'You do picture restoring, don't you?' Well," here Miss Mansfield lifted one shoulder, "it was on the tip of my tongue to say: 'Your father can surely enlighten you about that, Lady Helen?' But, since apparently she had no knowledge of *me*, I saw no reason why I should recognize *her*."

"Oh, ah. I see. And then?"

"She was carrying that portrait under her arm. I didn't know it was that particular portrait, of course; it was wrapped up in newspapers."

"Yes, miss! Go on!"

"She put it down on the counter here and said: 'This is from Severn Hall. It will be called for.' Then she hurried out of the shop. I . . ."

Miss Mansfield stared at vacancy.

"Well!" she added. "I ran after her to the door."

"Why did you run after her to the door?"

Miss Mansfield hesitated.

"I really don't know," she admitted. "My head was swimming. I felt simply beastly. Probably that was the

89

cause of it. And yet there was something so ... so unnatural about the whole thing.

"As I say, I went to the door and looked out. The rain
was splashing down. There was another flash of lightning
without any thunder. And sometimes, at night, near the
Cathedral, one imagines queer things. She had been there
a moment before, because I saw her go out. But now the
street was empty. Shall I tell you something absolutely
silly?" Miss Mansfield pressed her finger-tips on the glass
case. "It was as though I had been talking to a ghost."

A sharp *ping* from the bell over the shop door made them
all start.

The door closed. Against faint grey light through the
glass door and through bottle-glass windows appeared a
man's high-shouldered silhouette. Apparently noticing
nobody except Miss Mansfield behind the lighted case, the
new-comer walked forward with confidence.

"I beg your pardon," he said. "My name is Beaumont,
Leo Beaumont. I wonder if you could tell me ..."

And then he too, in his turn, stopped dead.

II

As though she had been talking to a ghost.
"My name is Beaumont, Leo Beaumont."
And—— ?

It formed a tableau which Kit recalled many times afterwards. The white-painted shop with its details emerging
as their eyes grew used to gloom. H. M., who had suddenly plucked off the fur cap as though its warmth were too
much for his ears, standing well back and peering at the
new-comer over his spectacles. And Masters, not turning
round, but stiffening vitally to attention as he heard that
name. And Julia Mansfield, her right hand again at her
throat. And finally the stranger, standing poised before
the counter as he removed his hat.

In Mr. Leo Beaumont you were conscious of a personality, a strong and compelling personality, relieved—as most
strong personalities are not—by humour.

Yet there was nothing obtrusive about him. Mr. Beau-

mont had a strong nose and strong jaw, with defined bones.
He was of middle height and middle age. His thick, glossy
black hair, knifelike in its parting, was cropped above the
ears where it had begun to turn grey; a lighter colour of
skin, there, than the rest of the face. His eyes, cat-green
and with small wrinkles radiating from the outer corners,
reflected humour.

Brushed, groomed, and at ease, Mr. Beaumont wore a
light Burberry with the collar turned up, and carried a soft
hat in his gloved hand. He spoke like an American.

Miss Mansfield, who clearly had never seen him before,
woke up.

"I'm so sorry," she said coldly. "The shop is not open.
This police officer," she emphasized the word, "is here on
business."

The stranger smiled.

"As a matter of fact," he said, "I did not wish to buy
anything. Though I'm sure," his eyes rested on Miss
Mansfield, "there are many treasures and rarities here."

"Well!" said Miss Mansfield. For the green, smiling
eyes clearly intimated that the greatest treasure would be
that lady herself.

"I only wanted to ask," pursued Beaumont, "how I get
to Severn Hall. There are no shops open to ask directions
at, and the only person I met in the street was an old grandfather who yammered at me in a way I couldn't understand."

Masters shut up his notebook and swung round.

"Going to Severn Hall, sir?"

"Yes," replied Beaumont. His lifted eyebrows added
politely: 'Who wants to know?'

"I'm a police officer, sir, as this young lady says. Here's
my warrant-card. C.I.D., New Scotland Yard."

"Scotland Yard, eh?" repeated Beaumont. His eyes
narrowed slightly.

"Yes, sir. I've been looking into this matter of Lady
Helen Loring's disappearance, but I came down here
about . . . other things. I understand, Mr. Beaumont, you
were acquainted with Lord Severn in Cairo?"

"How do you come to understand that?"

"Were you?"

"Very much so, Mr. . . . ?"

"Masters, sir. Chief Inspector Masters. And did you
get 'em?"

"Did I get what?"

"The gold dagger and the gold perfume box," returned Masters, "out of the old Thinggummy's tomb. We understand you offered big prices for 'em, but that Lord Severn couldn't sell because the stuff belonged to the Egyptian Government."

Beaumont nodded. He did not pretend to misunderstand. Amusement-wrinkles deepened at the corners of his eyes, which seemed to acquire an extraordinary penetration as they fastened on Masters. He stood motionless, a reposeful quality of stillness, and nodded again.

"Yes, Mr. Masters. That's true. But I don't want those articles any longer, in view of what happened on Thursday. No, believe me! My interest lies in something else altogether!"

"Oh?"

"I am very much in the market to buy the bronze lamp. I will pay fifty thousand dollars for that little bit of bronze" —suddenly Beaumont brought his hand down, but softly, like a pounce, on the edge of the glass case— "and think it very cheap at the price."

"May I ask what in blazes you want with the lamp sir?"

"Ah! I'm afraid that's my business, Chief Inspector." Masters was beginning to lose his temper.

"And you came down here just to buy it? Eh?"

"I did."

"From a young lady who's disappeared?"

"Pardon me," corrected Beaumont. "I read yesterday that Lord Severn himself was expected back in England to-day. So I came down here last night. I'm putting up at The Bell. And did you hear the nine o'clock news on the radio this morning? No? You should have. Lord Severn's plane got in early to-day. You may say and you're probably right, that it's vulgar and in bad taste of me to approach him with a business offer so soon after his daughter vanishes . . ."

From the lips of Miss Mansfield there was a small, sharp, impatient bleat.

"But that's absurd!" she protested. "I mean, it's utterly absurd to speak of Lady Helen's having vanished, when I was talking to her in this room an hour after it's supposed to have happened!"

This was the point at which Beaumont dropped his hat.

A small action, which may have been caused by no more than his bumping his elbow when he swung round towards her. Beaumont bent down to pick up the hat, and, when he straightened up again, they saw that the blood had rushed into his face as though from the exertion. But Chief Inspector Masters received the impression that Beaumont was utterly taken aback.

"I beg your pardon?" Beaumont said.

Masters laughed with a stuffed, unreal, hypocritical laugh.

"Now, now, sir! It's all right! No call to get excited! I'm afraid this young lady has got a bit mixed up in her times, that's all." Masters turned round, and his murderous eye warned Miss Mansfield to be silent or see trouble. He turned back again to Beaumont. "Er—you're staying at The Bell, sir?"

"That's right."

"Odd," ruminated Masters, "that nobody at the hotel could give you directions for Severn Hall."

"Wasn't it?" agreed Beaumont. His greenish eyes twinkled under their heavy lids. "Particularly since I didn't ask them."

"How's that, sir?"

"Come now, Inspector! That was not a very crafty trap, was it?"

(What the devil, Kit Farrell wondered, was that unnatural pedantic note in the man's voice? A heavy, slow-speaking voice, as though the mouth were synchronized with the eyes that fixed on you. What did it remind you of?)

"I went out," continued Beaumont, "for a morning stroll in a fine old English town, meaning to see the place where Bishop Hooper was burned at the stake. And I completely forgot to ask for directions at the hotel. How *does* one get to Severn Hall, by the way?"

"Take the Sharpcross bus in Southgate Road," said Miss Mansfield very rapidly. "Or hire a car at Miller's in Spa Road. Or you can walk it if you feel like some exercise."

Beaumont inclined his glossy dark head.

"Thank you. I don't intend to go out there, actually, until Lord Severn returns. But I thank you. Will you want to see me again, Chief Inspector?"

"Very much so, Mr. Beaumont. Oh, ah! Very much so! But that can wait. In the meantime..."

"In the meantime, you want to jump with hob-nailed boots all over poor Miss ... Miss Mansfield, is it? I wonder why."

"That's neither here nor there, sir."

"No doubt. And I can take a hint." He looked at Julia Mansfield. "If you have any treasures for the amateur, please save them until I return. Good morning."

Not once had Mr. Leo Beaumont glanced towards H. M. or Kit Farrell, standing back in the shadows. In fact, it may be doubted whether he had even noticed them.

Putting on his light tan-coloured hat, he drew the brim slightly over one eye. He bowed to them pleasantly, and left the shop with the door pinging in a decisive sort of way after him. Through the crooked window-panes, a distorting-glass, they saw him stop to light a cigar before he sauntered off in the direction of the Cathedral.

"Lummy!" muttered the chief inspector. He looked at H. M., who still stood silent with his arms folded. "What do you make of that gentleman, now?"

It was Miss Mansfield, ready to weep, who intervened.

"I have a cold," she burst out—the voice through her nose made it sound like 'code'—"and I still feel beastly, but this is really a little too much. Please, will you tell me what all this means? Why did you shut me up when I tried to speak? Don't you believe what I've been telling you about your precious Lady Helen?"

No reply.

"Will you please be good enough to answer me, Mr. Masters? Don't you believe what I've been telling you?"

Masters looked her straight in the eyes.

"Frankly, miss," he answered, "I can't say I do."

Kit Farrell's heart went down with sickening effect.

"But you've got to believe her, Chief Inspector!" Kit roared. "Why should Miss Mansfield say Helen came here, if Helen didn't come here?"

"Ah!" said Masters, with a sinister inhalation.

"And who brought that picture here, if Helen didn't?"

"Ah!" Masters said again. "I'll tell you what it is," he went on grimly. "It's a very pretty little story this lady tells us, about a ghostly figure coming in out of the rain. But I'm not much on ghosts, as Sir Henry will tell you. *If* Sir Henry ever says anything." He glowered at H. M.

94

"I've got to go on what's probable, young fellow. And is this story probable?"

"Why not?"

"First, because the whole caboosh of witnesses swear Lady Helen never left Severn Hall. All right!" Masters held up his hand. "We'll pass that. Just take the story itself."

"Well?"

"In here," resumed Masters, "comes somebody that Miss Mansfield positively identifies as Lady Helen Loring. Admits she's never seen the lady close up or heard her voice, but identifies her in spite of a hood partly drawn across the face."

"But it was Helen Loring!" cried Miss Mansfield. Then a horrified suspicion seemed to strike her. "Just exactly what are you saying? Do you think I invented the whole thing? And that nobody came in at all?"

Masters shook his head.

"Not necessarily, miss. I'm only saying that if anybody came in here—*if*, mind you, and it's a big if!—that person wasn't the lady we're looking for. Let me go on. You next say the visitor had what you call a 'common' voice. Oh, ah." He turned to Kit. "Did Lady Helen have a 'common' voice?"

"Good lord, no! I mean ...!" Catching Masters's sardonic and sceptical eye, Kit stopped.

"Then there's the hooded cape she was wearing. If this person was Lady Helen, where did she get that outfit or any outfit? Her own mackintosh was left behind on the floor of the main hall. Her luggage hasn't been unpacked or even unlocked up to this very minute. There's no clothing missing from the hall, or we should smacking well have heard of it. It's a funny thing, Miss Mansfield, that you couldn't remember anything else about the clothes."

"Wait!" put in the other sharply. Then she quietened down. Still not looking at Masters, but with an offhanded and aloof air addressed to a Venetian mirror on the other side of the room, Miss Mansfield added: "As a matter of fact, now I come to think of it, I did notice something else."

"Oh?"

"You mentioned shoes. Now I come to think of it, Lady Helen was wearing scarlet and black patent-leather shoes, size about fours."

"And you don't even need to look at your notebook, Chief Inspector," Kit Farrell said with ferocious geniality. "*I* can tell you that's right. I remember noticing those red and black shoes when we drove up to the house. Doesn't this prove Helen was here?"

Apparently it didn't.

A still more sinister expression pinched down one of Masters's eyelids as he studied her. Some theory, clearly, had begun to take form in his mind.

"Oh, ah?" he queried, and pounced. "Why didn't you tell me this before, miss?"

"I... I didn't think of it."

"*Answer me, miss. Why didn't you tell me this before?*"

"Just a moment, son," interposed H. M. very quietly.

It was the first time H. M. had spoken since they entered the shop. Masters whirled round.

At the back of the room there was a faint, slanted line of light where the door to Miss Mansfield's living quarters still stood open as she had left it. For some seconds H. M. had been contemplating this door, surveying something inside the door and beyond it, with a look for which 'interest' would be far too weak a word.

Now he lumbered forward, unfolding his arms and thrusting the fur cap into the side pocket of his baggy ancient suit, to address Miss Mansfield.

"Ma'am," said H. M., leaning one hand on the glass counter and putting his other fist on his hip, "I'm the old man." He let the grandeur of this sink in. "This weasel Masters hasn't got any courtesy. Now me—I'm never discourteous. Would you like to tell *me* why you didn't mention the shoes at first?"

"I..."

"Was it," continued H. M., looking very hard at her, "because for some reason you already didn't like Helen Loring much? And then, when she came in here and didn't recognize you or pretended not to recognize you, it made you so mad you weren't goin' to admit you'd bothered to notice *anything* about her?"

(Bull's-eye, thought Kit. Whang in the gold.)

"Really," cried Miss Mansfield, "I had no reason either to like or dislike her. I'm sure I'm not interested in her fine clothes and her archæological expeditions and her lo—"

Kit could have sworn she was going to add 'love-affair', but she checked herself.

"But I do think," Miss Mansfield added, "it would have been only common courtesy to have said: 'Good evening ; I'm Helen Loring'. Instead of behaving in that queer, shivery kind of way, as though she suspected me of something. Especially considering how kind Lord Severn has been to me in the past. And . . . and the other gentleman." Surprisingly, Miss Mansfield blushed. "I mean, I think it would have been only common courtesy. Don't you ?"

"I do, ma'am. I do for a fact. What do you mean by sayin' Lord Severn has been kind to you in the past ?"

The blue eyes opened wide.

"Good heavens !" cried Miss Mansfield. "Not what you are thinking !"

"Well, now. How do you know what I'm thinking ?"

"Naturally I don't know. Naturally ! But . . ."

"I got a low mind," said H. M. apologetically. "Haven't you ?"

"No ! Certainly not !"

H. M. looked depressed.

"What I meant was," explained Miss Mansfield, "that Lord Severn has been good enough to write to me two or three times in the past year. He occasionally sends me one or two things from Egypt." Her finger indicated the lowest shelf of the display case. "Nothing really valuable, but at least I can assure intending purchasers that the articles are real and not made in Birmingham."

After a pause she put her hand to her throat again.

"I . . . I even used to do picture restoring *at* Severn Hall," she went on. "I worked in Lord Severn's study. It's on the ground floor, with a private door to the outside, and you can go in there without traipsing through the house and being looked at by servants. That was where I . . ."

"Where you what, ma'am ?"

"You really must excuse me," said Miss Mansfield. "I feel simply ghastly."

She came out from behind the counter. Her fingers pressed hard on her neck, pinching it up in the scarf; the soft brown hair looked oddly disarranged. Then, before H. M. could speak, she almost ran towards the door at the back of the shop. It closed behind her with a slam. Two seconds later it opened again.

"And please," Miss Mansfield called to them with icy sarcasm, "stay as long as you like."

For the second time the door slammed, and a key turned in the lock.

Vibrations of the noise quivered in this scrubbed white-painted room, with its brocaded chairs and Venetian mirror and the ancient grandfather clock that wouldn't work. H. M. sniffed. He peered at Masters.

"No, son !" he commanded warningly. "Don't say it !"

"Don't say what ?"

"Don't say," explained H. M., "whatever it was you were goin' to say. You'd be miles off the mark. Can you guess what it was that made her fly off the handle and dash out of here like that ?"

Masters looked ponderously satiric. "It wouldn't be a guilty conscience, by any chance ?"

"Oh, my son ! It was relief." H. M. nodded. "Sheer, pourin', overwhelming relief. That's what it was. Y'know, Masters, I'm beginning to understand a lot of things about this business I didn't understand before. There's only one thing, burn me, I don't understand."

"I'm happy to hear it, sir. What might that be ?"

"How in blazes," said H. M., "Helen Loring disappeared out of that house."

"But that's the only thing that matters !" said Kit. "And was Helen here on Thursday night, or wasn't she ? H. M., what do you believe ?"

"Son, I don't know."

"When you were talking to Miss Mansfield, you sounded as though you did believe her. But the chief inspector seems to think . . ."

Masters snapped a rubber band round his inevitable notebook, snapped it against the leather, and put the notebook into his breast pocket.

"If you don't mind, young fellow, whatever I think, I'll keep it to myself. We can't—excuse me !—we can't have you going off the deep end again."

"Look here," said Kit quietly. "Let's have something out now."

He paused for a second, trying to find words. The blackness of that morning crowded back on him.

"It's been difficult," he said, "to look you two in the face for the past hour. I know now I was within one whistle of

98

". . . well, of doing something idiotic this morning. On the tower. I went loony and nearly jumped over."

The others did not comment.

"Believe me, I didn't know it at the time. I honestly thought the blood had gone to my head. But I realized afterwards. Going down the ladder. Maybe I wouldn't actually have jumped. I like to think so, anyway, because it makes me feel less ashamed of myself." (How the hell *could* he get the words out of his throat?) "What I want to tell you is that that's all finished. I won't be the same kind of ass twice. As I say, I thought the blood had gone to my head. . ."

"It had, son," H. M. told him. "There's nothing to apologize for." He glared and glowered. "Just remember it's that little blind-flash that causes suicides. . . . And murders," he added.

"Why do you say murders?"

"Ask Masters."

"Well, Chief Inspector?"

Masters cleared his throat.

"Let's face it, Mr. Farrell," he said. "I'm bound to tell you now I think your young lady is dead."

"I see," said Kit.

"That little point about the shoes . . . oh, ah. Yes. It wouldn't surprise me if that clinched it."

"How so?"

"Somebody—I'll give Miss Mansfield that much—seems to have been here in this shop at six o'clock on Thursday. Not Lady Helen, but *somebody*. Wearing Lady Helen's scarlet and black shoes. Why? Lugging in a picture for no apparent reason. Why? I'll tell you. To establish that Lady Helen Loring was alive and outside Severn Hall at six o'clock on Thursday. Whereas, you can bet your shirt, she was actually dead and inside it."

Close at hand, heavy and slow-clanging, the bells of Gloucester Cathedral began to ring. Kit Farrell scarcely heard them.

"Dead," he repeated, "and inside Severn Hall. I see. But where inside Severn Hall? Why wasn't she found?"

"Ah!" said Masters grimly. "I've got a bit of a theory about that too. The only thing, as I blooming well ought to have seen from the start, that could explain the whole mess. It's a good thing, a very good thing, the local

Superintendent's kept that house under observation every night since Thursday." Masters raised his voice above the clangour of the bells. "Don't you agree, Sir Henry?"

H. M. was not listening. His eyes were fixed on the closed door to Miss Julia Mansfield's living quarters.

"Oh, ah?" the chief inspector muttered abruptly. "A little while ago you seemed to be a good deal interested in something inside that room. when the door was partly open. Mind telling me what you saw there?"

"Only another picture." The big voice sounded far away. "A tiny little picture this time, in a silver frame on a table. That's all."

"Never mind this business of pictures, sir! Listen to me for a second! Don't you agree about the other thing? About what the murderer or murderers have got to do now? And ... finding the body?"

Still H. M. did not reply. It was not until five o'clock that afternoon, when the last terror gathered and struck at Severn Hall, that he answered Masters's question.

12

IT was now, as they were well to remember later, a quarter past four.

"Kit," said Audrey Vane, "don't you think it's about time we were hearing from Lord Severn?"

"Is it? Yes, I suppose it is."

"His plane got in early this morning. He was interviewed at Croydon, and quoted in the one o'clock news. He said ... Kit, what's the matter with you?"

"What do *you* think's the matter, Audrey? More tea?"

The day, which began in such mild weather, had changed towards afternoon after the fashion of April days. Gusty rain-spatters ticked against the windows. whose curtains had not yet been drawn, and caused uneasy upheaval among the leaves of the park.

Kit Farrell leaned back in the cretonne-covered easy chair, and closed his eyes. Tea had been brought up to these two before the fire in Helen's room—that long, cheerful, now poisoned room with the white marble mantelpiece on whose top still rested the bronze lamp. Across from him, beyond a silver tea-service on a low table, Audrey was curled up on the sofa.

So Kit leaned back and shut his eyes. If he opened them, he reflected, he would be looking up at the thrice-accursed bronze lamp. The heat of the fire fanned him, scorched him, seemed to rock him drowsily. He had only to relax, and his head swam.

His companion's voice seemed to come from far away.

"Little Audrey," observed the Audrey who was not little, "is seriously annoyed with you, Mr. Farrell."

"Is she, Miss Vane ?"

"You rush out of here this morning on a mysterious errand, and don't even bother to knock at my door..."

"I thought it was better to let you sleep, Audrey. You needed it."

"You're a one, aren't you, to talk about needing sleep ?"

"All right."

(Very peaceful, keeping the eyes closed. A dull red glow in front of the lids. The heat of the fire searched him, probed into his being, muffled him against rain-gusts and thoughts.)

"Anyway, Kit, where did you and the others go ? Why won't you tell me ?"

"Because I can't."

"Honestly, Kit ! Why not ?"

"Because for some reason they say it would help Helen's murderer if all the facts get out."

"Helen's murderer ?" There was a gasp of indrawn breath; a rustle and stir as though Audrey had moved sharply on the sofa.

"Yes. They think she's dead, just as you do. All I can tell you is that we went to the shop of a woman named Julia Mansfield, and heard several things. Oh, and met an odd cove named Beaumont. If you'd like to know who they think the murderer is, on the other hand, I can tell you that because..."

Roused out of torpor, dragged back by facts to real life again, Kit partially opened his eyes. And for an instant he thought he must be dreaming.

Audrey was not looking at him. She was gazing at the other side of the room, gazing at nothing at all; but on her face was such a white and concentrated look of hatred, such a glassy blind furious expression in the dark eyes, that her scarlet-fingered nails might have been ready to rip across the cretonne cover of the sofa.

God Almighty! Had he been dreaming? For an instant later, as his sanded eyes opened fully, there was the old sympathetic Audrey regarding him. Her face was a trifle pale under the lacquered make-up, yes, and the long dark eye-lashes lowered. Her hands shook when she bent to pour out more tea that was almost cold. But this might have been the effect of his announcement about murder.

"Yes, Kit?" Audrey prompted him. "You were saying you could tell me who they think the . . . the murderer is?"

"Because it's only my own guess. Masters, I'll take my Bible oath, believes it was done by Benson and Mrs. Pomfret working together."

Audrey upset the milk-jug, and then mopped at it hastily with a napkin.

"Benson! That's absolutely silly!"

"I know it is."

(*Had* he been dreaming, about that look in Audrey's eyes? Couldn't you trust anybody in this infernal business?)

"Mrs. Pomtret," declared Audrey, "might be anybody or anything. But Benson! My dear Kit! What makes you think Masters believes that?"

"Certain things that were intimated at the antique shop. And one other point, when we were coming back here to lunch." Kit struggled with temptation, and yielded because of the utterly fantastic nature of the accusation. "H. M. said"—here he gave a very fair imitation of the old maestro's manner—"H. M. said: 'Did you find out what I asked you to find out—who picked the daffydils on Thursday?'"

"Picked the what?"

"Daffydils. His version of the word. And Masters said: 'Yes, sir, it was Benson'. "

"Daffodils!" echoed Audrey. As though uncertainly, her eyes wandered over to the bowl of yellow daffodils, now withering, on the centre table in the grey-and-gold room. "But what's a bowl of flowers got to do with this?"

"Don't ask me."

"And what would Benson and Mrs. Pomfret have to gain

from doing ... well," Audrey shivered, "what they shouldn't ?"

"What would anybody have to gain from it, except Alim Bey ? I was wrong, of course," growled Kit. "I thought, and told 'em so, that this whole thing was a piece of dirty work managed by Alim Bey. Who except a blasted seer and fortune teller *would* profit by it ? Who else could make capital out of the bronze lamp ? But Alim Bey is in Cairo, and ..."

"Kit." Audrey sat up straight as though flicked by memory. "Did you say you'd met a man named Beaumont at this place you went to ?"

"Yes, whoever he is."

"You mentioned the name before." Audrey nodded. "You said somebody called Beaumont had come to the Semiramis Hotel to enquire after Helen. But I never connected the name with ... Kit !" Her voice was a small scream. "You don't mean *Leo* Beaumont ?"

"Yes ! What about him ?"

"You mean to say you've never heard of Leo Beaumont ?"

"Never. And neither has H. M. or Masters—I'll swear to that. Who is he ?"

"He's the most famous seer and fortune teller in America. Makes millions out of it. He's got an Egyptological Temple in Los Angeles, and runs it like a big business concern."

Emily, the stout parlourmaid, tapped softly at the door and came in to draw the curtains. Rain had so thickened outside that it flickered past in fine sheets like blown dust, bringing its own early twilight. Lightning silhouetted it, and then came a crash of thunder distantly rolling.

"So that's it !" said Kit. All his somnolence rolled away. It brought back the twitch of shaking nerves. He jumped to his feet.

"How do you mean, that's it ?" demanded Audrey.

"That's why Beaumont had that funny way of talking ! And the eyes fixed on you ! And the whole atmosphere ! It's the up-to-date version of the Gothic romance. You got the impression that Beaumont would only have to snap his fingers, and women would jump through hoops." Kit broke off. "H. M.'s got to hear about this, Audrey ! Where's H. M. ?"

Again thunder rumbled. There was a soft rattle of

rings as Emily drew the curtains on the long line of windows.

"If you please, sir." The parlourmaid suppressed a giggle. Emily was a Yorkshire girl, not at all alarmed by any occurrences here. "If you mean the stout gentleman, he's having his tea with Mr. Benson in the butler's pantry. The police inspector's there too. They're comparing scrapbooks."

Kit and Audrey exchanged a glance.

"They're comparing what ?"

"Scrapbooks, sir."

But any idea that placid, patient Mr. Benson might be in course of being subjected to a third-degree was dispelled as soon as they hurried downstairs.

They crossed the echoing main hall, where the two suits of armour stood in the glare of two roaring fires. They opened the green-baize door, leading into the long, narrow, fusty-smelling passage carpeted with coconut matting. Other doors to backstairs quarters—kitchen, store-room, larder, servants' hall—opened off this passage as well. But, even if they had not known where it was, there could be no mistaking the door to the butler's pantry.

It stood partly open, and a voice issued from inside. It was a bass voice pitched in a strange, high-falutin tone of false modesty. The voice coughed deprecatingly.

It said: "Now this here picture of me, son, is not half bad. It was taken—lemme see !—yes, when I won the Grand Prix motor-car race in 1903. What do you think of it, hey ?"

"It is an extraordinarily fine photograph of the car, sir."

"Not the car, dammit ! Me !"

"Well, sir . . ."

A very domestic scene was in progress in the snug butler's pantry. At one side of a scrubbed table, tea-things pushed away, sat Sir Henry Merrivale with a large leather volume bulging from its contents of badly glued press cuttings. On the other side of the table sat Benson, with a smaller volume of the same kind.

In the background stood Chief Inspector Masters, maddened to frenzy by this dilatory way of doing business.

"Sir Henry, listen !" Kit began. "We've found . . ."

H. M. merely lifted his head and gave the two newcomers a glare of such malevolence that they both subsided. Then he became all milk and honey again as he addressed Benson.

"Now here," he pursued, holding out the scrapbook and pointing, "is one of me christening a battleship. There was a spot of bother there, I can't think how, with the champagne bottle. Instead of hittin' the battleship, it conked the Mayor of Portsmouth and knocked the poor blighter cold."

"Indeed, sir? I trust there were no serious consequences?"

"Oh, no. Only a clout over the onion. But he looks kind of cross-eyed in that picture, don't he?"

"Extremely, sir."

"And the bottle didn't break, so we used it again. That's me on the left. Newspaper photographers say they like takin' my picture."

"I cannot in the least doubt it, sir. I should fancy you must have provided them with some memorable photographs."

"Oh, well!" said H. M., waving this away with the same stuffed false-modesty which would not have deceived a baby. "Now here," he bent forward in absorption, "here's somethin' really choice. Full-face and close up. I had it taken when I was standin' for Parliament. East Bristol. The idea is to express nobility and sternness, d'ye see?"

Evidently it did. The effect was such that even Benson started slightly and shied back.

"What's the matter, son? Don't you think it does me justice?"

Benson coughed.

"Candidly, sir, I can't say it does."

"Aha!" said H. M. "You hear that, Masters?"

The chief inspector did not comment. Perhaps Masters was incapable of it. He merely pressed his hands firmly to his bowler hat.

"And why don't you think it does me justice, son?"

Benson coughed again.

"Well, sir. There is about your countenance a certain quality, a certain *je ne sais quoi*, if I may so express myself, very difficult to define. Indeed, I doubt whether it could be recorded by a photographic plate."

H. M. looked very hard at him, as though suspicious of some ulterior meaning in this. But the tactful butler hastened to explain.

"I mean, sir, that it is a quality often found. Now I have here"—undoubtedly determined to get in his own innings, Benson thrust forward his own scrapbook—"photographs of her ladyship taken over a period of a dozen years. You will no doubt observe . . ."

"Sure, sure ! But I was showin' you . . ."

" . . . that her ladyship," said Benson firmly, "though very beautiful, is not what is called photogenic. It is a matter of colour and expression, I fancy. Her photographs . . ."

"This is me at the Taj Mahal."

" . . . are execrable or unrecognizable. If you will glance at this picture taken recently in Cairo, with a certain Mr. Beaumont, you will note . . ."

"Here is me impersonatin' Peter the Hermit in a pageant of the Crusades."

Benson closed his eyes.

"Yes, sir. That brings me to my next point with regard to getting a good likeness of you. I refer, sir, to your evident fondness for being photographed in false beards."

H. M. sat up.

"What's wrong with false beards ?" he demanded. "I like false beards !"

"Exactly, sir," agreed Benson with a serene smile. "I like them myself, especially in Christmas charades."

"Well, then !"

"But in no less than four instances here, notably as Shylock and Father Christmas, you appear in false beards so luxuriant, sir, that it is difficult to tell where the beard ends and the face begins. You will concede this as being something of a barrier to what is known as a speaking likeness ?"

"Yes," H. M. was impressed. "Yes, I, s'pose that's true."

"Exactly, sir. On the other hand, take the case of his lordship. I have here a photograph of Lord Severn which . . ."

"Looky here, son. You seem determined to talk about your family, and not let me get a word in edgeways. All right. We'll *talk* about your family. You've got a lot of pictures of Lady Helen Loring. But I'll bet I've got one that you haven't got."

"Sir ?"

H. M. flipped open the back of the big scrapbook, into

which had been wedged a thick bundle of cuttings not yet fastened in. He began to sort through these, muttering to himself and spilling a considerable number on the floor.

"The one I'm lookin' for," he said, "was taken outside the Main Railway Station in Cairo close on three weeks ago. It's really a picture of me gluing a five-pound note to a taxi-drivers' face."

This nearly shook Benson's nerve.

"I beg your pardon, sir ?"

"He cut my necktie off, so I glued a five-pound note to his face," H. M. explained carefully. "But the gal's in it too, and you can see her face quite clearly in the foreground." His voice grew querulous. "I know I got the ruddy thing here somewhere, because . . . ah ! Here we are !" He disengaged the newspaper-photograph, which was a good-sized one. "Like to have it for your collection ?"

"I should deeply appreciate it, sir."

"Right," said H. M., holding the picture beneath the overhead light to study it himself. "This is me without the tie, and my mouth open. This is Lady Helen, and you can see that she . . ."

Then it happened. Something in the whole emotion and atmosphere of that room altered, as clearly as it altered in H. M.'s face.

H. M. had partly got up from his chair, in the act of handing the photograph across the table, when he looked at that photograph more closely. Something in the picture riveted his attention, caught it and held it fast. He remained motionless, staring down.

They heard the rain drive against the pantry windows. They heard the wheezing of H. M.'s breath. They saw the polish of his bald head, the gleaming spectacles, the gold watch-chain that ornamented the waistcoat across his corporation. He was not now thinking of himself at all, or of any vanities and foibles he may have possessed.

Abruptly H. M. sat down again, with a jar that shook the chair and seemed to shake the linoleum-covered floor as well. On his face, the mouth pulled down, was a look of dazed realization.

"Oh, my eye !" he murmured. "Oh, lord love a duck ! To think I never noticed that before !"

Now this was a mood that Chief Inspector Masters understood very well. Masters said sharply: "Got anything ?"

"Lemme think, now," protested H. M. "Lemme think !"

Propping his elbows on the table and his fists at his temples, he studied the idea in his mind, while nobody spoke. Once or twice he nodded, as one point after another occurred to him. Presently his forehead smoothed itself out. The hall clock was beginning to strike five when he lifted his eyes and addressed Benson.

"I say, son." He spoke very gently. "That bronze lamp, now. If memory serves, it's still upstairs on the mantelpiece in the gal's room. Just nip up and fetch it down, will you ?"

A stir ran through the group. Benson hesitated, as though wondering whether he ought to be here. But long habit won.

"Very good, sir."

Benson turned round and left the room, closing the door carefully after him. H. M. contemplated the air in something like admiration.

"What a dunce I've been !" he said hollowly. "What a star-gazin' cuckoo to think it wasn't possible ! I say, Masters. If I turn my behind round, would you like to kick it ?"

"There's nothing I'd like better," the chief inspector assured him sincerely. "But that can wait." His voice roared out. "What is it, sir ? What have you got ? Why do you want the bronze lamp ?"

"Well," H. M. sniffed. "To be strictly honest, I don't want it at all. But I thought it was better to have friend Benson out of the room while you and I had a little *causerie*. Because, d'ye see . . . ."

"Because what ?"

"I know now," answered H. M., "what happened to Helen Loring."

13

Kit Farrell glanced at Audrey, who shrugged her shoulders. Kit' heart began to beat suffocatingly.

"Ah !" said Masters, with rich satisfaction. "I rather

thought you'd hit on the truth, sir.   And is it what I think it is?"

"No," said H. M.

He raised his hand, forestalling objections.

"Once you've tumbled to one thing, Masters—just one little thing!—the whole business falls together with each part in its proper place.   It explains how that gal disappeared smack out of the main hall .."

"She *did* disappear out of the main hall, then?"

"Oh, yes.   It explains how the footsteps came to 'stop' in mid-air.   It explains why the mackintosh came to be thrown down on the floor along with the bronze lamp.   It explains ... oh, burn me! it explains ..."

Drawing a deep breath, H. M. looked at Kit.

"You've had a lot of heart-burning over this, son," he said gently.   "And it's only fair to tell you something now. Here it is, short and sweet—you can stop worrying."

Kit took a step forward.

"Helen's alive, sir?"

"Uh-huh.   And I can tell you something else.   The mysterious girl who appeared at Julia Mansfield's antique shop, the gal who wore the hooded cape and carried the painting was .."

"Well?   Was whom?"

"Was Helen Loring herself.   Just as Mansfield said."

"That's impossible!" shouted the chief inspector.

"Oh, no."

"Wouldn't it be simpler," suggested Masters, putting himself under strong restraint and getting out his notebook, "if you just told us what you think happened to Lady Helen?"

"I can't do it, son.   Not, at least, until Lord Severn gets here.   Then I'll tell you fast enough."

"And why can't you tell me until then?"

"Because it's not my secret."   H. M. spoke with deep earnestness.   "Because I haven't got any right to.   Burn it all, Masters, you'll understand what I mean when you do realize exactly what happened!   I'm not askin' you to wait very long, am I?   Only until ..."

That was when the telephone rang.

It may be doubted whether either H. M. or Masters, each profoundly sincere in his own way, even heard it ring.   In the absence of Benson, Kit Farrell might not have bothered to answer if the insistent peal of the bell had not been distracting his thoughts, and making him want to shut it off. He hurried over to the sideboard by the fireplace—where a fateful call had been received at this time just three nights before—and picked up the phone.

Out of the receiver came the voice of Sandy Robertson.

"Sandy!" said Kit, with his mind still on a certain long-distance conversation. "Are you still in Cairo?"

"Cairo?" yelped Sandy, taken aback. "I'm in London, you fat-head! I got here with His Nibs this morning, and I've been running my legs off all day! Listen: take a message. Tell the old man..."

"What old man?"

"Lord Severn! Who else would I mean? Tell him I've been to Scotland Yard, and the Assistant Commissioner says..."

"How the devil can I tell Lord Severn anything? He's not here."

"He's... *what's that?*"

By this time both H. M. and Masters had roused themselves, catching the import of this. Masters hurried over to the sideboard, and H. M. followed him. Both of them had all along been close enough to hear Sandy's penetrating voice. Audrey Vane remained where she was, with a face suddenly panicky.

"He's not here, Sandy."

"Listen!" said Mr. Robertson, in a tone of reasonableness. "He's got to be there! He borrowed my car—you remember, the red Bentley?..."

"Yes?"

"And he left town well before lunch time. Not much past noon, anyway. He's got to be there, unless he's had a break-down."

Instinctively Kit Farrell did just what Benson had done on receiving disturbing news three nights before. He stood back to look at the little white-faced clock above the fireplace whose hands now stood at two minutes past five.

The phone was still talking when Benson himself returned to the pantry. Benson closed the door with a sharp click which attracted their attention. His bland pinkish face wore a hesitant expression.

"I beg your pardon, sir," he said to H. M., "but I was

unable to execute your order. May I ask whether anyone has moved the bronze lamp?"

"What's that, son?"

"The bronze lamp, sir," returned Benson, raising his voice, "is no longer on the mantelpiece in her ladyship's room."

Audrey Vane, her slim body rigid, pressed her hands to her mouth. Intuition seemed to flash through her mind as clearly as the lightning that lifted outside the windows, or the shock of thunder that followed.

"No!" cried Audrey. "No, no, no, no!"

She did not explain what she meant, she did not define the cold fear which rang in her voice. But they all understood.

"Is anything wrong down there?" piped Sandy's voice out of the phone. "I'll get a train down there as soon as I can, but the old man told me to. . . ."

"It's all right, Sandy," said Kit, and hung up the receiver.

"That bronze lamp," Kit added, putting the phone down on the sideboard, "was definitely on the mantelpiece in Helen's room when Audrey and I came down here about a quarter of an hour ago. We can both swear to that."

They all looked at each other.

"Easy, now!" roared H. M., as he caught Masters's suggestive eye. "We're all right. I tell you! It's no good gettin' the wind up just because a feller's been delayed, or stayed too long over his lunch, or . . ." He broke off to address Benson. "*Did* Lord Severn get here, by any chance?"

Benson's eyebrows went up.

"His Lordship, sir? Not to my knowledge. May I ask why you think his lordship should be here?"

"That was young Robertson. He says Lord Severn left town in a car five hours ago. Burn it all, son, you'd have known it if he had got here?"

"I should certainly have thought so, sir. And his lordship could scarcely have arrived in a car without the lodge-keeper's knowledge. If you will allow me to ring through on the house-phone . . . ?"

"I'll do that," Chief Inspector Masters snapped. "It's this box thing on the wall, I'd guess? Just so!" After surveying Benson with a suspicious and doubtful eye, Masters attacked the house-phone. He pressed the button marked 'Lodge', he listened, he pressed it again, he jiggled the hook, and finally he turned round with many emotions boiling inside him.

"This line's dead," he announced.

Benson, they all noticed, was as white as a ghost.

"It works," the butler said, "on a different mechanism from the outside phone. Perhaps the weather——" He conquered a shaky throat. "In a matter of such importance, Mr. Masters, may I take liberty of going down myself to the lodge and seeing Leonard?"

It proved to be unnecessary. Benson was taking overshoes and umbrella from a cupboard when a hesitant tap at the door preceded the arrival of Bert Leonard himself.

The lodge-keeper, a big stringy elderly man with work-stooped shoulders and a cadaverous face, wore dripping oilskins and carried a sou'wester hat. His thin grizzled hair stood up like a goblin's, and he seemed discomfited to find so many people in the butler's pantry.

"Shouldn't 'a' troubled 'ee . . ." he began in a hoarse voice.

"But your phone's out of order?" said H. M.

Bert seized at this. Very uncomfortable under Benson's eye, he was utterly at ease with H. M. He gave the latter a comradely grim.

"Ah," he agreed. "Out of arder"—in the speech of Somerset, 'order' becomes 'arder'—"and I can't make 'ee work. *That's* not too bad, thinks I. I'd me arders to keep them gates open, look, and let everybody in that wanted to go in. But this gentleman . . . !"

"What gentleman?"

"Comes up to the gate, look; and hangs about and hangs about; and I thinks to meself: 'Dash my buttons, mister, *you're* up to no good.' Tries to come in. No go. Says 'e wants to see Lord Severn. 'Ah,' says I, 'not in residence.' Won't believe me. Wants to write a note. This is it."

With a whirl of oilskins that sent raindrops across the room, Bert produced a white envelope.

"Says his name's Mr. Beaumont," Bert added.

"Listen, son! Never mind Beaumont! Did you see Lord Severn?"

Bert was taken aback.

"Who?" he demanded.

"Lord Severn! Did he drive through those gates this afternoon?"

"Now how could I recognize Lord Severn?" Bert asked with hoarse reproachfulness. "Never set eyes on the gentleman in me life."

H. M.'s voice abruptly grew very thoughtful.

"Let's get something straight," he suggested. "On Thursday afternoon Lady Helen got here with that gal there," he pointed to Audrey, "and this feller here," he indicated Kit. "You rang through to say Lady Helen was on her way up. How'd you know it was Lady Helen?"

"I didn't," Bert retorted argumentatively. "But the lady's *expected*, look. And here's a fine car with two ladies inside and nothing but trunks and suitcases all over the place—I ask you, what do I think?"

It was Chief Inspector Masters who sailed in here.

"We're asking," Masters snapped, "about Lord Severn. Did any car at all drive in? He'd be driving . . . ?"

"He'd be driving," supplied Kit, "a red Bentley two-seater—I can't remember the number—with a Mercury figure on the radiator cap."

"That?" exclaimed Bert, in uneasy surprise. "That one? I seed 'ee right enough! Elderly-looking gentleman in a cap and raincoat. Shot past at fifty mile an hour. Lord Severn?"

"Then he did get here?"

"Ah."

"What time was this?" asked Masters.

" 'Bout ha' past four. Ah, that'd be it! 'Bout ha' past four."

Benson, who had been standing motionless with a pair of overshoes in one hand and an umbrella in the other, carefully put them back in the cupboard. He closed the cupboard door.

"You had better return to the lodge, Leonard," Benson instructed, with a shaky return of his old authority. "That will be all."

"What about this note?" Bert held up the envelope. "And Mr. Beaumont?"

"I'll take charge of the note," said Masters, putting out his hand for it. "Just keep Mr. Beaumont at the lodge for a while. Cut along, now!"

For many seconds after the door had closed behind Bert

Leonard, Masters stood weighing the envelope in his hand. But he was not thinking of the envelope.

"Half-past four!" Masters said—not loudly, but in a dangerous tone. "Half-past four! And you and I," he looked at H. M., "have been in this blasted pantry since four o'clock. Did anybody else see a car drive up here?"

No one answered.

"Or hear a car drive up?"

"Kit and I," observed Audrey, seizing Kit's arm, "were having tea upstairs in Helen's room. But we certainly didn't hear anything."

"With all this rain and thunder, Miss Audrey," suggested Benson, "it is unlikely that you would have hea..." Benson stopped. "May I point out, Mr. Masters," he added in a louder tone, "that I also have been in this pantry since four o'clock?"

"Oh?" said Masters. "And why do you think you need to point that out?"

"Because it seemed to me," Benson stood his ground, "you were looking at me in a very odd way."

"Maybe I was, at that," said Masters. "Maybe I was at that. Have you had any message from Lord Severn?"

"No, sir."

"Sure of that?"

"Perfectly sure."

"He'd drive straight up to the front door, wouldn't he?"

"No, sir. Not necessarily."

"What do you mean by that?"

"His lordship has a study on the ground floor. You have undoubtedly seen it. There is a side door, an outer door, that gives on to the drive. It was often his lordship's practice in the old days..."

Masters did not wait for the completion of this. He was across the room in five strides, with Kit and H. M. after him.

Together they hurried along the narrow, fusty passage with the coconut matting underfoot. It was the same journey that Benson and Mrs. Pomfret had made on Thursday; and again the lightning winked along that passage, showing the darkened paintings—with one still gapingly missing—on dingy-papered walls. But, when they plunged past the green-baize door into the main hall, they met no unpleasant sight to bring back terrors. The main hall lay swept and empty.

"I tell you, Masters," roared H. M., "you're barkin' up the wrong tree! At least . . ." And his eyes wavered, uncertainly, and he rubbed a hand across his forehead.

"Just so, sir. You could be wrong."

"Yes. I could be wrong. And, my God, Masters, if I am wrong—— !" He let the sentence trail off.

"It's even worse than we thought it was ?"

"Yes," agreed H. M. "In that case, it's even worse than we thought it was."

"Lady Helen Loring," said Masters implacably, "has been murdered. Her body's hidden in this house. I mean to find it. Or let others find it for me." His glance was significant. "In the meantime. . ."

"In the meantime, son ?"

"If I've got my geography straight, that's the library over there. To get to Lord Severn's study, you go through the library, turn left to a little door at the back, and that's the study. Come on, sir."

The library was dark, since no fire had been lighted here to-day. Its great stained-glass windows, nearly drained of colour between the lights, showed as pale pointed arches against gloom. The gurgle of rain, its clamour in gutters, sounded louder here. Masters, groping his way across in the lead, found the door leading into the study. He turned the knob and flung this door open.

No fire in here, either. A smell of damp. And a faint aromatic odour, hardly perceptible . . .

But the first thing they noticed was not in the dark study at all. In the north wall—that is, the wall towards their right—were four clear-glass windows, two on either side of a modern-looking door. This door stood an inch or two open, with a shimmer of rain dancing at its edges, and creaked with a very slight movement in the brush of the wind.

Two stone steps outside the door led down into the gravel driveway, which curved past the house on the north side. Through rain-blurred windows they could see a two-seater Bentley car, dark red, its top up and dancing with rain, standing empty in the drive. It was a lonely sight, one door still partly open, against the sodden tossing trees of the park.

Masters spoke out of the near-darkness. "So he did get here, eh?"

"Haven't we got any lights in this place?" demanded Sir Henry Merrivale. Kit did not like the strained tone of his voice. "Haven't we at least got any lights?"

"That's all right, sir," Masters assured him. "Switch here on the left of the door. I just press it down, and . . .

"*God!*" cried Masters uncontrollably. And he jumped backwards as though he had been burnt.

Subdued light showed them the long, rather low-ceilinged room, so crowded and overflowing with archæological relics that at first the eye could not take in details.

You were caught, of course, by the three mummy cases, one large and two smaller, the sort known to archæologists as wooden coffins, dully painted in black and gold and blue and brown with a lifelike image of the swathed dead inside.

The eyes of these figures, brown and staring eyes sharply outlined with black, gave some semblance of life in a room where there was no life. You noticed the pottery ornaments, dull brown or greenish. You noticed the ibis head over the fireplace. You noticed the framed photographs on the walls, the little cat figure on the writing table. But always you came back to the brown staring eyes of the mummy figures, eternally pencilled out in black.

"Lord Severn!" Masters shouted wildly. Only the rain answered. He made a trumpet of his hands and bellowed: "Lord Severn!"

"It's no good, son," said Sir Henry Merrivale. "I doubt if he'll hear you."

In H. M.'s dazed expression Kit Farrell saw all his new hopes crash down, all his universe again upset.

For the room was empty. Of John Loring, fourth Earl of Severn, there was now no trace.

In the middle of the room, against a frayed old carpet, lay the disreputable tweed cap, with its crumpled peak, which Kit had so many times seen Lord Severn wear. It rested on top of an equally old coat, a combination raincoat and topcoat, flung down to the floor with one of its sleeves turned inside out.

Just beyond them, rolled over on its side, lay the bronze lamp.

14

AFTER a space of time during which many possibilities might have been imagined, Chief Inspector Masters walked forward. He walked slowly. As though it required a little effort, he bent down to pick up the coat in one hand and the cap in the other. And it is to be recorded that, for a split second, Masters wavered.

"Sir," he burst out, "you don't suppose there could actually *be* anything in old Thingummy's curse?"

"Easy, son! Wake up!"

"Oh, ah. Yes. Sorry."

Masters shook his head as though to clear it. With an effort he glanced at the inside of the tweed cap, and dropped it back on the floor. He turned the coat over in his hands, pulling down the brim of the inside pocket so as to inspect the tailor's label.

"You don't need to do that," Kit told him. Kit's muscles felt numb, his head heavy. "The coat belongs to Lord Severn."

"And you, sir," Masters said bitterly to H. M., "you had the whole thing worked out, didn't you? We'd got nothing to worry about. Oh, no! You'd tell us the whole story as soon as Lord Severn got here. By the expression on your face I'd say you had something to worry you now."

"All right, all right!" howled H. M. "Clout the old man over the head again! Kick me in the pants as usual!"

"It wasn't your secret, you said," continued Masters. "But you could explain it. Can you explain this?" Masters dropped the raincoat on the floor.

"No," admitted H. M.

"And you got your whole inspiration from a picture of you gluing a five-pound note to a taxi-driver's face. God's truth, sir! A joke's a joke; but this is serious! Where does it leave us?"

"For the love of Esau, Masters, gimme time to think!" H. M. blinked at Kit. "I expect you want to slosh me one too, son?"

But Kit, who had faith in the old maestro and wouldn't see him let down, only gritted his teeth and tried to grin in reply.

"If you say Helen's still alive, H. M., that's good enough for me."

"Ah ! But does he still say that ?" inquired Masters.

"Yes, I do !" roared H. M. "This thing's just caught me a bit off balance, that's all." He pressed his hands to his temples. "Curse it all, there's some very simple explanation of this too, if only . . ."

"You bet there's a simple explanation," Masters agreed grimly. "It's another murder, that's what it is."

H. M. hesitated.

"Are you still harpin' on the idea, Masters, that the gal was done away with by Benson and Mrs. Pomfret ?"

(So, Kit reflected, his own guess had been right about that.)

"I'm doing more than harping on it," Masters retorted. "See here !"

Diving into his inside breast pocket after the notebook, Masters produced along with it a square white envelope, sealed down. This envelope surprised him a little. Immersed in other matters, a flustered chief inspector frowned at it. 'Now where.' his expression said as clearly as words, 'did I get this ?'

"You got it," Kit answered his thought, "from Leonard, the lodge-keeper. It's a note written to Lord Severn by Leo Beaumont."

"Oh, ah ! Yes ! To be sure !"

"Beaumont," Kit continued, "refused to believe Lord Severn hadn't come down here. Probably he saw the old boy drive in—he knew Lord Severn in Egypt, remember—and that's why he wrote the note. What I really wanted to tell you both—I've found out who Beaumont is."

H. M. shaded his eyes with his hand.

"What's that, son ?" he demanded.

"Beaumont," explained Kit, "appears to be a famous American seer and fortune teller. Makes millions out of it. If anybody would be interested in curses that blow people to dust, it'd be Beaumont. I thought I'd better tell you."

"So !" said H. M.

Masters. scowling with doubt, plainly considered this something of an irrelevance. But, after studying the envelope, he slit it open with his finger.

"It's not a note," the chief inspector announced. "It's a visiting card. Hrrum ! On one side is printed, 'Leo

Beaumont'. Down in the left-hand corner, 'Temple of Sakhmet, Los Angeles, California'. On the other side . . .''
Masters turned the card over. "Writing. Just so. 'You are in grave peril. Could we not forget past differences and meet? Yours sincerely, L. B.' "

Masters ticked the card against his thumb, still scowling. H. M. turned round, with a very thoughtful brow, and stared towards the windows. You would have said that he was remembering something, which also came to him with a great blaze of light.

"Mr. Beaumont," Masters dismissed this, "can wait. I'm not interested in any ruddy fortune tellers. We've got two disappearances, that's what we've got. And there's only one thing that could possibly have happened."

"Oh, my son! *You* say that? After the cases you've been through?"

Masters's colour went up.

"I repeat," he snapped, "that in this case—this case, mind you!—it's true. This smooth cove Benson . . ."

"Haven't you forgotten, Masters, that Benson was with you and me in the butler's pantry when Lord Severn disappeared?"

"Just so," acknowledged Masters, with a slow and significant nod. "But where was Mrs. Pomfret? . . . Excuse me just one moment!"

Before the others could speak, Masters had hurried out of the room into the library, closing the study door behind him.

"H. M.," said Kit, "what's on his mind?"

"A whole lot, son." H. M. turned round. "And, d'ye see, I can easily understand why he thinks what he does think."

"Murder?"

"Yes. Somebody"—making a face of emphasis, H. M. pointed to the floor—"somebody had to bring that bronze lamp down from upstairs. It can't be coincidence or chance that the house telephone to the lodge was out of order bang at the time Lord Severn's due to get here. I can see how Masters's mind is working, right enough."

"But if Benson and Mrs. Pomfret are a pair of murderers —and that's fantastic!—where did they hide the bodies?"

"Secret hiding place. If everything else is eliminated, Masters thinks it's got to be."

H. M. was surveying the crowded room, turning slowly from one side to the other. His gaze encountered that of the largest mummy case, a dull burnished-gilt shape beside the fireplace in the wall facing across to the wall of the outer door and the four windows. To the right of the mummy case hung a heavy brown curtain. H. M. lumbered across to this curtain. Sweeping it aside on its brass rings and rod, he revealed still another door.

This was fastened with two bolts on the inside. H. M. knocked his knuckles against it.

"What's this, son ? Where does the door lead ?"

"To an inside staircase," replied Kit, readjusting memories of the house. "Corkscrew staircase. Goes up between the less walls to a door on each floor. Why ?"

"I dunno," admitted H. M., testing the bolts and finding them solidly fastened. "I was only grubbin' in the dust."

Beating his hands together, a picture of indecision, H. M. swung round again in the direction of the wall with the four windows and the partly open door. Rain-spatters had already formed a pool below this door. Little gusts of air would flutter in with a breath of cold damp as the door creaked.

"I can prove I'm right about one thing," he declared, "in a very short time. But will that help, with the other things pilin' up on us ?" He seemed to be gabbling away to himself. "What happened to *this* bounder ? The same thing ? And why ? And how ? And will it upset the whole apple-cart if I show . . ."

Then his tone changed. He spoke softly but sharply.

"Put out that light, son !" he said. "Put it out, quick !"

The jab of the voice across that quiet room took Kit Farrell off balance. He reached the light-switch in two strides, and pressed it down. Dusk blurred the room again. Making a gesture for silence, H. M. went to the window immediately at the right of the outside door. Kit followed him, and they looked out.

Immediately in front of them stood the deserted Bentley. To their right the gravel drive curved eastwards towards the front of the Hall. The drive was lined on its far side with oak-trees, their new leaves greasy with rain. They formed a background, with the leaden sky between their stems, for the figure of a woman who was walking towards them up the drive.

The woman wore a shapeless brown felt hat. She walked slowly, her eyes on the ground, so that they could not see her face. But there was something familiar about that figure, about its poise and carriage. In her right hand she carried a narrowish parcel, done up in paper and string.

And there was somebody following her.

Behind the line of oak-trees parallel with the drive—soft-stepping, quick-footed on sodden grass—somebody hurried, unseen, to get ahead of her. It seemed to be a man's figure, shadowy beyond the trees. A moment more, and it over-took the woman. Then it stepped out abruptly into the drive, facing her, and touching a hand to its hat.

The woman stopped short, raising her eyes. Her mouth opened to scream. The narrowish parcel dropped out of her hand and fell on wet gravel

"Easy, son !" murmured H. M.

H. M.'s hand clamped down on Kit's shoulder.

Since the woman was now twenty or thirty feet away, they recognized Julia Mansfield. But no word could they hear of the brief conversation that ensued. It appeared to them as a furtive little pantomime, carrying with it an atmo-sphere of evil—at least, on the part of the man who stood with his back to them.

The man, who wore a Burberry with its collar turned up, bent over to pick up the fallen parcel. But, instead of returning it to the woman, he slipped it into his pocket. The woman seemed to be protesting; they saw her lips move, and fear in her eyes. The man said something in reply.

It was then that Sir Henry Merrivale raised the window, with a screech of warped wooden frames.

"It's pretty wet out there," he shouted through the window. "Hadn't you better be comin' in where it's a little bit more comfortable ?"

The woman stiffened, again suppressing a cry. The man's head jerked round over his shoulder, as one who is surprised but has surprise under control. It needed no extra light to show them, between down-turned hat brim and upturned Burberry collar, the greenish eyes and fixed, mechanical smile of Mr. Leo Beaumont. There was a brief silence, while the rain splashed.

"Thank you," Beaumont called back.

Miss Mansfield, Kit could have sworn, was ready to turn and run. But Beaumont, politely gesturing her to precede him, marched her straight up the drive and straight across to the window. It was a low-built window; their heads and shoulders were only a foot or eighteen inches below H. M.'s.

Beaumont spoke with a sort of pounce.

"Your face, sir, is vaguely familiar."

"Of course it's familiar!" said Miss Mansfield. "That's Sir Henry Merrivale! He was with the police officer in my shop this morning."

"Indeed. Sir Henry Merrivale." Beaumont drew in his breath. "He is familiar to me by reputation. But I never thought . . . !"

"Neither did I," observed H. M. "I mean, I never thought you were the joker you turned out to be. High priest of Sakhmet, ain't it? Somethin' in the more rarefied line of hocus-pocus?"

Beaumont's eyelids rose and fell briefly.

"During my present trip abroad," he said, "I have been careful to keep my identity a secret. Especially from Lord Severn and Lady Helen in Egypt. They might not have understood my motives. How did you learn who I am?"

"Your card."

"My card?"

"The visiting card you sent to Lord Severn in a sealed envelope."

"Ah!" said Beaumont. "Then Lord Severn *was* at home!"

"That doesn't surprise you, does it? Didn't you see him drive up here?"

Beaumont's eyes, powerful in their intensity even under the shadow of the hat brim. seemed to retreat and grow evasive.

"See him . . . drive up?"

"Lord Severn," continued H. M., motioning Kit to go towards the light-switch, "got here from London at half-past four. He was drivin' that car. The car you see behind you now." Beaumont's eyes turned briefly. "He seems to have been drivin' like a lunatic, dead-set on gettin' here. He came in by that side door on your right. And then . . ."

"And then?"

"The lightnin'," said H. M., "walloped down like a load of bricks through a glass roof. Old Herihor got him and blew him to dust. Anyway, he vanished out of this house as clean as a whistle.   Just like his daughter before him. Turn on the lights, son."

Kit Farrell pressed the switch.

With painful intensity, despite their subdued glow of pink shades, the lights showed that grotesque heap in the middle of the carpet—the tweed cap, the crumpled raincoat lying asprawl, and the bronze lamp.

"No !" cried Julia Mansfield.   "No !"

Beaumont's head and shoulders, framed in the window, turned partly sideways.   Snakily, his gloved hand came through the window like the lunge of a boxer.   Leaning his elbow on the sill, fingers twitching, he stood there rigid; the lights emphasized his tautened muscles, the twitch of the lip, and the sudden glitter in his eyes.

H. M. spoke insistently.

"You saw Lord Severn, didn't you ?"

Then Beaumont woke up and smiled, a quick, serene smile, which they were to remember long afterwards. Raindrops blew past him and spattered on the floor.

"Yes," Beaumont assented.   "I saw him."

"At half-past four ?" inquired H. M., in a very curious tone.

"At half-past four."

"Then come on in !" roared H. M., with a violence difficult to understand.   "Haven't you been tryin' to get in all afternoon ?"

"Thank you," said Beaumont, still staring at the bronze lamp.   "I did grow rather tired of waiting at the lodge, when the gate-keeper was so long about returning with an answer to my card.   That was why I ventured to . . ."

Breaking off, he disappeared from the window, came up the two outside steps, opened the creaky door, and confronted them.   With the relics of all Egypt looking on, he breathed deeply.

H. M. made no reference to the parcel in Beaumont's pocket, or to Miss Mansfield still standing outside in the rain.   The old maestro was playing some game.   Kit felt it; it made the air electric.   Under every word he spoke to Beaumont ran a hidden muffled significance, scratching at the nerves.

"Listen !" said H. M.   "Do you still want that bronze lamp ?"

Beaumont walked forward and inspected it.   Unlike

Alim Bey, he did not throw back his head and speak in deep, thrilling tones of unholy influences clustered round this room. He seemed merely practical.

"Want it ?" Beaumont said. "Of course I want it. I am a business man."

"It'd be pretty valuable to your Temple of Mysteries, wouldn't it ? The lamp that annihilated two scoffers ?"

"Undoubtedly."

"Would you still pay fifty thousand dollars for it ?"

"If necessary, yes."

"Suppose," said H. M., "I told you you could get it for nothing ?"

Beaumont looked at him quickly. Something shrewd, something of-the-earth-earthy, peered out of the green eyes before they were veiled. It overlaid a kind of professional glee.

"On whose authority ?" Beaumont asked. "Lady Helen is gone. Lord Severn is gone. Or apparently so. On whose authority could I get it ?"

"Mine."

"May I ask what the catch is ?"

"There's no catch. . . . Steady !" said H. M., his voice rapping out as Beaumont bent down to pick up the lamp. "Don't touch it ! Not quite so fast !"

"You imagine," said Beaumont, "it would be dangerous to touch the lamp ?"

"Stolen relics are always dangerous to touch, son. Unless you got the proper authority. You'll be spendin' to-night at the Bell Hotel ?"

"Yes."

"I'll see you there," H. M. told him, with a glance of powerful meaning, "in an hour or two. I got an idea we can strike a very satisfactory bargain. In the meantime," he cocked an ear, "I think I hear Masters comin' back. You'd better cut along. And you too, ma'am."

H. M. swung round. Miss Mansfield, her pink mouth partly open, had not moved from the mud outside the window. Under the shapeless brown felt hat, the broad, pretty, and rather stolid face was a mask of sheer terror. Whereupon H. M. did something which his friends would have seen as hilariously comic. He extended his hand, and when the girl mechanically took it, he raised her hand to his lips.

"You're not to worry," he told her, with furious concentration. "Got that, my wench? You're not to worry about Lord Severn or anything else! Off you go, now."

"I wasn't worrying!" said Miss Mansfield. "I only . . ."

Whether Kit Farrell felt a breath of air, or whether it was H. M.'s reference to Masters, Kit never afterwards remembered. But he glanced round towards the library door. That door was now open.

It wasn't Masters who stood in the aperture. Audrey Vane stood there, well back where the study lights hardly touched her. Once again, for a flash as brief as the flicker of a camera-shutter, Kit surprised on Audrey's face that look of blind and helpless rage. Once more he could hardly be sure he saw it, for Audrey backed away and closed the door.

Cross-currents! Cross-currents! Cross-currents!

Kit had not even time, when Miss Mansfield and Leo Beaumont were tramping away down the drive, to ask what this new move was all about. Chief Inspector Masters, grim but triumphant, did march into the study.

"I've got it, sir," Masters announced.

"Eh?" said H. M. blankly.

"I said I've . . . Sir Henry! Are you listening to me?"

"Sure, son, sure!" said H. M., who had been doing nothing of the kind. He made bothered gestures, as though to keep away an invisible fly. "What's up now? Where have you been?"

"Servants' hall."

"Oh? And did *they* see or hear anything of Lord Severn?"

"Not so's you could notice it," returned Masters bitterly. "They were all having their tea together between half-past four and five; usual thing, usual time. See anything? Oh, no! This business was much too carefully planned."

"I agree with you, son."

"They were all having tea," Masters explained slowly, "except Mrs. Pomfret."

"So. And where was she?"

"In her room. Been there all day. Says she's ailing. No more alibi for half-past four than . . . than . . ." At a loss to find a comparison, Masters flung the idea away. His colour came up. "The point is, sir, what do we do now?"

H. M. considered.

"I'm glad you asked that, Masters," he said. "I'm goin'

to tell you exactly what you're to do. You're to take Benson and Mrs. Pomfret along to the local police station."

Dead silence.

H. M. made another fussed gesture as Masters hurried forward.

"Now wait a minute, son!" H. M. urged. "Don't go runnin' away with any ideas, Masters! Mrs. Pomfret had no more to do with any part of this business, either the disappearance of the gal or the disappearance of the old man, than you had. She's exactly the harmless, middle-aged scion o' respectability she pretends to be."

"But look here . . . !"

"I don't ask you," H. M. silenced him, "to arrest Benson and Mrs. Pomfret. I don't ask you to put 'em under restraint. I simply ask you to hoick 'em off to the police station, on any pretext you like, and keep 'em there out of the way for a couple of hours." He turned to Kit. "Just as I ask you, son, to take Audrey Vane out to dinner, anywhere you like, and keep her at the pub until ten o'clock."

Masters studied him from under sinister eyebrows.

"What's the game, sir?"

"I think you're right about one thing, Masters." H. M. spoke heavily. "I'm pretty sure it's murder. And it's as nasty as hell."

Masters smote his hands together.

"Very decent of you to agree with me," he said with some dryness. "Oh, ah! But I still ask, what's the game?"

H. M.'s expression was fixed and far away.

"Listen, son. I want a little while to investigate something in this house. I want to look for what I expect to find, burn me, without anybody to watch me! Yes, son, includin' you! I also want to pay a visit to the Bell Hotel. And after that . . ."

"After that?"

"I can tell you everything that happened," replied H. M. seriously.

With an effort, due to the impressive size of his corporation, H. M. bent over and picked up the bronze lamp. He held it in two hands, gingerly under the staring Egyptian relics.

"In the meantime," he said, "I'll just keep this bounder with me." A spasm of ghoulish amusement crossed H. M.'s face, making him rock back and forth as he handled the lamp. "If anybody disappears next, it's got to be me. But the hocus-pocus can't go on, son; I tell you that gratis! We're headin' for a smash, Masters. We're headin' for a smash."

15

HEADING for a smash.

In front of the car-lamps, shining white and far ahead, an asphalt road unreeled beneath the wheels of the Riley as they swept back from Gloucester towards Severn Hall. The night, clear and moist-scented now, was lighted by an uncertain half-moon. It was warm and snug inside the Riley, with a black uncertain world about them.

Kit, at the wheel, kept glancing at the illuminated clock on the dashboard.

"Twenty minutes past ten," he said.

"My dear old boy," protested Audrey, and the bundle of silver fox furs stirred on the seat beside him. "I shouldn't think you'd be in such a dreadful hurry to get back. What's all the fever, Kit?"

(Don't tell her anything! You've been warned not to tell her anything!)

But Kit could not help himself. The necessity for talking to somebody burned too strongly.

All through dinner *à deux* with Audrey at the New Inn, and playing darts afterwards in the smoke and beer-dampness of the saloon bar, that fire had increased. Kit had found himself throwing darts so violently at the scarred board, not much caring where they landed, that onlookers had been moved to remonstrance. Now he put on a burst of speed, carrying the car skimming over a rise and jolting Audrey like a switchback.

"H. M. admits it's murder," he said. "And something's going to happen to-night."

Slight pause.

"What's going to happen, darling?"

"Catching the murderer. Or at least . . ."

"Was your idea right, Kit?" Audrey stole a sideways glance at him. "Do they honestly and truly think Benson and Mrs. Pomfret . . . well, killed Helen ?   And killed Lord Severn too ?"

"Masters does, anyway."

"But why ?"

"What really sent Masters off the deep end," Kit exploded, "was that infernal picture. You remember the painting that disappeared ?"

"Well ?"

"Mrs. Pomfret, you also remember, very pointedly called our attention to the fact that a picture *was* missing. Benson, on the other hand, swore he didn't know anything about it. Masters says, and I agree, that old Benson is a martinet who can tell you the position of everything in that house down to the smallest teaspoon or ash-tray."

"He certainly is. Kit ! You ought to know that. But . . ."

"Let me finish. I can now explain the mysterious references to Helen that H. M. made this afternoon in the butler's pantry. They must have been gibberish to you at the time.

"Early this morning, Audrey, Mrs. Pomfret sent us a pointed note to say we could find the missing picture at Julia Mansfield's antique shop in College Street. We went there, and found the picture. When we asked Miss Mansfield what about it, she told us the painting had been brought there, on Thursday evening just before six o'clock, by Helen herself."

Audrey's mouth opened.

"*What's that ?*"

"But that," pursued Kit, "is clearly impossible unless you can explain how Helen first got out of a house watched and guarded like a prison. Which I, personally, can't explain.

"Masters's contention is that the picture has no point, no meaning, no place in the business at all, unless you see it as a blind to create an alibi. Who engineered the whole business ? Mrs. Pomfret and Benson. They sent somebody to impersonate Helen, to prove Helen was alive at six o'clock and well away from the house. Whereas actually she died at soon after five, and her body's rotting away in a secret hiding place in the wall. Some place that only Benson knows."

Kit paused.

"For the last three nights, Audrey, I've had a dream. . . ."
Again he stopped.

"What dream, Kit?"

"Nothing."

The car hummed drowsily. Ahead of them a rabbit scuttered across the road. The beam of the head-lamps caught its eyes, which winked like glass before it disappeared.

Kit Farrell raised a hand from the wheel and pressed it to his own hot eyes. He dreaded the night, dreaded it with that physical terror which only victims of insomnia can know. The aching hours. The hypnotic clock. The dreams, brief bubbles of horror, that come and go amid snatches of sleep.

Dreams of familiar faces turned to ogres in an ogre's castle. Dreams of people who sat beside you and turned into something else. Dreams of . . .

"But H. M. says," he continued doggedly, thrusting such things away, "that Mrs. Pomfret has got nothing to do with this. And that clears Benson as well; at least, of being concerned in anything that happened to Helen."

"Does it, Kit? Why?"

"Because Benson and Mrs. Pomfret were together the whole time when Helen disappeared! If one of 'em's not guilty, it provides an alibi for the other. You see that?"

"Yes. I see it."

"Consequently, we must . . ."

"*Kit! Look out!*" screamed Audrey.

Brake and clutch bumped the floor. Kit yanked the hand-brake over hard. As the car swerved, slithered, and bumped to a stop with a crunch of its wheels on gravel, Kit saw that the warning had been none too soon. Swinging the car round in a broad right-hand curve, he had been about to drive slap into the closed barred iron gates of Severn Hall.

Yes. Closed and barred, now.

Around them in the darkness rose up a murmur of voices. Kit and Audrey were conscious of motor-car lamps, of bicycle lamps, of electric torches, and, a moment later, of many dark shapes closing in on them. Somebody tapped on the window at Kit's right hand. When he turned the handle and rolled down the window, the white blur of a face appeared there.

"Sorry to trouble you," said an apologetic voice. "I'm

Andrews of the *Evening Record*. And we can't get in." A chorus from behind assented in this. "Sir Henry Merrivale said we could always get in. But we can't get in !"

"I'm sorry," said Kit, touching the starter and setting the car throbbing again. "You'll have to see Sir Henry about that."

"Where is Sir Henry ?"

"I'm afraid I don't know." Kit leaned his head out of the window and shouted for Leonard to open up.

"You're Mr. Farrell, aren't you ?"

"Yes. That's right."

"Is it true, Mr. Farrell, that Lord Severn has gone too ?"

"Yes. It's true enough."

A single expletive, breathed and blurted by someone in the darkness, followed a stunned pause of perhaps three seconds. Then the murmurs began, a rising tumult of excited sound which would sweep out from this small corner to blare in headlines on the following morning.

It was sensationalism, it was the last knife-twist, it would overshadow all England with horned gods and shapes of nightmare. Herihor, high priest of Ammon, loomed as real as the granite of his tomb. There was a thud and creak, swaying the car, and three more figures jumped on the running-board.

"*I* saw Lord Severn," an isolated voice rose behind the tumult, "in town this morning. He laughed fit to burst. He said if I'd come down here to-morrow morning—Monday morning, mind you !—he'd give me a story that'd bust the curse wide open."

"He told me that too."

" 'Curse Strikes Again as Peer Hurls Defi.' "

"Nuts ! I still don't believe it !"

"Well, where is he ?"

Kit was trying to stem a flood of questions through the window.

"Look, Mr. Farrell," urged a still more insinuating voice, whispering at his ear like the devil out of darkness. "You can answer this one, I'm sure, because it's about Thursday evening."

"See the police. I can't give out any information. See the police !"

"Somebody," whispered the tempter, "phoned three newspapers and the police—the man with the foreign accent, remember, Mr. Farrell ?—to say Lady Helen Loring was missing. Have the police traced those calls ?"

The man with the deep voice and the foreign accent, yes. Kit remembered having asked the same question of Masters that morning, and Masters had replied that they hadn't traced those phone calls. Kit said as much now.

"Then do you mind my saying, Mr. Farrell, that it's damn funny ?"

"How so ?"

"Because *we* traced one of 'em fast enough. Not a sausage on two. But the third, Mr. Farrell, was to the Bristol *Evening Post*. A toll call, see ? So the Exchange had to keep a detailed record. The man with the foreign accent was phoning from Severn Hall."

Kit exchanged a glance with Audrey.

"Severn Hall ?" he demanded. "Are you sure of that ?"

"Here," cooed the tempter, "is a full list of all outgoing and incoming toll or trunk calls between Thursday and seven o'clock to-night. Thursday: one outgoing to Bristol, one to Cairo. Nothing Friday or Saturday, but one outgoing, also to the Bristol *Evening Post*, Sunday evening. The man with the foreign accent phoned again to say Herihor had got Lord Severn too."

"That was also from Severn Hall ?"

"I'm telling you, Mr. Farrell. Care to see the list ?" A piece of paper fluttered through the window on to Kit's lap. "Now, if you'd care to make a statement about who might have been the man who . . ."

Ahead, in the beam of the head-lamps, the tall iron gates were pushed open. Bert Leonard, supported by Lewis the chauffeur and a uniformed inspector of the local police, emerged to make a path for the car.

Its revving motor drowned out whatever else the tempter was saying. They shot through, and the gates clanged again. Then they were speeding up the shadowy drive, the tyres slurring on gravel.

"Did you hear that, Audrey ?"

"Yes," said Audrey, picking up the piece of paper and studying it by the glow of the dashboard lamp.

"The phoning was done from Severn. And Masters must have known it all along, in spite of what he told me. That means . . ."

"Well ? What does it mean ?"

"Probably another reason why Masters suspects Benson. But it still doesn't make sense !"

Kit was silent until they drew up outside the Hall. Monstrous in half light were the shapes of box and evergreen clipped to resemble animals and chessmen. The stone flags of the terrace looked bone-white. Black and dim except for a shining of coloured glass windows, the Hall ran up into irregular battlements printed against a moonlit sky, with the battlements of the big square tower predominating.

That was when Kit had, most strongly of all, the sensation of being watched.

A police car already stood in the drive. Leaving Audrey's car behind it for Lewis to take round to the garage, Kit followed Audrey up to the terrace. That feeling of hidden watchers, of a ring of eyes, grew stronger. He turned round and round with quick movements, as though to surprise it.

"Kit, what's wrong ?"

'Nothing !"

But, as he twisted the iron ring to open the front door, Kit glanced upwards along the sheathing of ivy on the house's face. And he could have sworn there was somebody standing on top of the tower, looking down at him.

He almost pushed Audrey inside ahead of him, closing the door with a hollow slam which echoed in the vault of the main hall. The first person they saw was Chief Inspector Masters.

There were good fires in both chimney-pieces of the main hall. Masters stood by the left hand one, stretching out his hand to its warmth. The stand of black armour loomed up behind him. Masters's bowler hat was on his head; his congested blue eyes looked strained and uneasy.

"Mr. Farrell," he said, "where's Sir Henry ?"

Nobody answered. The thought which flashed through Kit's head . . .

"Now, now !" urged Masters, seeing that thought. He extended his hand mesmerically. "Don't go getting any ideas ! All the same. where is he ?"

"Isn't he with you ?" cried Audrey.

'Mr. Farrell can tell you," Masters said bitterly, "he insisted on my taking Benson and Mrs. Pomfret along to the police station for informal questioning. Lummy, that was a do!" A weight of trouble rested on the chief inspector's red forehead.

"Mrs. Pomfret," he added, "screaming she was socially ruined for life. Benson not turning a hair, but with a funny kind of smile I liked less than anything else. Then, when I brought 'em back here . . ."

"When did you bring them back here?" asked Kit.

"About an hour ago. And I'll tell you something else, Mr. Farrell. Something's got to be done about the servants. They're leaving in a body to-morrow morning, and lord knows what they'll tell the press."

"But I thought," Audrey said, "they were taking this as good clean interesting fun?"

"Oh, ah! They were at first. When they thought it was a fine thing, romantic like, to be mixed up with a great family that's got a curse on it. Then Lord Severn goes. I have to tell 'em it's murder, and . . ."

Masters drew a deep breath.

"Parrot-house!" he said. "Parrot-house! The housekeeper pitched into the cook. The cook pitched into the parlourmaid. The parlourmaid pitched into the housemaid. The housemaid pitched into the kitchenmaid. The kitchenmaid pitched into Little Orphan Annie, the betweenmaid, who's fair game for everybody. Annie said she'd seen Sir Henry prowling about in the dungeon . . ."

"Dungeon?"

"A joke dungeon," said Masters, who was not amused, "that old Augusta had built. With manacles and all kinds of tommy-rot. You lift one of the flagstones on the south terrace, outside the dining-hall, and go down into it." He broke off. "You've heard about the dungeon, haven't you?"

"Yes," answered Audrey, with her eye on the staircase across the hall. "We've heard of it. And seen it."

"But Sir Henry," demanded Kit, "isn't there now?"

"No. If he ever was."

"Have you tried the Bell Hotel?"

"Yes. He's not there either."

Masters smote his hands together.

"All I can tell you," the chief inspector went on, "is that he borrowed my brief-case. He stuck that bronze lamp in it. He walked away somewhere into the house, and . . ."

Masters made a gesture.

"*No !*" cried Audrey. "It can't be !"

"I'm not worried, mind you !" Masters assured them, so hastily that Kit realized he was good and worried. "Not one bit of it ! No ! The old man knows how to take care of himself. And, anyway, I can't stop here any longer."

Masters stamped his feet on the stone floor as though they were cold. He dragged a big turnip of a watch out of his waistcoat pocket.

"There's a man coming down from London, by the ten thirty-five train, that I've got to meet. And I'm late already."

"From London ?" repeated Audrey quickly. "You mean Sandy Robertson ?"

"No, miss. Though I expect Mr. Robertson's coming by the same train, and I want to see him too. The other man"—replacing his watch in his waistcoat pocket, Masters looked significantly at Kit—"the other man, Mr. Farrell, is an expert who's going to end all this foolishness. Yes, so help me !"

"End it by doing what ?"

"Ah ! That's a bit of a secret."

"Like the secret," said Kit, "of the man with the foreign accent ? The man who telephoned from this house ? You knew that all along, didn't you ?"

Masters regarded him blandly, a faint smile creeping round his mouth.

"We coppers, Mr. Farrell, don't tell all we know. This world 'ud be a happy hunting ground for criminals if we did." His tone changed. "Where did *you* learn about that, by the way ?"

"From one of the reporters."

"Reporters !" snarled Masters. "Oh, ah ! Those gentlemen'll muck up the whole show, if we're not careful. Sir Henry's last order . . ."

"Last order ? Do you think H. M.'s gone for good too ?"

"His last order," continued Masters, ignoring this, "was to keep 'em out. I've got the grounds patrolled. Anyway, there's broken glass on top of the walls, and there's a little back gate in the west wall, but that's locked now. All human precautions——"

"Then where's H. M. ?"

Masters's look said that he would waste no time on argument about this. He strode across to the front door. With his hand on the ring, about to open it, he turned round again.

"I can't tell you much, young fellow," he declared, "but I can tell you this." Then Masters exploded. "I'm fed up with what's been going on in this place, and that's a fact! Ever hear of beaters, young fellow? Beaters that go through the brush and stir up game when it won't come out for the guns? Oh, ah. Just so. That's me. Good night."

The door closed after him with a hollow slam. Audrey looked slowly round the hall; at the cavern stone staircase, at the two suits of armour—one black, the other inlaid with gilt—standing cold and remote and cruel on their pedestals.

"Now what," she murmured, "did he mean by that?"

Kit shrugged his shoulders. Audrey went to the fireplace where Masters had been standing. Though she held herself rigid, Kit could see that she was breathing quickly. With every appearance of casualness, Audrey opened her handbag, took out a compact, opened it, and studied her reflection in the mirror.

And with her eyes still on the mirror, moving her head to get a better light, she spoke.

"Kit. Do you know what night this is?"

"The thirtieth of April. What about it?"

"It's May Day Eve," said Audrey. "The night that evil spirits are supposed to walk."

"For the love of Mike, woman, don't *you* start too!"

"I wish Sandy were here," said Audrey, with her eye still on the mirror. "That dirty dog, that unspeakable swine, has more brains than all the rest of us put together! I'd give odds, you know, that *he* could find out what... what..."

"Audrey. Look here." Kit hesitated. "Are you very much in love with Sandy?"

"He's in love with me too. Only... I haven't got enough money for him." Audrey laughed and shut up the compact with a click. "Oh, it's quite true! Why deny it? Sandy's head rules his heart with a vengeance."

"Audrey, listen! It's none of my business, but... haven't you been hurt enough already?"

Audrey's eyes blazed at him.

"Haven't you been hurt enough too? By Helen?"

"That's a different thing! Helen cant' help it if... if..."

"Somebody cuts her throat?"

"I suppose that's what I meant, yes."

"Don't misunderstand!" The dark eyes softened. "What *I* mean is, Kit, aren't you sorry now?"

"Sorry for what?"

"Sorry for what might have been," said Audrey. "Sorry you didn't speak out. Sorry you didn't tell Helen how you felt about her, while you still had the chance. Aren't you, Kit?"

"Yes."

"Does Helen's money, does all the money in the world, make one pennyworth of difference now? It doesn't, Kit. You know it doesn't. It's a flea-bite, it's nothing at all, when something really serious happens. But you were a stiff-necked idiot. You wouldn't admit you loved her. And now she's gone."

"*Stop it, damn you!*"

There was a pause.

"I'm—I'm sorry, Kit."

"That's all right."

"But I wish," Audrey dropped the compact into her handbag, and closed the bag with a snap, "I wish I could make Sandy realize it too. That the question of money isn't the important thing he thinks it is. Sandy really loves me, Kit. But he's an actor and a dreadful liar. He was in love with Helen's money, and in the meantime he amuses his sense of superiority by going about with dreadful little tarts like . . . like . . ."

"Like whom?"

"Judy Mansfield," answered Audrey. "Judy the oh-so-refined, who dislikes stuffy places like Gloucester and yearns for the great world."

(And now, with a shock, much was made clear. Fortunately, Miss Mansfield was harmless enough.)

"Was that, Audrey, why you glared like a basilisk when I as much as mentioned her name? And then, later, when you saw her at the study window? Wait a minute! Where are you going?"

"Up to bed." Audrey spoke languidly. "How very shame-making that I can't control my feelings any better!" Her tone changed. "No, you needn't come with me! I can get to my room safely, thanks! I'm going to lock myself in and drink whisky. Just tell me if . . ."

"If what ?"

"If H. M.'s disappeared too," said Audrey.

He heard the high heels tap on stone, he saw the jaunty swing of the silver-fox cape and the defiance of the dark glossy head, as she marched across to the staircase. Audrey went upstairs without haste; but, by the time she reached the landing, he knew she was crying. Silence, except for the crackling fires, again held the hollow vault of the hall.

May Day Eve. When evil spirits are supposed to walk abroad.

Kit Farrell stood for a long time with his hand on the stone ledge of the chimney-piece, staring at the fire. Then he tramped slowly up the stairs to his own room.

His bedroom was up on the first floor, on the north side and roughly above the study. Kit went in, closed the door, and leaned his back against it for a moment without switching on the light.

The windows of the room faced north: small-paned windows, woven in the centre with the colours of the Severn arms, and now set open like little doors because the night was mild. Through them the light of the half-moon painted the floor white. It showed duskily the big canopied bed, the tall claw-footed chairs, the one easy chair —a solitary concession to comfort—beside the left-hand window, a fire laid ready for lighting under the stone hood of the chimney-piece.

Sorry for what might have been.

He wouldn't think. Curse it, he'd stop himself from thinking !

Kit stretched out his hand for the electric switch, and then realized that he didn't want light. Light would show too clearly the room and the truth. In the dark you could crouch down, you could hold a shield over yourself, you could half stultify the mind.

He groped his way across to the easy chair beside the window and sat there, bolt upright, while the clock in the tower clanged out eleven.

Sorry you didn't speak out. Sorry you didn't tell Helen how you felt about her, while you still had the chance.

Relax ! Got to relax !

What's the good ? You can't sleep.

Kit got up. Pyjamas and dressing-gown were laid out for him on the bed. He undressed, hanging up his clothes with a dull slow-moving care he never ordinarily used; he got into the pyjamas and the heavy wool dressing-gown; he thrust his feet into slippers. Then he returned to the easy chair under the window.

Beside the chair stood an oak table with ash-tray, cigarettes, matches, and the piles of soporific books with which he had tried to deaden his imagination on previous nights. Kit groped in the dark for a cigarette, and lighted it.

But you were a stiff-necked idiot. You wouldn't admit you loved her. And now she's gone.

This was going to be the worst night of the lot.

The tip of the cigarette, a tiny orange-glowing core, looked disembodied. It moved to his mouth and away again. The smoke was ghostlike, too. They said blind men didn't enjoy smoking The thing to do was conquer the sheer fear of insomnia, and then . . .

Kit leaned back deeply in the chair, trying to loosen his muscles. He half closed his eyes. He put the tip of the cigarette into the ash-tray, though still keeping hold of it.

Recite verse. Or at least think in the rhythm of verse, so that thoughts churned to drowsiness along with it. The trouble was that out of instinctive liking you chose some galloping rhythm, Kipling or Chesterton, and it only heated the fancy. Not that ! Something else . . . something . . .

Here, where the world is quiet,
Here, where all trouble seems
Dead winds' and spent waves' riot,
In doubtful dreams of dreams.

That was it. That was it ! Dimly he heard his own voice whispering, whispering on into the darkness, whispering to a night breeze. A monotonous whisper that hardly rose and fell as the seconds ticked on . . .

From too much love of living,
From hope and fear set free,

Helen ! Helen ! Helen !

We thank with brief thanksgiving
Whatever gods may be,
That no life lives forever;

138

That dead men rise up never;
That even the weariest river
Winds somewhere . . .

The words 'safe to sea' were inaudible. Kit's hand, palm upwards, rolled over with a faint rattle on the oak table. But he did not hear it.

A black anæsthetic lifted him and carried him far away. Soothingly he travelled, and this time there were no hurts in that world. No blunders to be made, no tongue-tied speech, no reminder of the things that might have been. But that was at first, for presently the landscape began to change. It grew darker. It grew cold. He knew that he was approaching a realm of monsters, the same nightmare as before. He couldn't draw back from it. He tried, but something impelled him on. Now he was on the top of a square tower, ready to jump. Now . . .

The shock of the Hall clock, striking one, clove through this mist.

Kit Farrell, cramped about the shoulders and chilled even under the wool dressing-gown, sat up suddenly in the easy chair. He felt the chair and found it was real.

Dreaming again.

He put out his hand for the cigarette, burnt out two hours ago. But his hand stopped in mid-air

The setting moon, deathly in its pallor, threw very faint radiance. It traced on the floor thin shadows of the little panes in the windows. These stretched as far as the bed, with its canopy and its heavy tapestry hangings.

Near the foot of the bed, looking full at him, stood Helen.

16

THIS must be a part of the dream.

For Helen was dressed—or appeared to be dressed, since you only imagined you saw her—in exactly what she had been wearing just before she disappeared.

There was the grey mackintosh, buttoned up to the throat. Colours were difficult in the moonlight, and red impossible;

yet he could have sworn anywhere to the tan stockings, and the scarlet and black patent-leather shoes.

She was bareheaded, the fair bobbed hair a little tumbled. One hand was at her breast. Tiredness, sadness, concern looked out of the brown eyes, worn with strain; it was as though she tried to smile, but the mouth refused. Very much as she looked when she ran through the rain into the house.

Then, standing motionless in the moonlight, this vision spoke.

"Kit," she said softly.

Kit Farrell, on cramped knee-muscles, got to his feet. At the moment he could not have spoken to save his life.

Again he pressed his finger to the oaken table-top, to reassure himself. He started to walk across to her, across a floor that seemed solid. He faltered once, but went on again when she smiled at him with a gleam of something like moisture in her eyes. Stretching out his hand, he laid it on her shoulder. He felt the rough texture of the mackintosh, and the flesh of the shoulder underneath.

Still Kit said nothing, though a kind of silent shout came from his heart. He put his arms around Helen—a real Helen—and held her with crushing force.

Then he tilted back her head to look at her eyes. He ran a finger along the soft line of her cheek, lightly touching the eyelids, and Helen's eyes brimmed over. He kissed her mouth, slowly but very hard, and her arms crept up round his neck as she returned the kiss.

"Kit, I am a fool !" Helen said. "I'm such a——"

"Don't talk. Not for just a minute."

Again he studied her face, committing every detail to memory. He touched her hair and ran it through his fingers; and Helen, half fainting from some emotion compounded of love and compassion and fear and perhaps something else, kept desperately trying to smile.

"You're alive," Kit said. "You're real. I love you better than anything in the world, and you're alive."

"I love you too," Helen said simply, and pressed him close. "That's why I couldn't stand it."

"Stand what ?"

"Seeing you like that. And then, when my father . . .

"Come over here."

Gently, as though she might break or again fly to atoms

under his touch, he guided her across to the easy chair by the window. He made her sit down there, and perched himself on the arm of the chair with an arm guarding her fiercely on each side. Still unreal as moonshine ! Still afloat in a mazy dream ! But Helen was alive.

"I've got you, Helen. And I don't mean to let you go ever again."

"No, Kit. Not after to-morrow. Never !"

"Not after to-morrow ?" A vague, terrifying doubt crept into him. He touched her hair again; and she seized his hand and pressed it against her cheek.

"Listen, my dear," Helen said. "I'm afraid something rather horrible has happened. I meant everything for the best ! Really I did ! But I'm afraid. . . . Will you help me ?"

"Do you need to ask that, Helen ?"

"But you haven't heard—what I've done."

"I haven't heard anything, Helen." He tried to keep the desperation out of his own voice. "What happened to you ? Where have you been all this time ?"

Again the uncertain look returned to the brown eyes.

"In the house," she replied. "And outside it."

"You got out of this house," Kit spoke carefully, "on Thursday when you disappeared ?"

"Yes, Kit."

"In spite of the fact that every side of it was carefully watched by honest witnesses ?"

"Yes, Kit. In spite of the fact that every side was carefully watched by honest witnesses."

"And your father did the same thing to-day ?"

Helen raised her head.

"No, Kit. That's what I meant by something horrible. At least. I don't know *what* happened to him ! But I'm afraid. . . . Listen !"

They had been speaking in whispers, aching little words that increased the dream-like quality of the scene, and could not have been heard even by someone listening outside the door. But Helen lifted her hand. Was there, somewhere in this sounding-board of a house, the stir of a footstep moving on a lawful or an unlawful errand ?

Helen started to get up, and all Kit's vague, terrifying doubts returned again. He held her back in the chair.

"Where are you going, Helen ?"

"It's all right, my dear ! I swear it's all right !"

"Yes; but where are you going ?"

"I'm taking you somewhere, that's all."

Helen, gently disengaging his arm, got to her feet.

"Only three days," she said, touching the sleeve of her mackintosh as though she too doubted its reality. "Only three days where I've been. But it seems like eternity."

"Helen," he said suddenly, "where did you get that mackintosh ? It was left behind when you disappeared. Where did you get it again ? And why are you wearing it, anyway ?"

"Because I don't want you to," she hesitated, "notice something. You'll understand, to-morrow morning. Please kiss me again. And then . . ."

She led him, both of them walking very softly, to the door. Softly turning the knob, she peered out.

The first-floor hall was a vault of darkness, relieved only by stray gleams of moonlight. Long ago Benson had locked up the house; long ago it slept. The beam of a pencil electric-torch, which Helen took out of her pocket, explored the side-wall.

She did not take him far. Close to his bedroom was a door giving on that interior staircase—Sir Henry Merrivale had asked questions about it during the afternoon—which was hollowed out of the wall. A spiral staircase of rusted iron, narrow and treacherous, it terminated on the ground floor in a door to Lord Severn's study; and it soared above their heads towards the second-floor hall.

It was down this stair that Helen led him now, with the tiny pencil-beam probing ahead. A current of air filled the hollow space between the walls. Even whispers, even the faint scrape of their feet as they descended, had echoes here. It was the most dreamlike time of all.

Cautiously Helen opened the door at the foot of the stair. That door, Kit remembered, had been bolted on the other side this afternoon; but evidently someone had drawn the bolts since. They emerged into Lord Severn's study.

"Don't make a noise," he heard Helen whisper. "It would spoil everything if someone heard us now."

Since Kit last saw the study, a fire had been built in the grate. It had sunk now to a fierce-glowing mass of red coals under a film of ash, but its core of red light gave dreamlike vividness to the room. The four windows facing them across the study, with the outer door between, were now covered by heavy brown curtains closely drawn.

Helen gave a little shudder.

"We can talk here," she said. "Is this . . . where my father was last seen ?"

"This is where we found the cap and coat, anyway. Nobody's seen him."

"I don't understand it ! I don't understand it ! H. M. says . . ."

Kit stared at her.

"Have you seen H. M. ?"

"Yes, Kit."

"When ?"

"To-night. Or last night, rather; it's morning now. I didn't want him to come to Severn !" she burst out. "I tried to keep him away ! I was afraid of him ! Even when I saw him on the train, weeks ago, I was afraid he'd guess . . ."

"And has *he* disappeared too ?"

In the red fire-glow, with the staring mummy cases looking on and the dim clutter of Egypt for a background, Helen's eyes grew enormous.

"What's that, Kit ?"

"Nobody's seen H. M. since early evening, when he seems to have been prowling about in the dungeon on the other side of the house. According to Chief Inspector Masters, he simply 'walked away'. Has he gone too ?"

"Oh, God !" whispered Helen.

She slipped across to the door leading into the library. Bolting this door, Helen pressed the electric switch.

And, with the appearance of lights, the dream dissolved. Here were the human things of everyday existence; even, if you included them, Lord Severn's cap and coat now thrown across a chair. The exquisite colouring of Helen's face, the tired frightened eyes, struck him to the heart again.

"Kit, listen. I can't talk to you much longer . . ."

"You're not going away again !"

"Only for a few hours, my dear ! Only for a few hours !"

She ran towards him, and he took her by the shoulders.

"Helen," he said in a normal voice, "hasn't this gone far enough ?"

"Please !"

"I'm not trying to force your confidence, Helen. If you

143

must go away again, I won't stop you. But practically everybody in the world thinks you're dead. Your friends think you're dead. I thought so too."

He saw her bite her lip, and the indecision of the brown eyes.

"If you must do this sort of thing, Helen—whether against your will, or however it is—don't you owe the people who love you anything at all ? Can't you make us feel easy about you for five minutes ? Can't you tell me what in God's name happened to you ? . And how you disappeared out of that hall ? And where you've been hiding yourself ever since ?"

" 'Hiding', " said Helen. "Yes, yes, yes !"

She ran her hands over the lapels of his dressing-gown, her eyes searching his face. All the intensity of her nature, that mingling of softness and strength with the vivid imagination which would not let her alone, shone out of Helen Loring now.

"I want you to forgive me, Kit," she cried. "But I had to do it, don't you see ? I had to do it ! And I do owe you the explanation !"

"Well ? The place you were hidden in ?"

Helen started to laugh. It was wry laughter, shuddering laughter; but she conquered the impulse to hysteria.

"It's so terribly simple, Kit, that you'll laugh too. I'm s-sorry, but there it is ! Anybody could do it ! The 'place I was hidden in', as you call it, wasn't what you think. I simply walked into the main hall, carrying the bronze lamp. And then, Kit, I . . ."

From somewhere close at hand, shattering the night-stillness, a new voice rose up clearly.

"*Mr. Masters !*" it shouted.

Helen's body stiffened. She jumped away from Kit, whirling around with a quick lithe movement.

"*Mr. Masters*," that unseen person cried, "*I've just heard Helen's voice. And I swear it came from the study there.*"

Then Kit Farrell understood. Heavy brown curtains had been closely drawn across the four windows, yes. But one of those windows still stood wide open: just as Sir Henry Merrivale had left it that afternoon.

He and Helen had been too engrossed to hear the footsteps of several persons crunching on gravel as they walked up the drive towards the side door. But Kit saw the movement of the curtain, a faint belling when the night breeze caught it; and the open window behind the curtain engulfed his thoughts.

Outside, the footsteps quickened to a run. One, two, three, four—four strides, four thuds, as they surged towards the door. Its handle rattled. The door was flung open.

In the doorway, breathing hard, stood Sandy Robertson. It was Sandy's voice that had cried out. Towering behind him loomed Chief Inspector Masters, with another man Kit had never seen before. They stood there, the same expression on all their faces, for about ten seconds. Straining eyes searched the room. And Kit Farrell turned round as well.

Except for themselves, the study was empty. Helen had gone.

Sandy was the first to break the silence.

"She was here!" Sandy shouted. "By the six names of Satan, she was here! I heard her!"

Masters shouldered past, head lowered like a bull's.

"Is this true, Mr. Farrell?"

"Yes," answered Kit. "She was here."

All the colour drained out of Masters's face, though his blue eyes looked no less congested and wicked. Masters nodded once. He darted to the door communicating with the library, and found it bolted on the inside. He raced across to the staircase door behind the brown curtain. Lifting the curtain, he found this door closed but not bolted. It showed him the spiral stair mounting into darkness.

Masters nodded again. He raced back to the outside door, put his head out, and blew a police whistle.

Running feet answered him.

"Now we've got her," the chief inspector said. "*Now*, by God, we've got her."

Kit woke up. "Masters! Listen! What are you going to do?"

"Where is she, Mr. Farrell?" The chief inspector ignored this. "Come on, now! Where is she?"

"I don't know!"

"Ah! But we soon *will* know!"

"How do you mean?"

"It seems I was wrong." Masters breathed heavily through his nose. "I was looking for a dead body. All right! A live body will do just as well."

He swept his arm out.

"This house is surrounded. I've got a man on the roof, and a man guarding the entrance to the cellars. Do you know why, Mr. Farrell?"

"Take it easy, Chief Inspector!"

"Because I thought," said Masters, "that sooner or later, under cover of dark, the murderer was going to try to smuggle a body out of the house. Because why? Because, thinks I, that body's in a secret hiding-hole, the only place it smacking well can be.

"But I didn't mean to wait for the muderer of murderers to move, Mr. Farrell. I was going to beat 'em out, smoke 'em out, just as soon as Mr. Rutherford got here. Mr. Rutherford"—Masters beckoned to the tall, grave-looking man behind him—"happens to be the foremost architect in London. He was interested. He promised to work a twenty-four-hour stretch if necessary, and find that damned hiding place for good and all. And in the meantime— got it?—the house would be surrounded, so the murderers couldn't get rid of that body while we were working around to their hiding place.

"That *was* the plan, young fellow. But it's a whole lot easier now."

Masters paused, choking.

"For the love of God, Chief Inspector, take it easy! Your blood-pressure..."

"My blood-pressure," bellowed Masters. "is going to be as right as rain."

He stuck his head out of the door again, blew another blast on the police whistle, and returned.

"So the girl's alive, Mr. Farrell," he said. "And you're in on this hanky-panky too?"

"No! I swear I don't know anything about it!"

"Oh? Then what were you doing here with her in the middle of the night?"

"I..."

"You *admit* you were with her? You admit that, don't you?"

"Yes! But..."

"Never mind," said Masters, "whether you were concerned in it or not. The point is, that girl's here. I've heard her voice with my own ears. She may be in a fine secret cubby-hole. But she's covered now. We've got

her.   She can't get away."   He swung round to the architect.   "Ready, Mr. Rutherford ?"

"Perfectly, Chief Inspector."

"I couldn't," said Masters, "I couldn't have asked for the
cards to be dealt better.   You can put 'paid' to Herihor's
curse, all of you, because I'm betting fifty quid to a lead
shilling it'll be all finished before we're an hour older."   He
lifted his voice.   "All right, boys !   All right !"

And then the police invasion—more policemen than Kit
Farrell had ever seen in his life—flowed over the house.

Masters would have lost his bet.

Five hours later, when the first streaks of dawn were in the
sky, Masters stood in the main hall.   The fires were all out.
Lamps burned bleak against the hush of morning.   And
Masters had attained a state not very far removed from sheer
lunacy.   Though at first he flatly refused to believe what his
companions told him, and mentioned every alternative from
bribery to blindness, they persisted in patient statements he
was at last compelled to accept.

There was no secret hiding place of any kind at Severn
Hall.

Lady Helen Loring had not left the house.   But she was
not in the house either.

17

It is pleasant to record the fact that Kit Farrell went down
whistling to breakfast.

For he awoke nearer to afternoon than to morning on
Monday, the first of May.   He had slept like a log, slept like
the dead.   He awoke to put his head out of the window and
breathe deeply on a warm day with a hot sun, a genuinely
hot sun.

Below him, as he looked out of the window, the countryside lay dark green, lush green, and dusted with gold.   Heat
brought out the odour of old wood and stone.   By craning
his neck out to the right, he could see eastwards across trees
to the slate roof of the gate-lodge, and sections of the mob
that appeared to be besieging the gates.

His brains, he noted with satisfaction, had ceased to feel as though they were frying in his head. He was a new man.

"I do not suggest," he said aloud, breathing the warm air, "that I have fallen in love with an authentic witch. I do not suggest that Helen can materialize or dematerialize as she chooses. This never struck me as being an essential facet of her character.

"But the fact remains that she's alive. She was here. There's the chair she sat in. She promised to return to-day. And she loves me, or says she loves me, which is the most mysterious fact of all.

"And don't, my subconscious self, give me any guff that I dreamed it. I didn't dream it. Masters didn't dream what happened to him.

"Otherwise, who cares?"

Thus he philosophized during the process of bathing, shaving, and dressing. But he was brought up with something of a jolt when he met Masters on the way down to breakfast.

Masters' room was next to his, and they met at the head of the main staircase under a brilliance of stained-glass windows. For a moment the memory of last night's upset and uproar held them both silent, as men with hangovers hesitate at the outset to refer to a drinking-bout.

The chief inspector, even more bilious under the colours of stained glass, looked bewildered enough and haggard enough to be pitiable. To indicate that he was a guest and not on duty, he had discarded his bowler hat.

He cleared his throat.

"Don't say it, don't say it!" he growled. "It's a quarter-past eleven. I overslept."

"So did I."

"But, considering everything . . ."

Kit, who this morning wanted to be friendly with the entire world, tried a gesture of friendliness.

"Will you for the last time," he said, "accept my word that I haven't been conspiring against you all this time?"

"Just as you like, sir. I accept it."

"That, so help me, I never set eyes on Helen from Thursday afternoon until she turned up in my room at one o'clock this morning? And that I still don't know what happened to her? Except that she's alive and not murdered, as you seemed to think."

They were tramping down the main staircase, under a still more fiery blaze of stained glass from the line of pointed windows over the front door. Masters stopped, and rounded on him.

"Oh, ah ! The young lady's alive, yes ! But what about Lord Severn and Sir Henry Merrivale ?"

Kit didn't answer.

"These," continued Masters, dragging a couple of folded newspapers out of his side pocket, "were sent up politely on the tray with my morning tea. Benson's work, no doubt of that. I swear, young fellow, I think the press has gone clean out of its mind !"

"There's a mob down at the gate now, anyway. I could see 'em from my window."

"Look here ! A four A.M. stop-press says it's reported on 'reliable authority' Sir Henry last took the bronze lamp, and hasn't been seen since. He's certainly not in this house. Where is he ?"

They tramped in silence to the foot of the stairs.

"And that," Masters whacked the papers into the palm of his left hand, "only follows the other string of headlines. 'Second Victim.' 'Lord Severn Gone.' 'Who Will Be Next ?' "

"Yes, I know."

"How in blazes, I ask you, can I tell 'em Lady Helen Loring is not a victim ? 'She's not a victim,' I say. 'Oh ?' they say, 'how's that ?' 'Because I've been close enough to her to hear her voice, and Mr. Farrell has actually talked to her. But the fact is, my lads, she's disappeared again.' "

"It does sound a little confusing."

"Confusing ? Do you think anybody will swallow that yarn ?"

"It happens to be true."

"I know it's true ! I simply ask you if the press will swallow it, if the public will swallow it, if—lummy !—my Assistant Commissioner will swallow it ?"

Kit glanced at him sideways as they stood in the warm fustiness of the main hall.

"What really worries you is H. M.'s disappearance. Now isn't it ?"

Masters lowered his defences.

"Yes," he admitted, "it is. Do you think we can get anything to eat as late as this ?"

"Yes, I should think so. Benson," Kit saw his companion wince, "will have seen to that."

And Benson obviously had seen to it.

In the immense dining-hall on the south side, which opened out on the south terrace, a sideboard bore a polished coffee-urn and spirit-lamps warming covered dishes. They found nobody in the room, but the remains of two breakfasts were on the table, and two chairs had been pushed back in disarray. Though the dining-hall remained shadowy, sunshine flooded the flagstones of the terrace outside, to which you gained access through a big oak door in a pointed arch. This door now stood wide open to warmth.

Masters's worry flared up again as he helped himself to bacon on a warmed plate.

"I don't like it, Mr. Farrell, and that's a fact! Many's the time, you know, I've warned that old bounder he'd one day tackle a case he couldn't handle. And if this is it . . . !"

"But you said he could take care of himself."

"Well! Maybe I didn't mean it in just that way. He's brilliant. Oh, ah! I admit that! But he's got no more practical common sense than a baby. Besides, take care of himself against what? The bronze lamp?"

In spite of himself, a sick lump rose in Kit's throat.

"Every time that infernal lamp is as much as mentioned," Kit said, "something unpleasant seems to happen."

"After last night, I tell you straight, I could almost believe in old Herihor myself. One minute the girl was there. The next she wasn't. And no joke about it, because I was there. I saw it happen. As for Sir Henry . . ."

Masters brooded. Then he lowered his voice.

"I wouldn't have him know it for a good deal, Mr. Farrell. But the fact is—I tell you straight!—I rather like the old devil."

"Certainly. He's not a bad scout."

Masters was careful not to let this concession be unqualified.

"Mind you!" he hastened to point out, "mind you, I won't say it wouldn't do him a lot of good to come a cropper. But we don't want him polished off, Mr. Farrell! We don't want him *dead!* I tell you straight, I wouldn't like it a bit if . . ."

Masters stopped suddenly.

He stopped because of a voice which appeared to come

from the air, but actually issued from the direction of the south terrace. This was a bass voice speaking as though in a trance. The voice gave a modest, hypocritical cough.

Then it said:

"Now this here picture, Benson, is me playin' Ivan the Terrible in front of the East Ruislip Cricket Club. Lots of people consider that my finest role."

"It must indeed, sir, have had a quality of the Terrible."

"Uh-huh. That's what everybody said. Would you 'a' recognized me from the photograph, now?"

"Only by reason of the spectacles, sir."

"Spectacles, son?"

"Yes, sir. Whenever I see in your scrapbook a false beard of more than Homeric size, I search for the accompanying spectacles and I can thereby identify you."

Chief Inspector Masters closed his eyes. Carefully he replaced the plate of bacon on the sideboard. It is a sober fact that his hand strayed towards a sharp carving-knife lying conveniently within reach. But he conquered the impulse, straightened his shoulders, and stalked out on the terrace.

A very idyllic scene was in progress there.

Seated at a small table with a crisp white cloth, which he had persuaded Benson to set up for him in the warm air, Sir Henry Merrivale basked at a breakfast of bacon, sausages, scrambled eggs, toast, and coffee. At intervals in gobbling these comestibles, he was turning over the pages of his scrapbook and illustrating the finer points with a fork.

In front of him stood Benson, also with a scrapbook.

"Aha!" said H. M., so interested that he put down his knife and fork. "Now here, son, I got something really choice!"

"Indeed, sir?" said Benson, patiently trying to get a word in edgeways.

"Yes. This is a series of press photographs dealin' with my last trip to the United States."

"I should imagine, sir, you found that nation highly appreciative of your talents?"

"That's just what they were, son. This is me officiatin' as Honorary Fire Chief. Take a dekko at the hat."

A slight frown creased Benson's forehead.

"I fancy, sir, you must be indicating the wrong photo

graph. This appears to be something in the nature of a riot."

"Well, now." H. M. sounded apologetic. "Things did get a bit hectic, yes. I wanted to lead 'em to a real fire, see?"

"The wish is perfectly understandable, sir. I myself . . ."

"And finally they said they would if it wasn't a big fire. We were havin' maybe one or two drinks—see what I mean, son?"

"Indubitably, sir."

"And then the alarm did go. And out we went clangin' and roarin' in noble style. Our progress through the streets of Garden City, Long Island, with me on the back seat of the hook-and-ladder, was somethin' really memorable. But it turned out to be a fizzle after all."

"Indeed, sir? I trust it was not a false alarm?"

"Oh, no. It was a real alarm all right. Only, when we got to the house and busted down the door with axes and turned the hose all over a bridge-party in the front room, we found we'd got the wrong house and there wasn't any fire at all."

"Most discouraging, sir."

"It sure was, son."

"And not, I should venture to think, entirely welcomed by the owner of the house?"

"His language was shockin'. I had to turn the hose on his stomach to make him shut up. Now here is me at Coney Island."

Benson, Kit could tell by the subdued twinkle in his eye, was enjoying this. The butler seemed to have not a care in the world.

And Benson's domain, here, was pleasant to look upon. On the flagstones of the terrace, with its blackened white-stone balustrade, wicker chairs gay in cushions had been brought out for the fine weather. A flight of shallow steps led down into the formal Dutch garden, where lines of early tulips were already in bloom, stretching away south-wards to the bowling green under hazy poplars, the grey of the park wall, and the winding river.

But Masters had no eye for this. He cleared his throat powerfully.

"Morning, Sir Henry," he said.

H. M., sitting with his back to him, craned around over

his shoulder. Then he began to shovel food into his mouth at a truly alarming rate, washing it down with an enormous draught of coffee.

"Haah!" said H. M., setting down the cup with an expiring sigh. "Morning, Masters."

The chief inspector stalked round to face him.

"And when," he demanded, "did you turn up?"

"Me? 'Bout an hour ago. Wasn't it, Benson?"

"About that, sir."

"And may I ask, Sir Henry, where you've been?"

"Me?" H. M. repeated innocently. "I wasn't here."

"Odd as it may sound," said Masters, "I already know you weren't here. What I'm asking you is, where in lum's name were you?"

"Oh, round about," said H. M., making a broad gesture with the knife and fork. "I had business, sort of."

"Are you aware," enquired Masters, rather like a barrister in a court-room, "that a lot of people thought you'd gone too? There was even a rumour in the press, in case you haven't seen it, that the bronze lamp had got you."

"That rumour, son, wasn't strictly true. The bronze lamp hasn't got me. I've got it." Diving down under the table, H. M. brought out an ancient brief-case. From this he produced the bronze lamp, which he put on the table beetween his plate and the scrapbook. "I took it with me, Masters. I had a use for it. Y'see, son, a good part of last night I spent at the Bell Hotel . . ."

"You damn well weren't at The Bell! I phoned there!"

"Sure, son, sure. But the reception-desk had orders to say I wasn't there. Because, d'ye see, I was locked up in a debate with Leo Beaumont. I knew it was goin' to be a long business and a tricky business. That feller's as shrewd as mustard. But I had to make him confess."

"Confess?" roared Masters.

"That's right."

"But you didn't spend the whole night at the hotel, did you?"

H. M. did not answer this.

"I understand from Benson," he pursued, scooping up the last remnants of sausage and scrambled eggs, "you had quite a party here last night." Inner amusement convulsed him. "I'm awful sorry, Masters, I wasn't here to see that."

"I'll bet you are," said Masters. "All right! Go on!

Laugh! I thought we had the whole thing taped when that architect got here. I was delayed, because Mr. Robertson got in by the same train as the architect, and we went along to the police station to get *his* story . . ."

"So. Anything in his story?"

"Not so's you could notice it. The press interviewed Lord Severn and Mr. Robertson first at Croydon and then at Lord Severn's flat in Hanover Square. Afterwards Lord Severn drove off in the Bentley. He promised the press faithfully he'd give 'em all an interview here at Severn Hall before lunch time to-day."

Here H. M. took out his watch and looked at it, with still more effect on Masters's blood-pressure.

"But I started to tell you, Sir Henry, about last night. It was one o'clock before the architect and Mr. Robertson and I got here. And then we found, or nearly found, Lady Helen in the study with Mr. Farrell here, who swears he wasn't in on the secret but won't tell us what she said to him. Did Benson tell you we got close enough to hear the young lady's voice?"

"Uh-huh."

"And then we searched. Lord lummy," breathed Masters, "how we searched! All right! Don't mind me! Laugh!"

"I wasn't actually laughing, Masters," H. M. assured him with great seriousness. "I do honestly wish I'd been here to advise you. Because you were wastin' your time."

"Wasting our time?"

"That's right."

"Can you tell me one inch or rat-hole of this house we overlooked in our search? Can you?"

"You were still wastin' your time."

"It's all very well to pretend wisdom, sir. But, considering Mr. Farrell's the only one who's seen the young lady or talked to her . . ."

"That statement, son, is very far from true." H. M. reflected. "*I've* talked to her, for one."

Masters stared at him.

"You found her?"

"Uh-huh."

"Where?"

"Exactly where I'd guessed she'd be when I tumbled to the dodge yesterday afternoon."

Masters got out a handkerchief and wiped his fore-head.

"Listen," he begged in a tone of mild reasonableness. "Fair's fair; a joke's a joke; and kicking in the pants is kicking in the pants. But do you understand the position I'm in ? A mob of reporters down at the gate, my office at the other end of a telephone line, and me with nothing to say for myself ? I've gone flat out on the assumption that this was murder. Blast it, you yourself said yesterday you agreed—at least, when we were talking about Lord Severn —that the design was murder."

"Uh-huh," agreed H. M. "That's quite right too."

An abrupt silence, of sinister quality even on that sun-flooded terrace, held them all for a little space.

Out of the corner of his eye Kit was watching Benson. It seemed to him that Benson was interested not so much in this conversation as in a certain wicker chair on the far side of the terrace. Which was curious, since nobody sat in the chair and it appeared no different from any of the others.

"For the last time," hammered Masters, "where were you last night ? And what's this about you prowling about in the dungeon ?"

"Well, now. I wasn't exactly prowlin'. I talked to somebody there because it's rather a quiet spot, that's all. And it gave me an idea, later on, for a little game this morn-ing. Take it easy, Masters ! First I was here. Then I went to the Bell. From there I went to Julia Mansfield's antique shop . . ."

"And stayed there all night ?"

"Oh, no. For the rest of the night I was at the hospital."

Quick, hurrying footsteps sounded on the terrace, in the eastern direction towards the front. Audrey Vane and Sandy Robertson, with something on their minds, ran to-wards the group at H. M.'s table.

It was plain to Kit that these two had made it up—it, indeed, they ever had anything to make up. Audrey, for the first time in days, looked happy. And Sandy, who seemed faintly shamefaced, touched her hand briefly as they rounded the corner of the house.

Kit had seen little of either of them during the trantic search of the night before. But even their summer attire— Audrey in white and Sandy in a blazer and white flannels—

argued reconciliation. Sandy, with his bump of a chin and his clever sardonic eyes and his old-looking face under the lined forehead, hurried up to H. M.

"This . . ." Kit was beginning introductions, when H. M. cut him short.

"That's all right, son. We presented ourselves to each other an hour ago. What's on your mind?"

"Listen, Maestro," Sandy began—a habit people had of addressing H. M. thus familiarly after shorter acquaintance than an hour—"we've just come from the gate-lodge. You or the chief inspector have got to do something about that rumpus down at the gates! In another ten minutes it'll be a fine old riot, and . . ."

"Now now!" Masters cut him off. "We'll attend to that! We know all about the reporters!"

"But it's not the reporters," Sandy told him. "At least, not mainly. It's an old friend of ours, a soothsayer, who swears he's got a right to get in. He wanted to have a shot at climbing the wall, broken glass and all; and he'd have tried it, too, if Inspector Davis hadn't threatened to clout him one with a truncheon."

H. M.' eyes opened wide.

"Oh, lord love a duck!" he murmured. "This is a new one. Has Beaumont gone off his chump?"

Sandy blinked at him.

"Beaumont?"

"Leonard and Inspector Davis have, anyway," said H. M. "I told them Beaumont was to be allowed in here as soon as he arrived. Burn me, what's got into everybody this morning?"

"Beaumont?" Sandy was repeating.

"Sandy, you won't listen!" Audrey plucked at his arm. "This man you and Helen and Lord Severn knew in Cairo as just an American who wanted souvenirs is really a fortune teller who conducts some crazy place called the Temple of Something! He's been in Gloucester since yesterday, anyway, and what on earth he really wants is more than I can . . ."

Sandy held up a hand for silence.

"But I wasn't talking about Beaumont!" he protested, with a kind of wild patience. "To hell with Beaumont, whoever he is. Will you, Audrey my pet, kindly put a sock in it until I explain what I do mean?"

Then Sandy turned to H. M.

"It's not Beaumont, governor," he added. "It's Alim Bey."

18

"ALIM BEY?" echoed Masters. "Stop a bit! That's the miracle merchant who started all this trouble?"

"Ho ho!" chortled H. M., rubbing his hands together in a very pleased way. "You're right, Masters. He did start all the trouble, he really did." Then H. M. frowned. "All the same, what's he doin' here?"

"From what I could gather," returned Sandy, "Alim Bey's stock as a prophet is now sky-high. His admirers in Cairo had a whip-round and raised the price of a trip to England by plane. Apparently so that he could preside," Sandy's face grew more ugly, "when the bronze lamp knocked 'em over like ninepins. That's the lamp there on the table, isn't it?"

"That's right, son." H. M. looked very hard at it.

"Anyway, governor, they want to know what to do about Alim Bey. What shall I tell 'em?"

"Tell 'em," instructed H. M., "to send the chap up here straight-away. You bring him. I didn't really expect him, but I'm very happy to have the blighter here at the finish. He'll be welcome."

Sandy was off at a run. Audrey, who had made a movement to follow him, turned back instead to H. M.

"Did you say," she hesitated, "'finish'?"

"Yes, my wench. There'll be no more disappearances." H. M. raised his voice a little. "And there'll be no more murders."

"*Murders?*"

"That's what I said, my wench."

"But that's imp... I mean," Audrey corrected herself, "I thought that was all over! They said last night, when they were absolutely turning this house upside down, they said—well, that Helen was alive. They said Kit had seen her!"

"So he did, my wench," assented H. M. "But who's seen Lord Severn?"

"By the Lord Harry," roared Masters, "so that's what you meant when you agreed it was murder! I don't want any more fooling, Sir Henry! Where's Lord Severn's body?"

"His body," replied H. M., as though choosing the words carefully, "is in this house."

The nightmare was back again.

"In this house?" repeated Masters, throwing a glance up across the south wall. "We searched every chink of it, and we didn't find Lady Helen Loring. Are you trying to tell me her father's body was here, and we didn't find that either? My God, can dead people as well as living people become invisible in this infernal house?"

Benson coughed.

Softly, with a murmured word of apology, Benson brushed past them and went into the dining-room through the big arched door. Returning almost immediately with a tray, he began deftly clearing the table in front of H. M. When he had finished, there remained only the bronze lamp. It stood there, alone and hypnotic, on the white cloth.

"Should you wish breakfast, sir," Benson said to Masters, "may I suggest that you avail yourself of it now? Food that has been too long warmed-over ..."

Masters remarks on the subject of breakfast at that time are not to be recorded.

"And I agree with him," said Kit Farrell. "Everything, no matter what it is, seems to start and finish in this house. But you can never see who does it, or why, or how! Even the telephone calls ..."

"What telephone calls?" H. M. asked very sharply.

"From the man with the foreign accent! One to say Helen was missing, and another to say Lord Severn had gone too! They were put through from here!"

The little eyes behind the spectacles bored into him.

"How do you happen to know that, son?"

"One of the reporters told Audrey and me last night. He gave us a complete list of calls to and from this house between Thursday and seven last night. Two calls were put through to a Bristol newspaper."

This time H. M.'s tone made him jump.

"Have you still got that list?"

"No. I—I don't remember what happened to it. I think Audrey took it."

"That's right," agreed Audrey, as bewildered as himself. "I put in it my handbag. Wait a minute: I left my handbag in the dining-room when I had breakfast !"

She was gone only a moment, returning with a crumpled slip of paper which H. M. smoothed out on the little table beside the bronze lamp.

"H'mf, yes. Very interestin'." H. M. looked up. "I take it, Masters, you haven't been in touch with the police station this morning ?"

"I overslept, sir, and I admit it !"

"Y'see, Masters, I was in touch with 'em. Both last night and this morning. With certain questions. You weren't interested in those questions, son; otherwise you'd have tumbled to everything. You've been hypnotized, that's all."

"Hypnotized . . . how ?"

"By a wrong interpretation of the right facts," said H. M. "Sit down, everybody. I'm goin' to reconstruct this thing for you exactly as it happened."

This was the point at which Julia Mansfield walked out on the terrace from the dining-hall.

What Miss Mansfield was doing there, how long she had been there, even how she had got there in the first place, Kit could not have told. But her presence seemed no surprise to Sir Henry Merrivale. Carrying less herself sturdily but a little self-consciously, offering no word of explanation, she moved towards one of the wicker chairs at a little distance from H. M. And then, unexpectedly, Benson's voice rang out.

"No, miss ! If you please ! Not that chair !"

Miss Mansfield started as though she had been struck in the face.

(Confound him, thought Kit, that's the same chair he was looking at so intently a while ago ! What about the chair ?)

Yet he had a creepy feeling that there were gathering on this terrace forces at variance with the hot sunshine, and the bickering birds, and the glistening ivy round the arch of the dining-hall door.

"Just as you like," Miss Mansfield said coldly. She plumped down in a chair close to H. M., arranged her skirt over her knees, interlaced her fingers, and began a pointed survey of the Dutch garden as though there were nobody near her. The blue eyes might have been miles away.

"Got a cigarette, Kit?" asked Audrey Vane in a loud voice.

"Yes. Here you are."

But Audrey didn't take the cigarette when it was extended to her. She didn't even seem to see it. Audrey also sat down in a wicker chair, which creaked sharply when she did so.

(Trouble coming! Be careful!)

"Take first," said Sir Henry Merrivale, "the disappearance of Helen Loring."

Odd, too, how small noises—the creak of that chair, the twitter of a sparrow—obtruded themselves at a time when for some reason every person on that terrace seemed to be holding his breath. Chief Inspector Masters stood as though transfixed. Then he too sat down.

H. M. took out a leather case, extracted from it one of his black cigars, bit off the tip, flicked that away with his thumb and forefinger, and put the cigar into his mouth. There was a sharp rasp as Benson, standing behind him like a familiar spirit, struck a match.

H. M. inhaled deeply, and slowly blew out a long cloud of smoke.

"The whole key to this mystery . . . thank'ee, son."

"Not at all, sir."

"The whole key to this mystery," proceeded H. M., "is in the workings of the mind and heart of a certain gal. I mean Helen Loring. I want you to imagine Helen Loring—very intense, very imaginative, the descendant and image of Augusta Severn. I want you to *see* Helen Loring, just as clearly as though," he nodded towards the arch, "she might appear in that doorway now."

Again H. M. inhaled deeply.

Nobody else spoke.

"I want you to throw your minds back to the eleventh of April, which was the day she left Cairo for Alexandria on the way home. And to Platform Number One at the Main Railway Station. I'd like you to follow the workings of that gal's mind as I followed 'em, or thought I followed 'em. You weren't there, any of you. But *I* was there. So was a osser named Alim Bey."

H. M. blinked at the bronze lamp on the table before him.

"Now what was the situation then? The story of a curse

was already well launched. First Professor Gilray dies of scorpion bite. It really was scorpion bite, as all the doctors testified, but that didn't stop the story. Next it's widely reported that Lord Severn is too ill to travel—Herihor's work again.

"Oh, my eye ! By the time Helen Loring left Cairo she was nearin' a state of nerves where she'd have done anything — *anything*, as Kit Farrell later said—to prove the curse was all eyewash.

"And then, at the station, up bobs Alim Bey. He weaves a really strikin' spell in front of the press. He tells her not to take away the bronze lamp, or she'll be blown to dust as though she had never existed. And that put the tin hat on it. The last thing she did, as that train was leavin', was to lean out and shout back at 'em: 'It's all nonsense ! I'll prove it's all nonsense !'

"Now she'd already told me she wanted to ask my advice about something. In fact, she'd booked the seat next to me in the train and the plane. But what did the gal want to ask my advice about ?

"Not about her love affairs; she admitted that. Not about any of the headaches and wrangles that'd come up during the opening of Herihor's tomb. Then what did she want to ask me about ? She nearly let the cat out of the bag when she looked at me with a rummy expression, a very rummy and curious expression, and said: 'But suppose something did happen to me ?' "

H. M. paused for a moment.

He contemplated the tip of the cigar with a far-off, sleepy look of pleasure.

"Y'see," he explained, "I'm the old man. I got a reputation, not undeserved, for knowing more tricks and dodges and hocus-pocus than the late P. T. Barnum. And that was it, of course. She wanted to ask me about hocus-pocus."

There was a sharp scraping as Chief Inspector Masters edged his chair forward.

"Wait a bit, sir !" Masters interposed. "I don't quite follow that."

"Oh, my son ! Suppose the curse of the bronze lamp apparently worked ?"

"Well ?"

"Suppose she came down here, just as Alim Bey prophesied, and, apparently, *was* blown to dust ? A supernatural disappearance, straight out of the world ! What would happen then ?

"I'll tell you, Masters—just what has happened. The press would have hysterics. Everybody on earth would be readin' about it. You'd have millions half believin', and a whole lot absolutely convinced, that Herihor's curse was a gilt-edged investment. Beware of the bogies—they're real ! Don't tamper with the evil powers of darkness !

"And then, just suppose, you allowed a week or so to go by, while people really get themselves into a lather. At the end of that time. when you've got to the psychological moment . . ."

The dawn of great understanding was in Masters's face.

"At the end of that time," he shouted, "Lady Helen Loring reappears ?"

"Exactly, son. She comes back and speaks as follows: 'There's your supernatural disappearance,' she says. 'Only a little trick that any of you could work. You swore it couldn't have a natural explanation; but it has. Now will you kindly stop talkin' flap-doodle about Egyptian magic or any other magic ?'

"*That's* what she wanted to ask me about in the train, Masters. Was there any possible way for her to work a disappearance-and-return ? Could the curse of the bronze lamp, as Alim Bey had just described it, be made to come true and then blown higher than a kite ? And could I, as the old man, think of any way ?

"There, Masters, was where somethin' else happened."

H. M. stared at the past.

"We were just runnin' out of the suburbs of Cairo," he went on, "and Helen Loring was delicately skirting round the subject, when all of a sudden an awful funny expression came over her face. She sat there lookin' out of the train window as though she'd been turned to stone. That was when she got the great idea.

"I couldn't guess then what had put the idea into her head, though I know now. I couldn't guess why she brushed the palms of her hands together, like this." H. M. illustrated, slowly. "I couldn't guess, burn me, what the idea was !

"But a minute later, while she kept noddin' to herself, she

turned round very briskly and said would I please forget everything she'd just said? She didn't want my help now; she didn't want it, she didn't want it! Naturally not, Masters. In fact, she wanted me as far away as possible. Because she'd just thought, all alone and off her own bat, of a way to work the disappearance trick."

H. M. here uttered a sound, surprising from him, which was remarkably near to a chuckle.

Kit Farrell, during this speech, had backed away until he found himself against the balustrade of the terrace, where he sat down. He noticed that Julia Mansfield still appeared to take no interest in the discourse. He noticed that Audrey Vane's lips were moving, though they made no sound.

Then H. M. lifted his voice until it boomed along the terrace.

"What I want to emphasize," he said, "is this. *Helen Loring disappeared voluntarily and of her own free will. She'll return voluntarily and of her own free will. The bronze lamp had no more to do with it than my left shoe.*"

Something, perhaps a noise of indrawn breath, made Kit glance to his right. Sandy Robertson was standing there. And beside Sandy stood Alim Bey.

Even if Alim Bey's photograph had not been so often published in the press, Kit would have recognized him by the red tarbush on his head. The Bey's long, cadaverous figure was made more gaunt by a chocolate-brown suit which did not improve the quality of his complexion. His bright black eyes seemed to protrude from their sockets. He did not speak, but the prominent Adam's apple moved spasmodically in his throat. Suddenly he lifted a hand, fingers outspread like claws, at a gesture of H. M.'s.

For H. M. absent-mindedly leaned forward and flicked the ashes of his cigar, as though he were using an ash-tray, into the bronze lamp.

"That, d'ye see, was my readin' of the situation when I got back to England. The gal had found some trick, and would probably try it on. If my idea was right, as I told you people here, then things were all right. But all the same, dammit, I wasn't just ten-tenths easy in my mind."

He gave them a sour look.

"I s'pose there's in all of us a little grain of superstition that keeps on saying, 'what if?' This thing's not possible, but *what if?* You follow me? I was sittin' and thinkin', and it bothered me. So, when they told me at the Semiramis Hotel that Helen Loring had just set off for Severn Hall, I drove down here myself on Thursday evening.

"It didn't knock me dead with surprise when Kit Farrell up and told me the gal had vanished. What did surprise me, what did rather put the breeze up me, were the circumstances of that disappearance. Cor! On the surface it looked like a sure-enough solid-gold miracle with knobs on.

"Y'see, I heartily approved of the gal's stunt if she'd done it voluntarily, as hocus-pocus. In that case I didn't want to queer her pitch by saying anything. So the first thing to do, as I told you people, was to get on to Lord Severn by telephone.

"You see why? Lord Severn had a groggy heart, and was pretty sick and dispirited already—I'll come to that in a moment. The gal was very fond of him. It didn't seem possible that she'd work a trick like that, lettin' it be thought she'd been struck by a magical lightning bolt, unless she'd already tipped him off about what she meant to do. Otherwise the news might have killed him.

"While she was in London, Helen had plenty of time to write to him by air-mail. She could either explain her great idea, or else, simply say: 'Whatever you hear, don't worry. I'm out to play a trick that'll scotch the curse for good.' So it struck me that if we talked to Lord Severn on the phone we could learn a lot, a whole lot, just by the way he took the news."

Audrey Vane stirred in her chair.

"Then that was it!" Audrey cried.

"Yes, my wench. That was it."

"But . . . !"

"Are you goin' to shut up and let me get on with this story," said H. M. sternly, "or aren't you?"

"All right. Sorry."

"In the meantime," pursued H. M., "I put a lot of questions to Benson up in the gal's room. And the more I talked to Benson, the smoother and blander he got when he answered me, and the more I became convinced of two things. This *was* a trick played by Helen Loring. And good old Benson was her accomplice. Benson was workin' in cahoots with her."

"Benson !" cried Audrey. They all looked at the butler...

On Benson's face, as he stood sedately behind H. M.'s chair, was a serene smile. He seemed to hold himself poised, dissociated from this. All he said, inclining his head with happy stateliness, was : "Very good, sir."

"First," continued H. M., "Benson was the old family retainer. She'd talked a lot about him. Second. Benson made a special trip to London to see her. Third, Benson clearly knew something about the eighteenth-century painting that disappeared. Fourth, Benson had definitely delayed Mrs. Pomfret for two minutes in the butler's pantry when Mrs. P. wanted to rush out and welcome the home-comin' Lady Helen .. "

The butler coughed. "It was unavoidable, sir."

"Fifth," said H. M., "there was the bowl of daffydils. Does anybody here remember the daffydils ?"

"*I* do," said Kit Farrell.

"One of the first things I saw, when I stuck my head inside that sittin'-room of Helen Loring's on Thursday night, was a bowl of fresh flowers on the table. Now Benson, the head of the household and the only person who knew anything about Helen's movements, swore he didn't expect her here for another week at least. But you don't order welcomin' flowers to be put out—and especially you don't pick 'em yourself in the rain, as I later found Benson did—unless you're pretty certain the home-comin' lady's due to arrive. It looked to me like a bad slip."

"I fear, sir," sighed Benson, "it *was* a slip."

H. M. gave him a dirty look.

"Finally, on that same night," he growled, "Kit Farrell had a phone conversation with Sandy Robertson and Lord Severn in Cairo. With me listenin' in. You haven't forgotten that either ?"

"Not a word of it," admitted Kit.

"That put the last nail in my conviction," said H. M. "You can't tell me that any fond father, a sick man and a nervous man, would ever in the world have treated his daughters' disappearance as Lord Severn treated it—unless he knew all the time it was a false disappearance.

"'Hello, Christopher,'" H. M. mimicked. "'Mr. Robertson is upset.' 'I can't understand what happened to Helen, but don't worry.' All in a cheerful tone as though he was talkin' about a picnic. At the end, if you remember, he could'nt prevent himself from busting out laughing in the telephone's face." H. M. looked at Sandy Robertson. "It even scared *you*, didn't it ?"

Sandy, with much enlightenment slowly becoming apparent in his eyes, rubbed his chin and gave a jerky nod.

"It scared the very devil out of me," Sandy admitted. "I couldn't understand what was wrong with the old boy. Damn him !" Sandy added suddenly. "He didnt't even tell *me !*"

"And that," continued H. M., "made me certain-sure of my theory. Lord Severn may not 'a' known exactly what the trick was but he'd definitely been tipped off there was a trick, and . . ."

Chief Inspector Masters got to his feet.

"If he didn't know what the trick was," Masters said in a powerfully restrained voice, "neither do any of the rest of us. For the last time, sir, *how did that girl disappear ?*"

"We're comin' to that," replied H. M.

"Even granting everything you've just said ! Even granting that Benson," Masters' glance at the butler became deadly, "was an accomplice. Benson didn't make her disappear, did he ?"

"Oh, no."

"It doesn't explain anything at all ! It doesn't explain how I searched this house twice, first on Thursday night and again last night, without setting eyes on the girl—even though I knew she was inside !"

H. M. took a deep inhalation and then blew out cigar smoke as though studying all sides of a problem.

"Are you sure, Masters, you'd have recognized her if you had set eyes on her ?"

"What's that, sir ?"

H. M. repeated the question. The tension on that terrace had now reached something like a point of mania. Even Julia Mansfield, Kit noticed, was gripping the arms of the wicker chair. As for Alim Bey, his red tarbush outlined against a blue sunlit sky and his countenance now paled to the colour of a sepia painting, he still had not uttered a word.

"Recognized her ?" bellowed Masters. "How do you mean, would I have recognized her ? You said yourself I'd seen umpteen-dozen newspaper photographs of the lady !"

"Aha ! Now we got it !"

"Got what ?"

"The thing," said H. M., earnestly flicking more ashes into the bronze lamp, "that held me blind and baffled and stumped until five o'clock yesterday afternoon. At which time my good old scrapbook, followin' a very revealing remark made by Benson, tore the mystery wide open. Helen Loring's not photogenic."

"Meaning what ?"

"Oh, my son ! Every photograph taken of her—Benson said it himself—is either execrable or unrecognizable.

"Now, Masters, the significance of that remark nearly slipped through my mind and got lost, because I was concentratin' on more important matters like pictures of me. But a minute afterwards I happened to pick up a photograph showin' me and Helen Loring outside the railway sation in Cairo.

"I saw it was true, Masters. That gal couldn't possibly be recognized by anybody who hadn't seen her before in the flesh. And then . . . oh, lord love a duck ! Then the clouds divided, the sun shone, and all was gas and gaiters."

H. M. got to his feet.

Carefully he put down his cigar on the edge of the white-covered table, so that it should not burn the cloth. He stood like a stuffed prophet behind the table and the bronze lamp.

"I will now," he announced, "perform an invocation."

"What the hell are you talking about ?"

"With your kind permission," said H. M., making a ducking motion of his stern rather than a bow, "I now perform a rite that ought to be of great interest to Alim Bey. By the use of the mystic words hanky-panky, jiggery-pokery, all-my-eye and what-goddam-fools-we-been, I'm goin' to make Herihor disgorge and the lightnings give up their prey. Look there !"

He pointed to the big arched doorway.

Audrey Vane cried out something that was unintelligible.

In the doorway, looking at them anxiously and with shame-faced hesitation, stood a slatternly girl in felt slippers and a neutral-coloured cotton dress much stained by soap-suds. Her harassed manners, the furtive air with which she peered back over her shoulder, the escaping lock of hair she pushed back with a small work-hardened hand . . .

"Masters," said H. M., "did you ever set eyes on that gal before ? Who is she ?"

"Yes, sir, I've certainly seen her before ! That's Annie, the between-maid. She . . ." Masters's voice trailed off.

"Oh, no," said H. M. "Lemme introduce you to Lady Helen Loring. Burn it all, don't you realize she's been masqueradin' as between-maid in her own house ?"

There was a small sigh like the rustle of a wing.

And Mrs. Pomfret the housekeeper, who had been following Helen out on the terrace, fell over in a dead faint just inside the door.

19

"I EXPECT," H. M. said dispassionately, "Mrs. Pomfret's had a bit of a shock. All the servants have been pitchin' into that between-maid something scandalous. Better slosh some water over her and bring her round."

Benson hurried in to the housekeeper's assistance.

While the others seemed held in a kind of paralysis, H.M. sat down and picked up his cigar as though nothing had happened.

"Didn't it ever strike any of you," he went on, "that in these big houses there are servants, like the kitchen-staff and the between-maid, never even *seen* by any guest ? And that a gal masqueradin' as one of 'em could easily keep out of the way of anybody who might recognize her ?

"Of course, Masters, I did catch a glimpse of the between-maid while we were standin' on top of the tower on Monday morning. If you remember, she was trudging out across the stable-yard with a bucket of swill. But it was an awful long distance off; and the closest that anybody except an investigatin' police officer was likely to come to her. . . . I say, my wench. hadn't you better tell 'em all about it for yourself ?"

He glanced at Helen, who was standing rather helplessly with her eyes fixed on Kit. Then Helen ran forward.

"I had to do it, Kit !" Helen cried. "Don't you see I *had* to do it ? Or they'd never have stopped talking about this ridiculous curse that... that..." She could not find words. "Do you hate me very much?"

"Hate you?"

"Yes! For doing this!"

Kit was so shaken by relief that he felt physically dizzy. It was a form of blindness; the blood beat in his ears, and, when he took Helen's hands, he had first to grope for them.

"Hate *you*?" he said incredulously. "You've got the words wrong. I love you."

"I did break down and come to see you last night, Kit. I got the mackintosh and wore it buttoned up because even the nightgown I wore as Annie might have given me away. And I didn't think it was time yet to... to..."

"That's all right, my dear."

"It's not all right. I was a fool. But I do lo—well, you know how I feel! And it seemed so grand to think I could make fools of all the people who talked about the curse. You see, Kit, I first had the idea in the train coming from Cairo. I got it by thinking about Benson."

"Benson?"

"Yes. About Benson engaging a new staff of servants who'd never seen me. The reporters had been questioning me about it at the station. And all of a sudden I realized how I could vanish by turning into a kitchen-maid or a tweeny. Because of my hands."

"What's that?"

Helen extended her hands, palms upwards. Her brown eyes were shining with a light of self-mockery; yet she was desperately serious and not a little proud.

"Look at them, darling. I've got hands like a navvy, as I told H. M., from working at the digging. Nobody without them could pretend to have done heavy housework before. But I did it here, and I think I did it well, as a servant to the servants. Even if they all did say," her eyes twinkled, "that I was the damnedest, silliest, clumsiest little slut that ever waited on them."

A shriek from Mrs. Pomfret, somewhere out of sight in the dining-hall, was soothed to silence by mumbled words from Benson. Afterwards Benson reappeared in the doorway. He slid forward a wicker chair.

"Will you be seated, my lady?"

"Thank you, Benson," acknowledged Helen. "Should *you* say, Benson, that I made such a bad between-maid?"

Benson considered this carefully, standing behind her chair like a guardian angel while Helen sat down with Kit still gripping her hand.

"Well, my lady, I should not myself have given you a very high recommendation, except perhaps for industry."

"No, I suppose not." Helen was philosophical. "But I got away with it, Kit. And, if you think for a second, you'll see how we managed it. Benson opened the Hall with a new staff of servants—when? On Monday the twenty-fourth of April. That was just three days before my disappearance, wasn't it?"

"Yes!"

"And, on those same three days, I did my first disappearing act when I was absent from the Semiramis Hotel in London?"

Now, with the inevitability of a picture-puzzle taking form, Kit began to see the design as each bit slipped into place.

"*You mean . . . ?*"

"Yes, Kit. Early on Monday morning I came down here, and was gravely installed by Benson. Benson and I had worked it all out in London, and I'd written to my father so he wouldn't worry. For three days I established my identity as Annie, the between-maid."

"Go on!"

Helen's eyes clouded momentarily as she mentioned her father. The fear, the indecision, were back again. But H. M. gave her an encouraging nod.

"On Thursday morning, at the first crack of dawn, I was off from here to London. I was waiting for you at the hotel, feeling horribly tired. But I wanted to be ready to drive down here again with you and Audrey, so that I could 'mysteriously vanish'. I . . . I . . ."

Benson coughed behind his hand. "If you recall, Mr. Kit, I stated in reply to Sir Henry's questioning that the between-maid had Thursday off."

"The actual vanishing," said Helen, "seemed to be the trickiest part but was really the easiest." She shivered. "Do you remember the drive down from London, Kit? Do you remember how we drove through those gates, in the rain?"

Did he remember? Momentarily the details of the sunlit terrace, the circle of staring faces, all faded away. Kit heard again the slur of wheels on gravel. He saw the open gates of Severn Hall, the lights of the lodge with Leonard peering out, the sodden trees of the driveway. He saw Helen sitting beside him, white-faced, her grey mackintosh pulled closely round her, holding the box with the bronze lamp. He saw her nervously smoking a cigarette . . .

"Benson and I," Helen went on "had already worked that out too. We chose a time when all the servants would be having tea together at the back of the house. On the way down I sent a telegram, timed to arrive shortly before I did; we knew old Mr. Golding, at the post office, would phone it through. In the meantime, Benson could invite Mrs. Pomfret to his pantry, and detain her there as a witness.

"My arrival had to be 'unexpected', you see, so that nobody was waiting to meet me.

"Bert Leonard the lodge-keeper had instructions to phone through the arrival of *any* car, so it didn't matter whether he guessed I was Helen Loring or not. The only very slight danger was that Bert, who'd already met me as Annie the between-maid, might recognize me as Annie when we drove past within a dozen feet of his windows.

"It wasn't very likely, on a rainy day and with me sitting on the far side of Kit. And clothes and trappings do make the woman; I've found that out. Still, I wonder if you can remember what I did?"

Audrey Vane, who was sitting bolt upright and contemplating Helen with dazed but fascinated eyes, spoke promptly.

"*I* can remember," Audrey said. "You were smoking a cigarette. Just as we shot through the gates, you dropped that cigarette on the floor and bent down to pick it up. Leonard couldn't have seen more than the top of your head."

Helen had been trying to avoid Audrey's eye. Now Helen turned round impulsively and stretched out her left hand.

"Audrey, I'm awfully sorry! I shouldn't have done that to Kit or to you either. I know I'm a fool! But I meant it for the best. Really I did!"

"Darling!" cried Audrey, lifting her thin arches of eyebrows and crowing with delight. "You're surely not apologizing? I never heard of anything so absolutely thrill-making in all my life! Dont' you agree, Sandy?"

"No," said Sandy Robertson calmly. "I don't."

"Sandy !"

Though he spoke in a calm tone, Sandy's poise was the poise of rage. He stood teetering back and forth, his hands dug into the pockets of his blazer. For minutes his eyes had rested on Helen and Kit—the eloquence of their gripping hands, the looks that passed between them—and Sandy's eyes were sick.

"Since you ask my opinion, Audrey," he said in an offhand tone, "I'm bound to say I think it was a damned dirty unfeeling trick."

"Sandy !"

"Not," his voice grew slightly shrill, "that my opinion has been called for by anyone intimately concerned in this. Not even a word of greeting for the Old Firm. However, I don't complain about that. I merely say, in passing and in an academic way . . ."

"Just a minute, sir !" interposed Chief Inspector Masters grimly. "This young lady's led us a fine dance, I agree; but I want to hear the rest of it. Go on, Lady Helen. You drove up to the house here with Miss Vane and Mr. Farrell. And then ?"

Helen hesitated, her eyes on Sandy.

"Tell him, my wench," said H. M. woodenly.

"On—on the way down from London, I was wearing my mackintosh over my maid's dress." Helen looked down at her dress, draggled and stained, with a disgust that was mental rather than physical. She seemed, now, to hate the whole masquerade. "That was why I kept the mackintosh pulled so tightly round me. When the car stopped in front of the house, I simply jumped out first and ran inside with the bronze lamp.

"The front door's never locked in the daytime; even if it had been, Benson would have seen to it. Benson had already put a lot of extra odd-jobs gardeners around the house—men from Gloucester, not house-servants—just to testify later I couldn't have slipped out.

"Once inside, I went on with the business of vanishing. I was so excited I said: 'Done it !' or something like that, not realizing how sounds carry in that main hall . ."

"Oh, ah !" Masters agreed bitterly. "A plumber named Powers heard you from upstairs. And then ?"

"What I did could be done in ten seconds. I put my

mackintosh down on the floor with the lamp. I stripped off my shoes and stockings, and put on the maid's felt slippers that were in my mackintosh pockets . . ."

Audrey Vane snapped her fingers.

"The footsteps that stopped," Audrey said.

"Then I went through the library, into the study, and up to the attic—where my cubby-hole is—by way of the corkscrew stair in the wall. I was carrying my shoes and stockings; and I left them in a locked bag under my bed.

"I was downstairs again by the back stairs to the servants' hall, where the others were finishing their tea, practically by the time Benson and Mrs. Pomfret reached the front door. Benson had delayed Mrs. Pomfret. of course, to give me plenty of time.

"Don't I know," Helen added vehemently, "that clothes and a name make the woman? Ten minutes later, when Benson came sailing in to say Lady Helen Loring was believed missing, and to get Lewis the chauffeur to help him search the house, nobody as much as glanced in my direction. Annie, the between-maid. had had a nice day out at the pictures—that was all."

Helen brooded.

"It would have been the end of my adventures, too," she said, "if it hadn't been for that picture of the first Countess of Severn. I made a dreadful slip over that."

Benson looked distressed.

"If I may correct you, my lady," he protested, "*no*. The error was mine. Being unused to the ways of deceit . . ."

"Ha, ha, ha," said Masters.

" . . . and somewhat flustered, I fear I blundered there just as I blundered about the flowers. May I speak, my lady ?"

"Of course."

"When Sir Henry Merrivale returned here this morning," explained Benson, "he taxed me with my part in the masquerade . . ."

"Half a minute !" Masters glowered at H. M. "When did you first twig it that Lady Helen was posing as the tweeny in her own house ?"

"Oh, Masters ! I'd decided on Thursday night, for reasons I told you, that the disappearance trick—whatever it was—was managed by Benson and the gal working together."

"Well ?"

"Well! And straight-away I hear about a between-maid who gets the day off, by special permission of the butler, at a time of rush-work and only three days after she's first come on the job.

"It would have been a brilliant dodge, I thought, if Helen Loring was the between-maid, or at least *some* maid. Because, d'ye see, it was a trick that any woman could have worked. It wouldn't call for any great acting ability, such as," H. M. gave a modest cough, "such as I show myself when I play Hamlet or Ivan the Terrible. All she'd need to do would be put on the clothes, drop her hoity-toity accent, and sling in a few words of dialect.

"But no sooner did I get the idea, Masters, than—oh, my eye!—I discarded it as absolutely out of the question and n.b.g. You see why?

"Even if none of the servants had ever seen Helen Loring, I thought, they'd certainly have seen her *picture*. Every newspaper, picture-paper, and illustrated magazine has been plastered for weeks with photographs of the gal. Up turns a so-called between-maid who's the image of a gal soon to disappear. They'd notice it; they'd mention it to the police; the police would start asking questions; and pop would go the weasel.

"That's why I stayed blinded and stumped until I suddenly realized nobody could possibly have recognized her just by lookin' at a photograph."

"Exactly, sir," agreed Benson. "But the portrait of the first Lady Severn was another matter."

The butler turned to Masters.

"That portrait, Mr. Masters, hung conspicuously in a backstairs passage constantly used by all the servants. Fortunately no one had yet looked at it closely. But there was great danger, especially when her ladyship disappeared and the police came in, that someone would see on the wall a huge speaking likeness of Annie the between-maid.

"I realized this, with horror, only in the middle of Thursday afternoon. In making our plans, Lady Helen and I had completely forgotten that picutre. So, between lunch and tea time, I took the picture down and hid it in the cupboard in my pantry.

"All would have been well if Mrs. Pomfret, at the worst possible moment, had not noticed the picture was mys-

174

teriously missing. This impressed her; she was certain to make an uproar about it later—as, in fact, she did. I confess, sir, I was more than a little distracted. . . ."

"Don't you see," cried Helen, "we had to get the picture clean out of the house?"

"Oh, ah," said Masters. "I see it all right! And so?"

Helen gave him a wry smile.

"I had an inspiration, or thought I had," she said. "I remembered there was a little shop in Gloucester where they did picture restoring. How could you more naturally hide a painting, where even the shop wouldn't suspect anything, than by taking it to be restored?

"Somebody had to take it there in a hurry. Benson couldn't do it himself without giving the show away; and, anyway, Benson had to be searching the house for me after I was supposed to have vanished. At intervals, in his pantry, he had to put through the phone calls to the press and the police, saying Herihor had got Helen Loring . . ."

Masters's rage was simmering again.

"So it *was* you, eh?" he said to Benson. "You were the bloke with the foreign accent, just as I thought?"

Benson radiated quiet satisfaction.

"A suitably disguised voice, sir. Her ladyship naturally wished the greatest possible notoriety for her disappearance to begin in the shortest possible time. But I fear, Mr. Masters, that everything I did in innocence . . ."

"Innocence, eh?"

". . . was interpreted by you as having some sinister purpose. May I beg you, my lady, to continue?"

"Benson couldn't take the picture away himself," said Helen. "But he could easily send Annie on an errand. Especially since the gardeners watching the back of the house had seen me mingling with the others as Annie in the servants' hall, and never dreamed of anything suspicious." Helen, biting her lip, moved the chair round so as to look past H. M. at the table. "You *are* Miss Julia Mansfield, aren't you?"

Miss Mansfield, with spots of colour under her blue eyes, presented an interesting study. All her appearance of aloofness had gone. She was tightly clutching the arms of her chair. It would be hard to say whether her predominating emotion was anger or—inexplicably, it seemed to Kit—fear.

"Yes. I'm Julia Mansfield." Her voice soared to a strange level before she corrected it. "I should have thought, Lady Helen, that would have been known to you."

"But that's just it !" cried Helen. "I knew you were a friend of my father, of course..."

"Yes," said Julia Mansfield.

"But I'd never seen you to speak to, and I didn't think you'd recognize me in a million years. Especially if I wore an old hooded cape that belonged to 'Annie', and kept the hood well over my face, and spoke in Annie's semi-cockney voice."

"I noticed the voice," said Miss Mansfield.

"At half-past five," Helen appealed to Masters, "I took a bus in to Gloucester with that painting well wrapped up in newspapers. When I went into the shop I didn't say I was Annie or anybody else. I just said the picture was from Severn Hall, and would be called for. Then I hared out again. I must have looked a bit furtive..." .

"You did," said Miss Mansfield.

"But," Helen looked at her curiously, "I never dreamed you'd think twice about it ! I never even dreamed you'd notice it. I thought the picture would be forgotten about, and..."

"Ordinarily," said Sir Henry Merrivale, "you'd have been right. That's where we meet the blinkin' awful cussedness of things in general. In an ordinary casual shop you'd have got away with it. But there was a very definite link between this antique shop and..." He stopped.

"Go on, sir," urged Masters. "A link between this antique shop and—what ?"

"A gold dagger," replied H. M., his voice rounded with ominous and terrifying distinctness. "A gold perfume box. And the murder of Lord Severn."

Silence.

The effect of that word 'murder' was extraordinary on everyone present. Helen abruptly rose from her chair, disengaging her hand from Kit's, and walked across the terrace with her back turned.

Alim Bey, his face the colour of coffee into which too much milk has been poured, but with his gleaming black eyes never wavering from H. M., swallowed twice. Slowly he moved forward. For the first time he spoke, in that deep cadaverous voice.

"I am a poor scholar," he said, upturning the palms of his hands. "I mean no harm. I do not know why I should be the victim of hoaxes." He swung his clenched fists into the air, the elbows crooked—a gesture that was not comic, but had a quality of the towering and the terrible. "*Bismillah!*" he shouted. "Would you have me mocked at by my friends in Egypt?"

Across the terrace from him, Helen whipped round.

"*Ahlan wa ʿahlan, Alim Bey!* We've met before, haven't we?"

"Yes. We've met before."

"You said I'd be blown to dust as though I had never existed! What do you say now?"

"I say, mademoiselle, that the dark powers are not mocked. Have you lost nothing by this jest of yours?"

"No!"

"You have lost your father," said Alim Bey.

Helen was very white. But, as H. M. gave her a warning glance of hidden meaning, she checked whatever reply seemed to be on her lips.

"It's true," said H. M., "that the joke got out of hand. The toy-pistol was loaded with a real bullet. Somebody went berserk and set a hand to murder. That person is among us now."

Sauntering footsteps sounded on the flagstones. Mr. Leo Beaumont, approaching from the front of the house, strolled towards them with a polite and affable air of ease.

He was hatless, and wore a well-fitting grey suit. He showed not the least surprise at seeing Helen, but merely bowed at her as towards the others. The quizzical lines at the corners of his eyes were offset by the wariness of his mouth.

"Good morning to all of you," Beaumont said. "I came to collect the bronze lamp."

Kit Farrell's muscles went rigid; he could not have told why.

"We now," observed H. M., "got two seers. The ancient and flowery kind," he indicated Alim Bey, "and the modern and businesslike kind," he indicated Beaumont. "Let's see if they can help us while we disentangle the problem of how Lord Severn disappeared."

H. M. was silent for a moment, turning the cigar over in his fingers.

"Yesterday morning, Sunday morning," he went on, "I was still gropin' blind with two sets of facts. First, how had Helen Loring disappeared? Second, what happened to a gold dagger and a gold perfume box?

"The dagger and the perfume box, worth ten or twelve thousand pounds together, were missing from the huge group of articles in Herihor's tomb-chamber. The Egyptian police said they'd been smuggled out of the country, on a complaint lodged by Lord Severn himself. I'd heard about the stuff before, from Helen Loring.

"She said there'd been some trouble over it, she couldn't say what trouble, but it was worrying her father. And Lord Severn himself, when we spoke to him on the phone from Cairo, said he was coming back to England not only because of his daughter's disappearance, but to attend to some 'unpleasant business' at home.

"Interestin'. Very!

"On Sunday morning, followin' the trail of the missing portrait, Masters and Kit Farrell and I went to Julia Mansfield's antique shop. Masters, by the way, got a bit of a shock when he first saw that portrait; he said he'd seen the face somewhere before. And I—still in my blindness!—said he must have seen it in one of Helen Loring's photographs. But Masters still wasn't satisfied. Of course he'd seen that face on Annie the between-maid.

"Anyway, I pressed the bell of the antique shop. And instantly—instantly, mind you, on a Sunday morning—Julia Mansfield came runnin' out in a hurry to answer it.

"She'd been expecting somebody, as her first words showed. Not us. But somebody.

"She wasn't much scared at first; only wonderin'. She didn't get scared when she first started to describe how Helen Loring delivered the picture. But she did start to get the breeze up when she saw young Farrell lookin' closely at some Egyptian trinkets, rings and lamps, in a show-case. He had no ulterior motive in starin' at 'em, but she thought he had. Why?

"Then the shop door opened. In came a visitor who couldn't see anybody except the proprietress. He announced in no uncertain manner that his name was Leo Beaumont, and he'd come to inquire . . .

"Bang! He saw us, and cut himself off straight-away. A minute later he was explainin' suavely that he'd come in by chance to ask the way to Severn Hall. That," said H. M. dismally, "was a very poor grade of eyewash. If I go into a shop to ask for directions, I don't wallop out with my name first.

"It looked very much as though Beaumont was the person she'd been expecting, especially as the first words she said to him contained a stressed warnin' that Masters was a police officer.

"And, burn me, she definitely did have the breeze up before we left ! So much so that she started babblin' about Lord Severn—how he'd written to her several times in the past year, how he sometimes sent her Egyptian trinkets that *weren't* valuable, and the rest of it. When we didn't ask any questions about that, she left us practically swoonin' with relief. When you added that to something else I saw there, it looked as though . . ."

Helen, whose features had a strain of bewildered concentration, pressed her hands together hard.

"What are you suggesting ?" Helen cried. "That Mr. Beaumont went there to get . . . ?"

"The gold dagger," said H. M., "and the gold perfume box." He added: "Somebody, at that very minute, was preparing to commit murder because of 'em."

It was now very hot on the terrace, with the sun overhead and westering.

Leo Beaumont, a shade pale, examined his finger-nails.

"Let's go on," mused H. M., "with the events of that revealin' day. Lord Severn, arrived back in England, was drawin' nearer to death every minute. Late in the afternoon it started to rain. A red Bentley, with a passenger, was somewhere on the road between here and London. Leo Beaumont, at half-past four, was hanging about the gates down there . . ."

He swept out his hand.

"Well ?" said Masters. "Get on with it !"

"Whereas you and I, Masters, were in the butler's pantry. At close on five o'clock, over a scrapbook, I got my inspiration and saw as clear as snow white just how Helen Loring 'vanished'. I was pleased, I was. I declared, with sweepin' assurance. that the gal was safe; her boy friend had got nothing to worry about.

"Immediately afterwards—panic-party. A phone message comes through to say Lord Severn left London before noon, and ought to be there now. The bronze lamp flits away from the sitting-room upstairs. Bert Leonard comes in to tell us the Bentley car arrived at half-past four. The cap, the coat, and the bronze lamp are all on the study floor. But no Lord Severn.

"Just when I thought I had the disappearance-bogey licked, the whole assortment of Grand Guignol horrors comes rollin' back again. Cor!

"I could prove, or believed I could prove in short order, that Helen Loring was harmlessly in this house as a maid. But the same thing, d'ye see, couldn't very well apply to her old man. You could'nt have two invisible cloaks cut from the same bolt of cloth. It was an awful shock, my fatheads. If I happened to be wrong . . .

"But I wasn't wrong.

"This disappearance had murder written on it. I saw the signature, I saw how the gold dagger and the gold perfume box fitted in, just as soon as Leo Beaumont and Julia Mansfield came creepin' up out of the rain. I had two minutes' conversation with Beaumont. I remembered the mechanics of telephone calls . . ."

Julia Mansfield sprang to her feet.

"I c-came here," she said, not very steadily, "to help you expose a perfectly foul trick that was played on me. I will not stand for the suggestion that I, or Mr. Beaumont either, had anything to do with Lord Severn's death!"

But H. M. was not looking at her or at Beaumont. He extended his hand and pointed a malevolent finger.

"That's the man you want, Masters. The sole culprit, the young swine who didn't care two hoots about strangling his benefactor. He's lookin' a bit sick now, and I hope he feels sicker before we get through with him."

Audrey Vane screamed.

For H. M. was pointing to Sandy Robertson.

20

"ARE you insane?" asked Sandy.
"Oh, no," said H. M.

Sandy was leaning with his back to the balustrade, his body arched forward, his hands gripping the stone on either side. His lips were so dry that you could see the cracked skin. The artifice of a stiff grin, moulded and stamped there, for the first time made unpleasant the face of Good Old Sandy.

"Standin' in front of you," pursued H. M., "are three women. Helen Loring. Audrey Vane. Julia Mansfield. Each one of 'em you've professed to be in love with. Each one of 'em you've made use of, in various ways, to put money in your pocket. That's your way of livin', isn't it?"

H. M. gestured towards Leo Beaumont.

"Now, son! Do you mind repeating what you told me at the hotel last night?"

"Not at all," answered Beaumont. Beaumont's manner was brisk and decisive; his cat-green eyes wary. "In Cairo, during the first week of April, I bought the dagger and the perfume box."

"Bought 'em from whom?"

"From Mr. Robertson there. He was to," Beaumont hesitated, "remove them from the large number of relics salvaged from the tomb. He believed it would be a long time before Lord Severn noticed this. Afterwards he believed he could convince Lord Severn—not a business man, and very absent-minded—that they had been lost."

"You couldn't do business with Lord Severn, so this feller here approached you with his proposition?"

"Correct!"

"What were the terms?"

Beaumont's face hardened.

"I was to pay him thirty thousand dollars on his assurance that he could get the articles smuggled out of Egypt for me. Half of this was to be paid when they were smuggled out. It has been paid. The other half, when the dagger and the perfume box were handed to me in England."

"And how was he goin' to get the stuff smuggled out of Egypt?"

"May I answer that?" cried Julia Mansfield.

H. M. surveyed Sandy.

"You're not goin' to say," he pointed to Miss Mansfield, "you've never seen that gal before? On Sunday, in the antique shop, she was talking about the kindness of Lord

Severn. Then she said: 'And the other gentleman', and stammered and went carnation-red.

"Other gentleman? There's a photograph of you in her living quarters, in the lovin' place of honour and a little silver frame. When I saw that picture I sort of felt your fine Italian hand behind this business of the dagger and the perfume box. I'd already seen you prancin' about the Continental-Savoy Hotel in Cairo; and I can't say I liked your looks."

Here H. M. glared at Kit Farrell.

"Couldn't *you* guess it, son? Audrey Vane told you that gal was one of Mr. Robertson's conquests. At least, Benson tells me that last night in the main hall he overheard Audrey sayin' . . ."

"Sir!" exclaimed Benson, in shocked reproachfulness.

"Anyway," said H. M., "with regard to smuggling the articles out of Egypt . . ."

Miss Mansfield would not look at Sandy.

She was still white except of the colour under her eyes. Her hands were down stiffly at her sides. Anger, humiliation, pouring embarrassment made her keep her chin high and speak over all their heads.

"Smuggling relics out of Egypt," she tried to speak in a level voice, "simply isn't possible in the ordinary way. Any suspicious parcel in the post, unless it's sealed by the Cairo Museum, and has a stamped invoice from the Department of Antiquities—well! it'll be stopped at the port of embarkation, that's all."

She faltered, but forced herself to go on.

"But all well-known archæologists, like Lord Severn, have what's called a licence to export. Often they send little things, not valuable, to their friends. As Lord Severn did to me. And in that case, as often as not, the authorities just put on the stamp and seal without even examining what's inside the parcel.

"Mr. George Andrew Robertson," she stressed, with hatred, Sandy's real Christian names, "was known as Lord Severn's right-hand man. He went to them with a forged description, in what was supposed to be Lord Severn's writing, and said those things were trumpery brass Lord Severn was sending to me. To *me*.

"That had happened before. They didn't even bother to open the parcel. Mr. George Andrew Robertson"—the name seemed to madden her—"told Mr. Beaumont it would be easy. He said there was a silly woman in England, meaning me, who'd do anything he asked."

Julia Mansfield lowered her head.

"Isn't that so, Mr. Beaumont ?"

"Yes," replied Beaumont, "that is so, I regret !"

Sandy Robertson found his voice.

"You perishing fools !" he said. He seemed less upset by the accusation than stupefied by their recklessness in making these statements. He could not understand it.

"Don't you know," Sandy screamed, "when to keep your mouths shut ? Do you want to go to jail, both of you ? You'll be charged with complicity in . . ."

Beaumont's voice, now very sharp, cut him off.

"No," said Beaumont, "I think not. I promised Sir Henry Merrivale to give certain evidence, in exchange for certain promises he made me. One of those promises was that there should be no prosecution of any kind."

Chief Inspector Masters jumped into the row with both feet. "Wait a minute, sir ! I'm a police officer ! I can't help compound a felony ! Sir Henry's got no authority to . . ."

"Oh, yes, I have," H. M. said calmly. "In a minute or two you'll understand why."

Again H. M.'s malevolent eye fixed on Sandy.

"From information received, son, I'll tell you just what happened. Lord Severn tumbled to the smuggling trick while you and he were still in Cairo. You denied it. He produced the Cairo Museum official who'd O. K.'d the parcel though he didn't betray your crooked work.

"Then you threw a scene. You begged him not to make a scandal and expose you. You said you were both going back to England in a few days; you said the stuff would still be at Julia Mansfield's antique shop, and you'd get it and return it—so help you, on your bended knees !

" 'Right !' says Severn, 'but I'll stick very close to you, young gentleman. We'll go to that antique shop together, to make sure you don't play any more tricks.' " H. M. peered round him. "I say ! Don't any of the rest of you remember how Severn sounded when he spoke on the phone from Cairo ? The blisterin' contempt in his voice when he talked about 'Mr. Robertson' ?

"You and Lord Severn left Cairo by plane on Friday

morning. The day before you left... well! Very rummy! Alim Bey turned up again, and made two more pronouncements."

Alim Bey took a step backwards.

"I've been wondering," grunted H. M., "just how much of a faker Alim Bey is. His first prophecy, that the gal would be blown to dust, I'll hereby affirm was no more than a modest stunt to get a bit of free publicity by jawin' away in front of the press.

"He simply, as fortune tellers have done before and since, took a chance. If anything happened to the gal, anything at all—even if she only tripped over a door-mat and had a bad fall—he could say later it was old Herihor shootin' out malignant rays. That's how these miracle merchants work.

"But on Thursday he made two pronouncements that were bang in the bull's-eye. He said Helen Loring had disappeared on Thursday, and she *had* disappeared on Thursday. He said Lord Severn would be the next to go, and..."

"Of what," said Alim Bey loudly, "do you accuse me now?"

"Of old-fashioned hokey-pokey," said H. M. "You said that because Lord Severn secretly tipped you off to say it. Now didn't you?"

"*I deny this!*"

"Sure, sure." H. M. was soothing. "Lord Severn, d'ye see, was building up the hoax his daughter had begun, just so he could help blow it to smithereens. He knew the gal was goin' to disappear on Thursday; she'd written to him and said so.

"He was returning to England with two purposes—to break the curse, and to get back the dagger and the perfume box. But, although he didn't know it, he was walking straight into a trap he'd helped create for himself. Because he really had been marked down as a victim—by Sandy Robertson.

"That smooth young feller," again H. M. pointed, "was in a corner. He couldn't let the old boy get home alive. In the first place, he still had fifteen thousand dollars comin' to him. In the second place, his chances of marrying Helen Loring wouldn't be much improved when the gal heard what he'd already done. In the third place, possible public exposure as a thief wasn't tasteful to him. From the time they landed on English soil, Lord Severn was as good as dead."

"Dead," whispered Helen.

She put her hands over her eyes. Sandy made an instinctive movement towards her; but she started back even though a long distance separated them.

"Christ !" said Sandy, as though from an anguish he could not express. "Helen, this is a lie !"

"Is it ?" inquired H. M. "Then just tell me this. Lord Severn apparently borrowed your car and came down here alone, arrivin' at half-past four. Where were you at that time ?"

"You ought to know where I was ! I was in London ! I talked to Kit Farrell on the phone at five o'clock !"

"So. Then you phoned from London ?"

"Naturally !"

"Uh-huh. I have here," said H. M., unfolding a slip of paper, "a list that Kit Farrell got last night from one of the reporters. It's a record of all toll or trunk calls—outgoing *and incoming*—between Thursday night and Sunday night at seven o'clock. If you talked from London, son, how is it the Exchange don't list a single incoming long-distance call ?"

He dropped the paper on the table.

"Phooey !" said H. M., honestly distressed at such clumsiness. "You ought to take a few pointers from the gal, son. She's really clever. When Lord Severn apparently disap peared bang out of his own study—leavin' behind the Bentley car, the discarded coat and cap—it didn't take long to remember that 'call from London' of yours.

"It didn't take long to remember that the Exchange, which always speaks first on trunk calls and says: 'Are you Muggleton 0001 ? London wants you,' didn't say a word. Your voice was the first that popped out of the receiver.

"The gaff was blown in another way, too. While Kit Farrell and I were waiting in the study after Lord Severn's 'disappearance'—Masters had gone out to chivvy the servants—we had visitors. Miss Julia Mansfield came up out of the rain, carrying a paper parcel . . ."

H. M. spoke more slowly. His voice had a prompting and prodding quality; it urged Miss Mansfield to take up the story.

But she only made a fierce gesture, sagged down in her chair again, and turned her head away.

"That parcel," said H. M., "contained the dagger and the perfume box. I couldn't know it for certain, but I could make a pretty shrewd guess. She was gettin' scared. She didn't dare keep the dibs any longer. She was goin' to sneak 'em into Severn's study—where, d'ye see, she'd first met Sandy Robertson years ago.

"Up out of the rain in front of her, all of a sudden, materialized our prowlin' friend Beaumont. Like a cat walking by itself. She dropped the parcel. He picked it up, and put it in his pocket. Dagger and perfume box? Yes, my children! Yes, for a fiver!"

"Mr. George Andrew Robertson," called Miss Mansfield, without turning round, "wrote to me and said Mr. Beaumont would call for them. He *said* it would be all right!"

And then, past control, she began to hammer her fists on the wicker arms of the chair.

"I'm not a crook," she cried. "Dear God, I'm not a crook!"

"Easy, my wench," said H. M. "I told you then it was goin' to be all right."

He addressed Masters.

"The revealing thing, Masters, was a conversation I had with Mr. Beaumont while he stood outside the study window. Now remember, Beaumont had been at the gates at half-past four. He must have seen Lord Severn drive through in the red Bentley. He even sent his card up, with a written message.

"And yet, when I mentioned that visiting-card to him, the first thing he said was: 'Then Lord Severn *is* at home?' with a quick breath and a whistlin' kind of surprise, as though he'd only sent that card on the offchance. And he was surprised, because he had to squirm and dodge the straight question I asked next.

"Why should he be surprised, Masters?

"I then said Lord Severn had got here only to disappear in a whiff of brimstone, leaving his outer clothes behind. We turned on the lights. Beaumont saw the clothes and the bronze lamp. He was very pleased—crouchin' at that window like a big cat, very pleased.

"So I next asked him the straight question: 'You saw Lord Severn, didn't you?' Whereupon, Masters, he gave a very rummy quick smile . . . look, he's smilin' like that now! . . . and said yes.

"He said so, of course, because this made a second apparently supernatural disappearance. It increased the reputation of the bronze lamp, which he wanted like billy-o to get. It gave the bronze lamp infernal blue glory. Beaumont's just as much of a faker as Alim Bey. . . ."

Beaumont made a short, slight movement. There *was* some-thing of the cat about him, and you could sense the claws.

". . . only," said H. M., " a bit more subtle. Because the man he'd seen drive through those gates in the Bentley wasn't Lord Severn at all."

"Wasn't... my father?" asked Helen. "Then who was it?"

"Sandy Robertson."

During a pause, while Sandy looked as though he were going to be literally sick, H. M. went on.

"At some time past noon yesterday, Lord Severn did start out from London in that car. But he wasn't alone. Robertson was with him. They were headed first—or at least Severn thought they were—for that antique shop in Gloucester, to pick up the dagger and the perfume box.

"Robertson knew he'd got to commit murder. But how in God's name was he goin' to get away with it? The only way . . .

"Cor, inspiration! If Severn also 'disappeared', like his daughter!

"Mind you, Robertson had no idea what had really happened to the gal. Severn under the circumstances wouldn't 'a' told him anything, and didn't. Robertson didn't actually *care* what had happened to her, except that it would dish his matrimonial chances if she did happen to be dead as most people thought.

"The point was, Severn had been named as the next victim. If he got caught by the bronze lamp, or whatever human agency was behind the bronze lamp, the one person nobody would suspect was Sandy Robertson, who'd admittedly been in Cairo when the gal disappeared.

"I think he'd been mullin' over the plan for days. Yesterday afternoon he carried it out.

"It was darkish, and raining hard. He drove like blazes for Gloucester, with Severn sittin' beside him. He took the river road, west of here. In the loneliest part of the river road he stopped the car. He strangled the man who'd protected him from the Egyptian police.

187

"It wasn't stranglin', really. Just a little pressure, a little suffocation, of a man with a groggy heart. He weighted the body with tools from the car, and sank it in the river where it'd be only unrecognizable bones if it ever happened to be found. And he chose a spot close to the back of the park-wall here. Close, in fact, to a little back gate in the park-wall. I think Masters has told you about that gate, if you didn't already know it.

"He'd kept behind Lord Severn's cap, his coat, *and his keys*. But he didn't use 'em, at first.

"He came in first on foot, for a little reconnoitre. Nobody saw him. The extra gardeners had all been withdrawn; they weren't necessary any longer. The police kept a watch only at night.

"So Robertson established what he'd expected to find, the lodge gates were open, as Severn had always kept 'em open. In the lodge was a keeper he'd never seen before. All he had to do was sever the connection between the lodge and the house—that is, cut the wires outside the butler's pantry window.

"All this took time, coverin' ground on foot. But he got back safely to the car. He drove round to the front, and shot through those gates at fifty miles an hour. All Bert Leonard could see, on a dark rainy day, was the flash of an 'elderly-looking' face—he does look fiftyish, don't he, if you disregard walk and hair and general youthfulness?—framed between a down-pulled cap and an upturned collar.

"Remember, there'd be nobody to identify later as the man who'd driven through. And Bert Leonard wouldn't be likely to connect him later with the obviously youthful feller in blazer and flannels that's prancin' about to-day.

"There's not much more to tell, except one rather darin' stunt. He drove to the house, opened the side door, and dumped hat and coat on the floor. All the newspapers had recorded one fact—Kit Farrell, carryin' out Lady Helen's first wish, had put the bronze lamp on the mantelpiece in her room—so he knew where it was. He nipped up by the cork-screw stair in the wall, got the lamp, and walked away from the house into the rain after he'd left it behind to indicate a bronze-lamp mystery again.

"By five o'clock he put in a phone call from an A. A. box in Gloucester. He could reappear when the night-train

from London got in.   I got only one more question to ask.
Mr. Beaumont !"

"Yes, Sir Henry ?"

"Did you see somebody drive in through the gates in that
Bentley at half-past four yesterday afternoon ?"

"I did."   Serene, smiling, seldom committing himself,
and somehow detestable, Beaumont inclined his sleek head.

"Who was the man you saw ?"

"It was Mr. Robertson," answered Beaumont.   He
extended his hand.   "And now, if you please, may I have
the bronze lamp ?"

A shock of something like horror went through Kit
Farrell.   It was not only at the wordless, blubbering cry
that came from Sandy.

"Sir Henry," explained Beaumont, "worked out his solu-
tion yesterday evening.   He found Lady Helen, but had to
confess he believed her father to be dead.   He then came to
see me at my hotel.   He—this is true, sir !—explained to
me that if I were to tell everything I knew I should be
immune from prosecution—and I should receive the bronze
lamp."

"The bronze lamp ?" repeated Helen.   Her voice was
breathless, her pretty face distorted with loathing.   "Do you
still want it ?"

"Why not ?"

"When I've proved—I've *proved*, I tell you !—just what I
set out to prove ?   That this curse is all nonsense ?"

"My dear lady," smiled Beaumont, "you have proved just
the opposite.   By defying a very real power, by playing
what will now appear in the eyes of the world a stupid and
dangerous joke, you have brought about the death of your
own father.   Alim Bey told you so a while ago; I heard the
words as I came round the corner of the house.   May I
have the bronze lamp ?"

"*Kattar Allah kheirak !*" cried Alim Bey, and beat his
hands in ecstasy against his breast.

"Catch," said H. M.

The bronze lamp, casually thrown, gleamed in hot
sunlight as it arched through the air.   Beaumont caught
it with tender care.

"There is blood on it," he said.   "There will be more
blood on it when that blubbering young man, Mr. Robert
son, is taken to the hangman at eight o'clock one morn-

ing soon. Does the Lord of the Gateway care what agency is employed, when the end is death and the design is punishment? That is what I shall tell the press. That is what I *have* told the press."

Sandy Robertson fell forward at full length on the flag-stones of the terrace. Writhing there in an agony of fear, beating his fists against the stones, he was a sight both grotesque and horrible.

"Don't let them get me, Audrey," they heard him say. "For God's sake don't let them get me!"

Beaumont looked at Helen. "*Your* doing, dear lady."

"What do you mean, son," asked H. M. in a soft, heavy voice, "about what you have told the press? I thought you were keepin' your identity a secret?"

"Up to the moment, true," Beaumont agreed blandly. "But this was really too good a business opportunity to lose. After you had left my hotel last night, the voice of a dead man spoke to me."

"After I'd told you all about it, you mean? After you knew Lord Severn was dead?"

"The dead," replied Beaumont, "spoke to me by powers beyond your comprehension. It is already in the press, I believe. *I* know how to use the power of the bronze lamp. Many revelations, which I fear you will not be able to challenge, were opened to me concerning Lord Severn." Then his voice changed, but not the smile of his mouth and eyes. "Thanks for the lamp, you old fool. Good day."

"Just a minute, son," called H. M. very softly.

There was something in the tone that made Beaumont whirl round. Alim Bey, beyond him, stopped in the act of formal salute.

"Benson!"

"Yes, Sir Henry?"

"You got a little something to attend to, haven't you?"

"Very good, sir."

With a kind of maniacal abstraction Kit noticed that Benson was going towards a certain chair, an empty chair, a wicker chair; the chair, in fact, at which Benson had kept looking surreptitiously from time to time.

Benson pushed this chair well back.

The smooth floor of the terrace was broken here. One of the flagstones, perhaps a yard square, stood tilted up some six or seven inches like the edge of a trap-door. It was held there by bricks propped inside; and hitherto it had been concealed by the chair.

It was the entrance that led down to the mock dungeon, beloved of Augusta Severn in the eighteenth century. Kit, who knew it well, had completely forgotten it. But it had a use now at which dead Augusta would have clapped her hands in glee.

John Loring, fourth Earl of Severn, climbed slowly up the steep-pitched steps inside. Lord Severn was pale under his leathery tan. His legs had a shaky look, and he kept his hand pressed inside his jacket over the region of his heart. But he was unquestionably alive.

There were nine persons standing or sitting in the group that faced Lord Severn, but not one moved a muscle, except that Sandy Robertson suddenly raised himself on his elbows. In that intense hush the sound of H. M.'s voice rose softly, heavily, innocently.

"Uh huh, son?" he said to Beaumont. "About the power of the bronze lamp. You were saying . . . ?"

Lord Severn—they could hear his whistling breath—walked slowly over to Sandy Robertson.

"Get up," he said, "There'll be no prosecution. But get out. Get out. *Get out!*"

H. M., sniffing at a dead cigar, still surveyed Beaumont.

"Y'see, son," he remarked, "when I left your hotel last night I really thought Lord Severn was dead. I did for a fact.

"So I went on to Julia Mansfield's antique shop, to ask her if she'd come along to-day and confirm things. While I was there, she got a phone message to say a middle-aged gent, whom somebody'd tried to murder, had been dragged out of the river by two farmers. He had a bad heart-attack, and was babbling something about her antique shop; they'd got him in the hospital.

"We went along there. Robertson hadn't made a good job of it, that's all. He'd been too scared. The doctors had fits, but Lord Severn insisted on comin' along here with me this morning when I arranged a little demonstration. The Mansfield gal came too; and I smuggled 'em in in a car with the blinds drawn. I hadn't time to do more than arrange things with Benson, and assure Helen her old man might be in rocky shape, but he wasn't dead."

H. M. bent forward, still very gentle as he watched Beaumont.

"Y'see, son, I rather expected you might try a little game like this. And young Robertson needed to have his hide tanned good and proper. Now you'll return the dagger and the perfume box to Lord Severn before you leave town, or you *will* land in jail. I say, after your revelations to the press, do you still want the bronze lamp?"

Beaumont stood motionless, weighing the lamp in his hand.

Turning slightly to his left, with a swing rather suggestive of a baseball-player than a mystic prophet, he sent the lamp flying out over the balustrade in a long arc. It landed with a faint thud, and rolled down the slight slope of the Dutch garden. Beaumont bowed slightly, turned his back to them, and stalked away with Alim Bey following behind.

Sandy Robertson, his hands pressed over his eyes, walked shakily through the arched door into the dining-hall. Audrey Vane gave the others a look of white-faced hatred before she followed Sandy. They saw Audrey slip her arm under his.

Helen came to the side of Kit Farrell, who put his arms round her. Lord Severn, smiling, extended his hand to Sir Henry Merrivale.

"Benson!"

"Yes, my lord?"

Lord Severn looked at the butler over his shoulder. "You may admit the reporters." he said.